Praise from Robert Joseph fans for the SHADOW series:

★ ★ ★ ★ ★ "Can't wait for his next book!!"

"Beautifully written, complex and unique storylines, intriguing characters, and a wonderful weekend read! Clear your calendar, you won't be able to put it down!!"

—Wes, Amazon review

★ ★ ★ ★ ★ "Well written storyline, character development and hope there is more to come by first time author!"

"Fantastic read. Layout of chapters meshes each one together seamlessly. I seldom find a book I want to skip ahead and find out what's going to happen but this kept me reading and eager to find out."

—JR, Amazon review

★ ★ ★ ★ ★ "Hopefully the beginning of a series..."

"I know every review has already said it- but I'm confirming it. You cannot put this book down!! It has suspense, love, deceit, mystery ... everything you need for a total page turner. The character development was spot on—especially with Reed Jackson. I really hope this is a new career path for Robert Joseph because I want MORE!!"

—JennacaBuster, Amazon review

SHADOW *of* VENDETTA

Robert Joseph

BANYAN TREE PRESS

Shadow of Vendetta

ISBN: 987-1-948261-65-4

Library of Congress Control Number: 2021924298

Cover design and interior layout: Ronda Taylor, www.heartworkcreative.com

Austin, TX • Denver, CO
www.BanyanTreePress.com

Reference Guide

SHADOW *of VENDETTA*—List of characters in order of appearance:

- Brando Bruzzelli—Son of Sophia De Luca, Son of Dante Bruzzelli

- Sophia Cairo—Brando's mother

- Lia Bruzzelli—Daughter of Vito Bruzzelli, friend of Brando

- Gina—Friend of Lia Bruzzelli and Brando Bruzzelli

- Vito Bruzzelli—Dante Bruzzelli's brother, underboss of Naples, Italy mafia

- Malvolio Bruzzelli—Dante Bruzzelli's son, Vito Bruzzelli's nephew, soldier in Sicilian mafia

- Dante Bruzzelli—Godfather of the Naples mafia

- Pascal Barone—Brando's partner in the wine operation

- Joseph Johnson, aka Tony Cairo—main character

- Claire McKinley—Joseph Johnson's girlfriend

- Amy and James McKinley—Claire's McKinley's parents

- Reed Jackson (from *SHADOW of DESCENT*)—Leader of THE AGENCY, a private security company

- Max Tobin (from *SHADOW of DESCENT*)—Brother of Anna and Sophie Tobin, Mandy's boyfriend

- Mandy (from *SHADOW of DESCENT*)—Max's girlfriend and Deshi's daughter

- Anna Tobin (from *SHADOW of DESCENT*)—Armando Ruiz's wife, Max and Sophie Tobin's sister

- Armando Ruiz (from *SHADOW of DESCENT*)—Anna Tobin's husband

- Sophie Tobin (from *SHADOW of DESCENT*)—Max and Anna's younger sister

- Bella (from *SHADOW of DESCENT*)—Anna and Armando's daughter

- Deshi (from *SHADOW of DESCENT*)—Reed Jackson's girlfriend and Mandy's mother

- Mario Cairo—Joseph Johnson, aka Tony Cairo's father

- Geno Cairo—Mario's brother, Joseph Johnson, aka Tony Cairo's uncle

- Traci Lorenz—Boston attorney

- Luca De Luca—Joseph Johnson, aka Tony Cairo's great uncle, Brando Bruzzelli's grandfather

- Isla Cairo—Joseph Johnson, aka Tony Cairo's sister

- Hans Breckman—Joseph Johnson aka Tony Cairo's personal Swiss banker

Chapter A

MY SCOOTER MADE A HIGH-PITCHED WHINE AS I WEAVED THROUGH THE slower-moving traffic of the Monday morning commute in Naples, Italy. My machine connected directly to my mind as I dodged oncoming traffic, bumper-to-bumper vehicles, and pedestrians in crosswalks. I anticipated three or four moves ahead and leaned Mario, the name I gave my scooter, through gaps in traffic that I knew would open up just in time to race through them. I was a Formula One driver, flying past the slower vehicles to the first day of class at my new school.

Scampia appeared in my rearview mirror. Scampia, the Naples neighborhood turned mafia-controlled ghetto over the years. The police had abandoned control and protection of its citizens there years before. Kids like me who grew up in Scampia grew up fast; many of us were forced into mafia drug trafficking and violence. My mother and I lived in the infamous Vele di Scampia, a huge public housing project that had fallen into complete disrepair.

Mario swept me up the hill to the more civilized neighborhood of Vomero. My appointment with the dean of the school was scheduled for eight o'clock.

My hair was wet. *It's going to dry sticking straight up in the air,* I thought. *I'll look like an actor from one of those old movies that Mama likes to watch.* I had agreed to wear this button-down shirt to make her happy. She wanted me to make a good impression with the dean. I didn't know how the rich kids dressed. If I showed up at my old school wearing this shirt, I'd be in for it.

I wasn't sure if Mario's more labored whine was because he didn't want to go to the new school or because of the steep slope. But Mario kept pulling me forward, as he always did.

Is this an escape, an escape from my life in Scampia? It can't be an escape if no one is chasing me. What is it? Carpe diem? Carpe diem, the Latin words

Mama wanted me to understand. She taught me the definition—"seize the moment." It wasn't until just now that I realized what Mama wanted me to understand was that carpe diem is more than a phrase; it's a state of mind. I need to seize the moment, forget about the slums where I grew up, and be prepared to take advantage of this opportunity.

Whoa! Is that my turn? I had come up here the weekend before to make sure I'd know where I was going. *There it is.* Left through a red light, then onto the sidewalk to avoid a turning car. Mario didn't like to slow down, especially for red lights.

I looked at myself in the rearview mirror and laughed. What a look for my first day. Mario's engine had misfired a couple of times going up that last hill. When I got home, I would use one of Mama's old emery boards to sand the tip of the sparkplug. The Bay of Naples looked pretty cool from up here. I tried to see my building in the heart of the slums, but had to lean away from the bay to avoid a parked truck.

I cruised past the school. *No reason to be early. Where do you want to park?* No scooter lot here. The rich kids drove nice cars.

I climbed the steps to the front entrance. Students gave me a weird look. Was it because they saw a new face, my goofy shirt, or the hairdo? I patted down my hair, but knew it wouldn't help. My reflection in the glass of the front door stared back at me and proved the obvious. *If I see a water fountain, I'll wet it down.* Inside the front doors was a large, open atrium with people all over the place. *This must be a big school.* I stopped in the middle of the turmoil and looked around. A couple of girls walked my way.

"Hey, where's the dean's office?" I asked them.

They clutched their books tight to their chest when they looked up at me. One of them said, "Right over there, under the sign that says Dean's Office.

"Thank you."

Inside the small office were three women behind a counter trying to take care of twenty or more students milling around. I was still a little early. Play it cool, let it happen. A few minutes went by. The commotion died down, and one of the ladies asked, "Can I help you?"

"I'm Brando Bruzzelli. I have an appointment with the dean at eight."

"Oh, yes. Have a seat over there. I'll remind him."

I looked at the row of chairs she pointed to. *I'm not sitting there.* I went back into the hallway and found a water fountain. I cupped my hand and splashed some water onto the top of my head. One didn't do it. I splashed several more handfuls of water onto my hair and tried to force it down. It probably looked worse now. My shirt was wet. I turned back to office. A group of kids were looking at me. All I could do was raise my hands and give them a smile.

I gave Dean Cassini's hand an extra-hard shake. Mama would have been proud. There was a pleasant-looking lady sitting next to the chair that seemed to be reserved for me. She said, "Hi, Brando. I'm Mrs. Greco. Welcome."

Dean Cassini had a puzzled look on his face. "Is it raining out?"

"No. I rode up here on my scooter with wet hair, and it went a little crazy. I tried to harness the beast with water from the fountain." After my eloquent explanation, he looked even more puzzled.

He picked up a file and scanned the contents. "It looks like you're a pretty good student." He looked over the top of his glasses at me. "But, you may find things a little harder here." He leaned back in his chair and crossed his arms. Still looking over the top of his glasses, he said, "Coach Moretti tells me that you're a good futbol player. He's desperate to get you on the team. What do you think about that?"

"My mother thinks it would be a good idea for me to go to school here. You know, get out of the slums and hang out with the rich people."

Dean Cassini looked at my file again and said, "You're only fifteen years old!"

The dean looked at the counselor. "Where are we going to put him?"

She said, "We should give him some tests and let his competencies place him in the appropriate classes. She looked at me as though I didn't understand what she had said. "Do you mind taking a few tests for us, Brando?"

"No problem."

"Just to get us started on the right path ... Do you get along with mathematics very well?"

"Yes."

"Have you taken any algebra classes at your old school?"

"No. But I know algebra."

"How about a foreign language? Have you taken any classes at your old school to learn a foreign language?"

I said in English, "No. My old school doesn't offer that, but I speak English well. Then in French I said, "I speak a little French, too."

"Where did you learn math and English?"

"My mother and I learned together. She thought it was a good idea, and I did it to make her happy."

Two men who were dressed exactly alike rushed into the office and interrupted us. One of them pointed at me and said, "That's him!"

Is he accusing me of stealing something?

The dean said, "This is Coach Moretti and Coach Ricci."

I stood up. One of them looked me up and down. He said, "I didn't know he was that tall." I could tell he was disappointed.

The other one said, "Glad you're with us, Brando. We'll see you at practice. Did you bring your shoes?"

I looked down at my feet. "Yes."

The two men laughed the exact same laugh. Then they looked at the dean. "Can we get him out a little early to get some gear for him?"

"Not today. He'll be taking tests the rest of the day and won't be done in time for your practice today."

"Okay. We'll find you and kidnap you sometime tomorrow, Brando." They both laughed the same cackle again and hustled out the door.

I finished all their tests before lunch. Someone led me to the cafeteria. I got in line and asked the nice lady on the other side of the counter for a few extra pieces of pizza. She looked around and put a couple extra pieces on my plate. I walked past all the students seated at tables and went out into the hall. I sat down on the floor. The pizza was excellent.

I wandered around the halls, trying to get a feel for the layout of the school. It was huge. A teacher stopped me in the hall and said, "Where are you supposed to be?"

"I'm not sure. I'm new here today. Where would those two futbol coaches be?"

The lady laughed, "You must be the new student from Scampia."

"That's me."

"First floor, all the way to that end." She pointed. "Go through the orange doors and look for the basketball court. They'll be roaming around there somewhere."

Chapter B

I ENDED UP IN CLASSES WITH KIDS OLDER THAN ME. THE SAME WAS TRUE on the futbol team. Everyone was pretty cool, though. It was easy living up here on the hill. I could tell the teachers had a chance, and so did the kids.

Vincent was a senior on the team. He took me under his wing and showed me around. That made a difference. His girlfriend was a year younger than he was and in most of my classes. She'd watch our practices, and the three of us hung out for a while after practice. Her name was Lia Bruzzelli. Down in Scampia, the name *Bruzzelli* meant something. It meant you were connected to the mob, and you were protected. Not sure about up here. She was nice and a knockout. Her friend Gina was, too. Gina started watching our practices and hanging out with us. It was hard to leave those guys, but I had things to do, and Mama wanted to have supper with me, so I left them early every day.

The four of us went to a Friday night party. There was booze and drugs everywhere. I told them I didn't touch that stuff. "I've seen too many bad things." They thought it was all fun. I knew better. I left the party early and let Mario coast all the way home. It was a dark, cool night with no traffic. A nice, quiet ride home.

The next Monday I went to Lia's home before school. She and Gina wanted to surprise me with something. The girls had bought me some new clothes. They made me try them on in the garage. It was funny to them, and they had a good time dressing me up. I didn't care. The new clothes were better than my button-down shirt. I told them that I couldn't wear the new clothes home, though. Lia said, "No problem, just come here after practice and before school." She gave me the passcode to the garage.

There was a sports car under a cover on the far side of the garage. The shape of it under the cloth made it look as if there was something fast hidden under there.

When it was time to leave for school, Gina took me by surprise when she said, "I want to ride with you." Who was I to disappoint her?

That was when Lia's father came out the door. He looked pissed at the sight of me in his garage. He asked, "Who do we have here?"

I got off my scooter and approached him. I could tell right away he was connected when I reached for his hand. "I'm Brando Bruzzelli." He ignored my hand.

"You live around here?"

"No, down in Scampia."

"Why are you up here?"

"I play futbol with Vincent."

"Come here." He motioned toward the far side of the garage. I looked at Lia, shrugged, and followed him.

He said, "With the last name Bruzzelli and living down in Scampia, I know that you know what's going on. I don't want you bringing any of that Scampia drug shit up here."

"I never touch the stuff. But you should know that it's all over their school."

"I figured it probably was. How the fuck did you end up here anyway?"

"They gave me a futbol scholarship."

He looked me up and down. "You must be really good, because the affluent fucks up here don't wanta even think about what goes on in the ghetto. You know you're going to have to start sending some money up?"

"Yeah, I know how it works."

"But I'll say it again, I don't want any dope around Lia."

"Like I said, I won't touch the stuff."

"How old are you?"

"Fifteen."

"Fuck you! How old are you?"

I said, "I'll be seventeen in a year and a half," and smiled.

He laughed. I could tell he liked me. "A wise guy, huh?"

I smiled again and tugged on the cover that I thought was blanketing a sports car. "What's under there?" I asked.

He said, "Are you connected to anyone yet?

6

"No."

"You are now. If anyone asks, tell them you're with Vito. Understand?"

I nodded.

"When you figure out a way to send some money up without selling drugs, I'll give you a ride in this Ferrari Tributo. I might even let you drive it."

I nodded and smiled.

"Figure it out, keep an eye on Lia for me, and we'll get along fine. He patted my face. A Bentley pulled up beside his house. He got into the backseat.

The ride to school with Gina holding me tight was exceptional.

Chapter C

OUR FIRST FUTBOL MATCH WAS A FEW WEEKS LATER WITH A GOOD TEAM from across town. I played the whole game, and the coaches yelled at me the entire time. "Pass it! Pass the ball!" I did what I was told, but it was getting old.

We were down two to one with less than five minutes left in the game. I said to myself and then out loud, "That's it!" I ran out of my zone and intercepted a pass. I dribbled through everyone the length of the field at full throttle, just like I drove Mario through traffic, and drove the ball into the back of the net to tie the game. I waited a minute or two later in the game and did the same thing again. I launched a rocket from the other side of the field with my left foot, and it whizzed past the frozen, flat-footed goalie. We won, and everyone went crazy.

That night we went to another party. Same scene. There was talk about a trip to Turin in a couple of weeks. I didn't get all the details, but it had something to do with a student visit to the university for the seniors. A girl and one of the players on the team schemed a way to blow off the trip and go to Capri for the weekend. They planned to party and screw all weekend while their parents thought they were on the student trip. I had an idea about how I could get behind the wheel of Vito's Ferrari.

Chapter D

THE LETTERS FOR THE NOTE WERE CUT OUT OF A MAGAZINE AND GLUED onto a piece of paper. The note delivered to the boy's parents read the same as the note delivered to the girl's parents:

> *WE HAVE SANTINO AND CARA. IF YOU WANT TO SEE THEM ALIVE AGAIN, CALL THIS NUMBER—83 767 628 AT NOON TODAY. DON'T MAKE US HURT THEM. DON'T CALL THE POLICE OR THEIR BODIES WILL WASH UP ON THE BAYSHORE. BOTH SETS OF PARENTS HAVE THIS SAME NOTE. WORK TOGETHER.*

I had checked on the kids' families. They were loaded but not connected. I'd seen plenty of old movies with this kidnapping plot, and it happened all the time in Naples. But they'd always ask for too much money. I wouldn't make that mistake.

At the Friday night party the day before, I found Santino's and Cara's cell phones and lifted their SIM cards. They had their phones, but the phones didn't work.

I figured their parents had tried calling them after they received the note, and I was sure their parents would have called the school, only to learn that Santino and Cara never showed for the field trip.

The phone in the phone booth rang at noon, right on time. I picked it up. "Listen closely. You only have one chance." I said in a low, disguised voice.

Someone was crying in the background. A voice said, "What do you want?"

"Let's make this easy. Do the right thing and you'll see your pretty daughter and son soon. Fuck it up and you won't. It's that simple. We have people watching you, so don't try anything stupid. You have time to go to the bank today and get twenty thousand euros for each kid. Put the forty K in a bag and throw it off the Via Luca Giordano railroad bridge where it intersects with the Line One at nine o'clock tonight.

"If the money falls on those tracks, you'll see Cara and Santino tomorrow by noon. If you disappoint us by calling the police or not dropping the forty grand off the bridge, you'll each receive the left ear of your child, and the new amount will be eighty thousand. Be smart." I hung up.

———◦———

At nine o'clock that night, a bag fell onto the tracks. Mario and I scooped it up, drove through the woods, and then on home. I knew that losing forty K wouldn't hurt them. Maybe they'd learn a lesson about caring a little more for their children in the future. Santino and Cara would come rolling home Sunday morning after their weekend of bliss and would have some explaining to do. But no one would be hurt, and no one would be blamed. The spoiled, rich kids would take a little heat. I could live with that.

———◦———

The next Monday morning I was in Lia's garage with the girls when Vito came out. A mean, dark-looking man and a young woman with big hair, who wasn't wearing much more than makeup, stepped out of the house after Vito. The man gave me a threatening snarl, and the woman offered a beckoning smile. The odd combination of the two characters creeped me out. I jerked my gaze away from them and said to Vito, "Got a minute?" As we walked to the far side of the garage, the black-cloud of a man went to the Bentley waiting in the driveway. The porn star-looking lady went back into the house.

I gave Vito twenty grand and the kidnapping story. I kept the other twenty for myself. Lia and Gina kept their distance while Vito and I laughed about my caper.

He peeled off two thousand euros, handed it to me, and said, "Do you want to see it?" He pulled the cover off a beautiful red Ferrari. "You'll get to drive this sometime. Nice work. And don't worry about sending any more up for a while. Go to school, play futbol, and keep your eyes open. Anybody asks, what do you say?"

I smiled and said, "I'm with Vito."

He laughed again and patted my face. "Beautiful. By the way, why are you here all the time?"

I nodded to the two girls who were watching us and said, "They like dressing me for school."

He cracked up again as he walked away. "Beautiful, beautiful."

I joined the girls and asked Lia, "Who were those guys?"

She said, "That guy is one of my father's associates. His name is Malvolio. He lives in Sicily with friends of my dad because he got in some kind of trouble with the law here. He can't go to his own home when he comes back because the anti-mafia squad is looking for him. I hate it when I'm in the house with him. I hate everything about him. He's a creep. He always has his hands on me and threatens me. That woman is my dad's current wife."

Gina slid behind me on the back of Mario. For some reason Mario took the long, slow way to school. Gina's touch felt different that morning, more caring. She leaned the side of her face against my back. I took one hand off the handlebars and pressed her hands against my chest.

Gina and I held hands for the first time as we slowly climbed the steps to school. We were a little late. My counselor was waiting. "Dean Cassini wants to have a word with you, Brando. Gina, you go on to class."

The three of us sat in our usual places in the dean's office. He was reading something while we waited. *What's this about?* I wondered.

He finally said, "How are you getting along, Brando?"

"Okay, I guess." I looked at Mrs. Greco and then back at the dean.

"Seems like you've made quite a splash here with your futbol successes."

I waited for something else.

He said, "You're hanging around with a much older crowd."

I waited.

He said, "Do you know what the word *plagiarism* means, Brando?"

"Yes."

"What does it mean?"

"It means to steal someone else's work and pass it off as your own. Referring to written work."

"That's right. It would be wrong to do that, wouldn't it?"

"Yes."

The dean pushed a piece of paper across the desk to me. It was my composition assignment. "Is this your work, Brando?"

"Yes."

He said, "You have me and part of the English department wondering where you found this work. Where did you find it?"

I saw where this was going. I looked at the dean's kind face. *The kind I wanted to smack.* Then I looked at Mrs. Greco for some direction and got nothing. *I won't lower myself to answer that question.* I waited.

"If it's yours, go ahead and read it to us then," he said.

I pushed the paper back to the dean and waited until he started to speak. Then I interrupted him. I looked straight into his eyes and recited my work from memory.

> *"Each morning started with the ringing of a bell. Her startle from asleep to awake was always the same. Morning came too fast; the bell didn't care.*
>
> *It wasn't that long ago when her son was her friend. She wondered what happened, where he got the new clothes and those headphones. What does he do at night?*
>
> *He made a sandwich with the eggs and toast she had prepared without joining her at the kitchen table. He put the sack lunch in his book bag that was always glued to his guarded shoulder and left without saying a word.*
>
> *She was running late, but checked herself in the mirror one more time and noticed the usual strain in her own eyes. She defended herself against the return look of those eyes with the repeating thought.*

"Don't confront me with my failures. I'm aware of them."

> *Another bell. Twenty-six pairs of eyes focused on her face. She wanted to make a difference, but her words drifted around the room. They floated in midair, not sinking into their minds. Their brains were full of things they didn't need. Bell after bell she tried and failed. The last bell of the day brought a welcome quiet.*
>
> *Two places were set; one plate was clean. She tapped her fork on the plate in front of her to disturb the unwelcome quiet at the kitchen table. The quiet brought the worry. The worry about when he'd be home, why he had changed, and about what she should do.*

She finished her day and planned her tomorrow. She tried to wait up for him, but the weight of her eyelids had the final say. She startled awake when he came blasting through the front door and went straight to his room without a word. She was relieved he was home.

They had made it through one more day.

Before she dropped her tired body onto her bed, she stood in front of the mirror.

She found her eyes in the mirror.

Do you see her eyes?

Do you care?

My eyes were still laser focused on the dean as I said those last words. Mrs. Greco said, "Who were you referring to in your paper, Brando?"

I turned to her. "I was thinking of the teachers I knew from my old school. I hadn't realized the strain on them until I noticed the difference in the eyes of the fine teachers here." I pointed to my paper and said, "That story is about the hard life of a good person who's lost her ability to influence the people she loves."

Mrs. Greco paused with her gaze on my face, reached for a tissue, and then said, "It's a beautiful story, Brando. You may go to class."

Chapter E

I FINISHED THAT YEAR OF SCHOOL AND SPENT A CAREFREE SUMMER WITH Mama.

The next school year Mario took me up the hill day after day. I hung out with Lia and Gina, played futbol, did my schoolwork, and let Mario coast me home at night. The Friday night parties turned into an opportunity for Gina and me to find some privacy and explore some of the more beautiful mysteries of life.

One Friday afternoon Vito came home early, which was typical for a Friday. I was with Lia and Gina in the garage. He wanted a word with me.

I was to tag along with two men from his crew, Enzo and Malvolio, to get some experience. *Malvolio, that's the dark-cloud that bothers Lia.*

⸺◦○◦⸺

The next day the three of us waited in a small Fiat at a highway stop about thirty miles out of town. The smell of their cigarette smoke was just one on the many things that annoyed me that morning. Enzo looked at me in the rearview mirror and said, "Vito told us to keep an eye on you, Brando. There's no reason for you to be scared. This is an easy job. The driver is in on it. He's going to give us his keys and then walk away, so keep your mouth shut and just stay out of the way." Enzo turned around and showed me his gun and said, "When you get to be a big boy, maybe, just maybe, we'll show you how to use one of these." Malvolio cracked up for some reason.

Malvolio said to me, "I've seen you sniffing around Lia at Vito's place. Are you tapping that smokin' friend of hers?" I didn't answer him. "I bet she likes it really hard. A guy like you will never keep a hot piece of ass like that happy. Don't worry, I'll be there to take over when the time comes. Until then, I'm gonna take Lia. She doesn't know how close I am to bending her over and finding out what's under her panties. She might try to fight me a little, but I know she wants it, and once she gets a taste of it, she'll be on her knees beggin' me to give it to her all day long." He and Enzo both laughed.

Enzo caught my eye again in the rearview mirror and said, "You know Malvolio is Dante's son. He can take whatever and whoever he wants, and there's nothin' you or anyone else can do about it."

I was in the backseat of the Fiat. I ignored them. *What would Vito do if he heard these thirty-year-old douchebags say those words about his daughter?* It was a gray day. The brilliant sun hid behind the clouds; that was where I wanted to be. Their cigarette smoke filled the car even though the windows were open.

The truck was late. Enzo and Malvolio talked smack about making the driver pay.

A white box truck pulled up close to us. They flicked their cigarette butts out the windows. The three of us got out. As the driver approached us, Enzo said, "Give me the keys." The man looked surprised. "That's not going to happen," he said

Enzo pulled the gun out from behind his back. "The keys!"

13

The man didn't move. Enzo hit him on the side of his head with the butt of his pistol. I expected the man to fall down, but he stood there and didn't flinch. His arms and shoulders were thick and looked strong. He was a workingman, not a truck driver. Enzo tried to hit him again, but the man grabbed his wrist before the strike landed. He snatched the gun from Enzo's hand and threw it away. Malvolio stepped up and pointed his gun at the side of the man's head.

The man said, "You're not taking this truck. That's my life in there."

Malvolio cocked the gun.

I held back, but saw the obvious. *Can't these two idiots see that this is the wrong guy?* "Hold on," I said. "I think we have the wrong truck. This isn't how this was supposed to go down." People looked at us, then looked away, not wanting to get involved. Another box truck pulled up. "That's probably our truck."

Enzo and Malvolio looked at each other and then at the man with blood running down one side of his head. "This guy still has to pay," Enzo said.

I stepped between the man and Malvolio and said, "We made a mistake."

Enzo said, "This is on you, Brando. Vito is going to hear what went down." Enzo retrieved his pistol and walked away. Malvolio snarled at me and said, "Find your own way home. You're not coming with us."

I inspected the side of the man's head. "It's not too bad. Do you have a towel or rag in the truck?" The guy sat down on the curb. He put pressure on the wound with a rag I gave him. The bleeding slowed, and he cleaned himself up a little as the other truck and the Fiat drove away.

The man sat there dabbing his wound. I said, "Are you going to be okay?"

"Yeah, I'm okay. Thanks for stepping in like that. Where are you headed?"

"Back to Naples."

"That's where I'm going. You can ride with me."

We drove along in silence for a while. Finally, he said, "My name is Pascal Barone. This is a rented truck, and the back is filled with cases of wine. My wine. Made from grapes that I hand-picked three years ago and bottled six months ago. It's all I have. Like I said, that's my life back there."

Eight hours later, Pascal dropped me off at Vito's house. My scooter was parked by the side of the house, and Vito was in the garage. He looked pissed. We walked to our usual spot by the Ferrari. "What happened?"

"We had the wrong truck, and those guys were about ready to cap that guy. I stepped in because there were witnesses everywhere, and there was no reason to take down a man like that."

"Enzo and Malvolio said you disrespected them."

"I don't know about that. We made a mistake. Besides ..." I reached into my back pocket and handed him five hundred euros.

Vito counted it. "What's this?"

"The guy is a one-man operation. He has a small vineyard up in Tuscany. We drove to wine stores all over town, and I helped him sell his wine. We sold it all. He said I was a good salesman and gave me a cut."

Vito laughed. He counted out fifty euros and gave them back to me. "You crack me up, Brando. I'll smooth things over with Enzo and Malvolio. Good work today." He patted my face. "I guess you work better alone." He laughed again as he walked away.

I said, "One more thing." Vito turned around. "I made a good connection with him. I think I could help his business. Would you mind if I work with him? It might be a good legitimate business for us."

Vito smiled. "For us?" He laughed again. "How could you help him?"

"I could help him out with money. I have some money saved. I could invest in his business."

"How?"

"He told me that if he could buy a few new French oak barrels, he could make some great wine and then make some real money. Right now he uses old, used barrels. It would be three years before the wine in the barrels would pay off. But I could help in other ways, like sales. Do you like good wine?"

Vito grinned at me. "How old are you?"

"I will be eighteen soon."

"Yeah, right. Soon, like in a year and a half." He laughed again. "Alright. I'm staying out of the investment, but go ahead. Let's see how it goes."

Chapter One

⊷◈◈◈⊶

JOSEPH JOHNSON FOUND HIS USUAL SPOT AT THE END OF THE BAR OF A trendy nightspot located in Palo Alto, California, on the edge of Stanford University's campus. The Friday night bartender walked over to him and said, "What's happening, my friend? Can I get you something?"

"Hi, Nick. Nothing now, thanks."

"Maggi and Kayla are here. He nodded toward the back of the room. "They asked for you when they came in."

Joseph smiled and twisted his wrist to check the time.

That was when she walked in with a group of friends. Nick said, "There's some new blood. Looks like it could be a late one for us tonight."

Joseph smiled again. The new girls all looked good.

Nick said, "I give you ten to one they'll be heading your way soon."

Joseph said, "Go ahead and shake me up one of my martinis." Nick kept a special bottle of Russian vodka behind the bar, exclusively for his favorite customer. "You got it," he said. Inside the vodka bottle was water. Joseph never drank liquor at a bar.

Nick poured Joseph's drink from the shaker right on cue as three of the coeds sauntered up to an open spot at the bar. She was one of them. The other two tried to get his attention, bobbing to the music and tossing smiles his way. But it was their friend that Joseph had his eye on. Her medium length auburn hair paired perfectly with her green eyes and light complexion. Her posture was feminine and elegant.

Joseph checked his watch again, tossed a twenty onto the bar, and said, "I have to run, Nick. See you later." After taking two steps toward the door, he turned around and walked past the two girls and up to the one that had caught his eye. He said to her, "Looks like you and your friends are having a good time tonight. That's nice to see. I have to take off now, but want to meet up with you sometime. Here's my card." He handed her his business card, then said, "I'll be at that little coffee shop next door this Sunday morning at ten. We could hang out there with a cup of coffee." He raised his eyebrows at her. "Enjoy the rest of your evening." Then he bent down and kissed her on the cheek.

⟞∘⟝

Her friends watched him walk away and turned back to the object of his affection. "Claire, what did he say to you? How do you know him? He looks exactly like those pictures we saw of JFK Jr."

Claire said, "He gave me his card. Look, he's a man, not a college kid. And he wasn't wasted like all the guys we know." She took a good look at the card and said, "Joseph Johnson wants to meet me for a cup of coffee Sunday morning."

⟞∘⟝

Joseph drove from the bar to his condominium complex, which was twenty minutes away in the center of San Francisco. His building had business offices and hotel rooms on the first twenty-five floors. Floors twenty-six through seventy-two were luxury condominiums. The building had two sets of elevators, one on the north side of the building and one on the south side.

A low growl from his mid-engine convertible echoed off the concrete walls as he downshifted on the ramp to the underground parking area that serviced the north side. He took the elevator up to the sixty-seventh floor and walked into his condo. His condo was immaculate. He had a cleaning service come in once a week to keep it that way.

Joseph undressed to his underwear and put those clothes in a hamper. He walked into the study, where he pulled an oil painting away from the cherry wood paneling.

He pressed five numbers on the wall safe keypad. The bookcase to his left clicked open. Through the bookcase was a secret room that he called his "dojo." The small room was filled with the tools of his trade. He pulled one of the backpacks off a shelf, then pushed open a door on the other side of the room and stepped into the bedroom closet of a different condo that he owned through an LLC with no ties to him. That condo was smaller than his and was decorated differently. He changed his appearance from a fit young man to an overweight, middle-aged man with long hair and glasses. After his transformation was complete, he left that condo through its front door and walked with a slight limp down the hallway to the south side elevators that serviced the south parking lot. Joseph always stayed in character because he assumed there were cameras everywhere.

He drove up the parking ramp in his eight-year-old GMC SUV, with his backpack on the passenger seat.

Forty-five minutes later, Joseph parked the SUV on a side street in a well-manicured residential neighborhood. He put on a black baseball hat and gloves, then snagged his backpack. It was after midnight, and all the houses were dark. The target's house was quiet, just as the research they gave him had said. He walked to the back of the house, picked the lock, and punched the key code of the security system that his handler had given him.

Upstairs was a man sleeping on his back next to a woman who was on her side, turned away from him. The smell of rank booze and the sounds of a fat man snoring filled the bedroom. For the first time that night Joseph noticed the moon. Its soft light poured into the room through half-circle windowpanes above the three bedroom windows.

Joseph took one step into the room, raised his Beretta Cheetah semiautomatic pistol with an attached silencer, inserted an imaginary red-and-white target on the man's head, and hit the bull's eye twice. The man jerked once. No movements from his lover.

Joseph picked up the shell casings, left the house, drove back to his southside condo, and tossed his clothes into the washer. He tapped a five-digit code on the built-in microwave and walked back through the bedroom closet wall into his dojo, where he replaced the backpack. He pushed open the secret bookcase wall and walked back into his northside condo. After taking a quick shower, he went to bed at 1:33 a.m.

His last thought of the night was a reminder of what the research they gave him detailed. It described the target as a Saudi militant and expert bomb maker who had dual citizenship in Saudi Arabia and the United States. His specialty was building bombs that destroyed western targets filled with innocent civilians. His background was chemistry, and he used

PETN in his bombs. PETN is an odorless white powder that even X-ray machines struggled to pick up.

The authorities were one hundred percent certain that he was responsible for many terrorist bombings over the last twenty years. They had not been able to prove their case in a court of law because it was his expertise and not his own hands that made the horrific bombs. They were now certain that he was passing his skills on to a new set of master bomber makers for al-Qaeda.

Joseph took comfort in knowing his actions may have saved countless innocent lives. He was asleep before the clock blinked 1:37.

Chapter Two

THE NEXT MORNING'S SUN WAS UP, AND SO WAS CLAIRE. SHE COULDN'T get back to sleep and take advantage of her usual Saturday morning sleep-in. She thought about the day ahead and reminded herself that she and her roommates had plans to spend the day and night with their boyfriends at a large resort home they had rented in the mountains. The event was their boyfriends' fraternity's end-of-the-year blowout celebration. Claire didn't want to go. She didn't want to fall in line and continue on the path with Hugh, but felt she was getting close to the point of no return. They had been dating for the last two years. Hugh had been accepted at Stanford Law School. His parents and her parents were good friends. He was a "good catch."

She pictured herself ten years in the future, chasing around two entitled brats while Hugh worked all the time and spent his spare time at the club, drinking with his friends. It would be a good life. But it was a life she'd already seen, and she wanted something else.

There was a knock on her door. Jenn peeked around the half-open door and said, "Are you awake? I can't sleep. What if it's cold up in the mountains tonight and we won't have the right clothes? You know they're going to want to build a fire again."

Claire said, "Come in. Pack a sweatshirt, just in case."

"I can't wear a sweatshirt. Tonight could be the night. It's too important. I have to look my best for Stu. You're so lucky, Claire. Hughie is crazy about you. Plus, you could get away with wearing a sweatshirt and still look perfect. Hey, did you throw away that business card from that guy who kissed

21

you last night? If Hughie ever found out what happened, we would all be in real trouble."

Claire said, "You can wear my teal jacket. You'll be the queen of the firepit."

"This is serious Claire.... Would you really let me wear it? Do you think it will be the same as last year? Those guys got really drunk. Remember how we didn't go to bed until the sun was coming up?"

"Yes, you can wear my jacket, and yes, it will be the same as last year. It will always be the same."

When Claire heard herself say the words *It will always be the same,* something clicked. She said to herself, *I'm not going to the party.*

———⊙———

Joseph's Saturday morning started at 6:30 a.m. He was outside, taking a quick jog through the park near his condo. The morning air was brisk, and the sky was clear. *A good morning for a run.*

Thirty minutes later he exited the park and nodded to three homeless men sitting on sheets of cardboard. Across the street and a few steps later he ducked into a small café. The man behind the cash register wore a white apron that was already dirty. He was as wide as he was tall, and when he looked up, Joseph saw that patented crooked smile with a toothpick dangling on one side. "Hi, Joseph. Nice to see you this fine morning. What's shakin' today?"

Joseph answered, "There's three of them today."

"Three of them you say?"

"Yes, sir. Thanks, Frank. I'll call you later to pay for their meals."

Joseph left the café, walked to the corner of the block, and then took off on a sprint straight up a long, steep hill. At the top of the hill, he slowed to a stop to catch his breath. He looked back down the slope of one of San Francisco's many steep hills. "What a beast," he said out loud.

The stairs leading up to the 2nd Street Boxing Gym were a piece of cake; he took them two at a time. The place was empty except for a custodian dancing with a mop on one side of the big room and a man walking away from the boxing ring, heading to the back of the gym. Joseph yelled at him, "Hey, Lenny, I know I'm early, but do you mind if I get some bag work in this morning?"

Lenny turned around. "Go ahead. Knock yourself out, kid." Lenny walked back to Joseph.

"How do you always get stuck with the early morning shift?" Joseph asked.

"You know those young guys can't get their ass outta bed before nine. What are you working on this morning?"

"I want to work the heavy bag with my hands and my feet. No weights today. I have to entertain some clients with a golf game this afternoon."

"Golf? You're the only guy I know who wastes his time on that pussy sport. I guess if you wanna play the big shot, you gotta have the moves." Lenny smiled, stepped close, and gave Joseph a quick combination of air punches to his midsection.

Joseph laughed. "Yeah, you know me pretty well. Hey, any chance you could get me a sparring partner for later tonight?"

Lenny said, "If you didn't make those fools look so bad, it would be a lot easier for me to set you up. Let me think … Joey's gotta comer he's been working hard. The kid looks like a real talent. He's a heavyweight, though. Those big guys are the only ones that will get in the ring with you these days. I'll try to set it up for eight tonight. But you better bring your A game. The kid's a real stud."

Joseph laughed. "I'll be ready. You got time to hold the bag for me?"

"For sure. But keep your damn feet on the ground unless you give me a heads-up. I'm too old for that fancy shit."

Four hours later Joseph and his three guests watched the female assistant pro walk away from them on the driving range. One of the men said, "I have to say, that lesson was way more fun than I've ever had on a golf course."

Joseph said, "I thought you guys would get along pretty well with Tess. She really knows her stuff. Come on, let's see if you guys were paying attention to her golf tips or to her other fine features." Joseph raised his eyebrows twice. The guys laughed, but their eyes swung right back to Tess as she walked down the line.

The three gentlemen on the range with Joseph were a team of managers brought in by a private equity group to run a large fabrication business that the equity group had purchased a few years before. Joseph had arranged a similar outing with them when he replaced the company's liability, property, and workers compensation insurance a year before. It was a big sale. The annual renewal of their policies included an audit that created an increase in premiums. He figured that he'd be able to smooth over the surprise those guys were about to receive by hosting them at the Olympic Golf Club. Joseph was a member of the club, and the day he had planned for them was off to a good start, with Tess's help. The three executives still had their eyes on her backside.

Joseph thought that the golf game and dinner should be enough to secure the contract for another year and a nice commission check for his efforts. Easy money. Anyone who was invited to walk the hallowed grounds of the exclusive Olympic Club and dine in the elite, members-only Chophouse would fall in line. They'd pay the higher premiums and love every minute, because at the end of the day, it wasn't their money.

After dinner in The Chophouse Joseph said, "Let me thank you guys again for spending the day with me. It's been great. I wanted to give you a heads-up about the results of the audit. There will be a bill from last year, and your premiums will be higher this year because of the great year you had. It's no problem. Just a result of how successful you are."

The three men fell over one another trying to speak first. One of them blurted, "No, no, it's us that want to thank you. It's even better than last year. Thank you, Joseph." The three executives raised their glass to salute him.

Joseph said, "That's nice to hear. I appreciate your business. I say we set this up again next year. Maybe I'll have another surprise waiting on the range for you." He raised his eyebrows again. The men all laughed. "But that's it for me tonight, gentlemen. I have to meet some people a little later. You guys stay here as long as you like. I'll keep the tab open and tell them you're my guests. They'll let you have the run of this place." Joseph stood, shook hands all around, and left the room.

As he drove away from the club, he called the boxing gym. "Hi, this is Joseph. Did Lenny get me a sparring partner for tonight?"

"Yeah, it's all set up."

The sparring session wasn't much of a match; Joseph didn't even count it as a workout. The young stud didn't answer the bell for the start of round two.

The third bedroom in Joseph's northside condo had been transformed into a workout room where Joseph finished a forty-five-minute kettlebell routine in thirty-nine minutes. He blended a protein shake, drank half of it, and hit the shower. The National's Boxer album was playing in the background while he finished the shake and messed around on his laptop. He got bored quickly, so he turned in for the night.

The last few thoughts of the night flowed through his mind. He wanted to search for a report on his work from the night before, but would never leave a trail on his computer. I wonder what I'll see in the Sunday paper? I'm glad I didn't have to deal with the girl. She was probably expecting her morning wood when she got an even bigger surprise. I'll hit the weights after my run tomorrow morning, then see what blows into the coffee shop at ten. I'd say there's an eighty percent chance the pretty girl shows. Sixty-five percent chance she comes alone. Those are pretty good odds. This one seemed different. I hope she shows.

Chapter Three

⟫⟩◇◇◇⟨⟪

THE NEXT MORNING JOSEPH WAITED IN THE COFFEE SHOP. THE FRONT wall of the shop was floor-to-ceiling windows that looked out on the nearly deserted Sunday morning street. He noticed an orphan newspaper on one of the small coffee tables and moved closer to have a look. The front page detailed his work from two nights before. There was no mention of the man's Saudi ties or his history of building terrorist bombs. The dead man, the story said, was in bed with his mistress. *There'd be no sympathy for that dude.* He twisted his wrist. It was 10:04. *Maybe I was wr—*

She walked across the street toward the coffee shop. Her hair looked lighter in the daylight. It was pulled back in a ponytail. She wore tan, casual slacks and flat white tennis shoes. Her longs legs accentuated her graceful, athletic gait. She had a slim waist and a nice rack restrained by a simple cream-colored, short-sleeved tee shirt, which was cut just above the top of her slacks. *Mercy!*

She walked through the door and spotted him right away. She smiled. *What a true knockout, man oh man,* Joseph said to himself.

Joseph waved her over and said, "Good morning. I've been thinking about you all weekend, and I don't even know your name.

She smiled again, stepped closer, offered her hand, and said, "Hi. I'm Claire McKinley. It's nice to meet you, Joseph Johnson."

"I can't believe you're here. This makes my day."

Claire said, "You have no idea. I can't believe I'm here either.

Her voice was a little lower than he had expected for such a feminine girl. "Yet here we are." Joseph flashed a smile. "Let me get us some coffee. Grab a table."

⋖◦⋗

He looks so different from anyone I've known, Claire thought. *He looks really young, but at the same time older. I might as well get straight to the point.* "So … how old are you?"

"I'm twenty-five. I know, I'm an old man, and I don't really look like a student."

"No, no, I was just curious. You do seem more mature than the students I know."

"I joined the marines right out of high school. I served my four years and then started working for the insurance brokerage firm where I work now. It turned out to be a good move for me. I really like my job."

His confidence showed in every word he said. *I should be suspicious of his charm.*

He said, "Now you know my life story. What's yours? It looks like you have some very good friends."

"Those girls you saw me with the other night are my roommates and sorority sisters. I will graduate in a few weeks. My parents want me to take a year off, then come back to Stanford to get my law degree."

"I like the 'take a year off' part."

"I know. My parents went to school here, and my father is a partner in a law firm down in LA. They just want what's best for me."

⋖◦⋗

Those emerald eyes of hers are amazing, Joseph thought. *I have to give it a try.* He put his hand on top of her hand and smiled when he looked into her eyes. *I'll be able to tell in an instant if she wants to take the next step. If she turns her hand over and squeezes mine, we'll be in between my sheets, giggling and whispering sweet nothings to each other in less than an hour.*

⋖◦⋗

28

Out of the blue and in mid-conversation he put his hand on mine. *I wanted him to touch me. I wanted to touch him.* I turned my hand over and cupped his. *His hand felt as if it belonged there. I felt the same as I did when he kissed me in the bar.*

I asked, "Is that your R8 Spider out there?

"Yes, it is. How do you know that car?"

"My dad is a car nut. He loves German engineering. That Audi is one of his favorites."

He said, "Do you want to go for a ride? I could give you a tour of my condo in the city."

I squeezed his hand a little tighter and said, "Thank you. But I'm not ready for that tour yet. Let's meet back here in a week and go for a run together."

"Sure. Can I see you before then?"

"Not this week. I have to stay focused on school, and I already have things on my calendar for Friday and Saturday."

"No problem. Let's at least get out of here and go for a walk around campus. It's nice out, and I've always wanted to get an insider's tour of the Stanford campus."

"That, Joseph Johnson, is a fabulous idea. We can take our coffee with us."

He pulled out my chair and opened the door for me. "This way, my new friend Claire McKinley."

Chapter Four

⟫⟫⟩◆◇◆⟨⟪⟪

A COUPLE OF WEEKS LATER JOSEPH HELD THE DOOR OPEN FOR CLAIRE as they walked into Sundance Steakhouse. The maître d' recognized Joseph right away, then said, "Good evening, Mr. Johnson. I was pleased to see your name on the reservation list for tonight. Please follow me."

Joseph and Claire followed the man past a long, darkly stained, traditional hardwood bar to the back of the restaurant, where he seated them at a small, candlelit table with a white table cloth.

They settled into their seats. Claire said, "This place is really nice. It seems they know you well. Is this where you take all the girls on the third date?"

"Very funny. I've only been here on business. Those high-tech guys say this is the best steakhouse in Palo Alto. And the reason we're here is to celebrate your last final. How did it go?"

"No problem. I was prepared. But it's nice to get all that behind me. Thank you for setting this up. I've been looking forward to spending more time with you."

"That's good to hear. I figured you'd want to celebrate with your friends. You know, doing shots and staying up all night."

"I've done all that and had fun along the way, but I would rather be here." She smiled. "I have something I want to ask you. It may seem a little weird, but here goes. Do you have any plans a week from today?"

"Not until later in the afternoon. I need to get on a plane and go on that business trip I told you about for a few days. Why, what's up?"

"My graduation ceremony is at noon, and I know it's kind of corny, but I was wondering if you would go with me."

"For sure I'll go with you. Thank you for asking. It will be a real privilege to witness Claire McKinley walk across the stage. My flight is at 6:30, so there should be plenty of time."

"There's one more thing … . My parents will be there, and it's assigned seating. The tickets I have are three in a row."

"Do you mean I would get to meet the famous Mr. McKinley and what I am sure is the very lovely Mrs. McKinley? I would be honored to be in their presence. Are you sure they're ready to meet me?"

"I'm sure they're not ready, but I'm certain that you will sweep them off their feet like you have me."

Wow. I wasn't ready for that proclamation. I better come up with something good. I better decide right now what to do. Now is the time to either go all in or let her go. Let her go back to the clean world where people like me don't belong. Keep her away from my world, where life has no value. She is too special for my world. If I don't let her go, I'll have to completely cut my family ties. I've proven that I can make it on my own in the real world. I want to be honest with her, but I haven't even kissed her, and I'm considering changing my life. That doesn't make sense. I need to let her go.

Joseph took Claire's hand and gave her his best serious look. He held her hand and her gaze and said, "I think I'm the one on the other side of the broom getting swept away here. We barely know each other, but I think about you all the time."

Claire smiled and put her other hand on top of his. *Man oh man, she is so beautiful.*

The waitress barged in and said, "Are you two lovebirds ready to hear the specials?" as she placed the menus on the table.

—◦◦◦—

By the end of dinner Joseph and Claire sat side by side with their hands all over each other. They could have been sitting in the same chair. A disturbance suddenly broke out near the front, by the bar. Three young men were acting a little too rowdy for the restaurant's fine dining atmosphere. Claire recognized them.

She was flustered by the situation. "I need to tell you something," she said quickly. "Before I met you, I dated another guy for two years. I broke it off with him the day before we met for coffee that first time. He's not happy. A few days ago, he made a scene on campus when I walked away from him. He's here now with two of his friends at the bar. Jenn must have told her boyfriend about our plans for tonight. He's Hugh's best friend, and he's here, too."

"That's no problem, Claire. We can take care of ourselves." He smiled as if he had everything under control. "We're going to settle up with our waitress and walk right past those boys. Don't worry about it. What did you think about the wine? It's from Paso Robles. They're making some fantastic wines down there."

Claire thought, *Maybe I should just leave now with them. Those guys are used to getting their way. They think they're tough guys, and there are three of them. I know they've beaten up people. They look drunk, and Hugh gets really mean when he's drunk.*

The waitress brought the bill. Joseph signed it and thanked her as if he didn't have a care in the world. Hugh and his friends had become much louder at the bar.

Claire said, "Do you think we should go out the back?"

Joseph grinned. "No. We're going to walk right past them and out the front door. Don't worry. I have this. Just stay by me."

There wasn't much space between the bar and the people sitting around tables. Joseph and Claire approached Hugh and his friends. Hugh stepped in front of them. One of his friends shifted around to the side.

Hugh glared directly at Joseph, but said to Claire, "So this is the reason you haven't returned my calls."

Joseph said, "Look, we've all had plenty to drink tonight. I can see you have concerns about Claire. This isn't the time or place to sort things out." He took a threatening half step toward Hugh. "We're going to walk out of here, and I'm going to drop her off at her apartment, where Jenn is waiting for her. You guys carry on with your evening." He gave Hugh his business card and said, "If you want to talk with me, just call. I'll meet you anytime, anywhere. I'll be waiting."

Joseph guided Claire past Hugh and his friends.

He gave Claire the keys to the R8 and said, "If they follow us, get in my car and leave. I'll take care of this."

Joseph and Claire walked across the street to where they had parked. No one followed them. When Joseph pulled away, Claire said, "I'm sorry about that. I never meant to get you involved with any of this. You handled it so well. I wasn't sure what those guys were going to do. I've seen them do some really ugly things."

"It's no problem. I'm just glad I was with you." Joseph smiled, shifted from second to third, and said, "He seemed like a good guy. I can't blame him for wanting your attention."

Chapter Five

—◦◦◦—

JOSEPH WONDERED IF HE WOULD BE ABLE RECOGNIZE CLAIRE WHEN SHE walked across the stage. His seat was at the wrong end of Stanford's Maples Pavilion. *I'll need a pair of binoculars to see her face from back here.* The graduates were filing into the large basketball gymnasium. The students all looked exactly the same to him. He stood up to get a better look, then realized he was blocking the people's view sitting on the bleachers behind him.

He saw Claire's parents working their way down the row to their seats. *Well, here we go.* There was no question the woman was Claire's mother. She looked just like Claire and way too young to have a child graduating from college. Her dad was a fit man who looked very distinguished. Mrs. McKinley led the way with her head down, trying not to step on anyone's toes as she walked his way. Joseph turned around to apologize to the people behind him before he caught Mrs. McKinley's eye. He reached for her hand to help her keep her balance as she stepped between the feet of people sitting in the row next to them. She accepted his hand and smiled. Joseph said, "You must be Claire's mother." Still holding her hand, he said, "It's nice to meet you. I'm her friend Joseph."

Mrs. McKinley smiled again and said, "Nice to meet you. Claire mentioned you would be here. Please call me Amy. This is James. James, this is the boy Claire told us about—Joseph." James gave Joseph a perfunctory nod.

The three of them sat down at the same time. The mass of students on the floor below them had found their seats. All Joseph and the McKinley's could see were the tops of hundreds of gray, square hats with red tassels hanging off to one side. Amy said, "Sorry we're late. We weren't prepared for the parking issues they're having out there. Which one is she?" Mrs. McKinley craned her neck, trying to find her daughter in the sea of graduates.

Joseph pointed randomly at the mob and said, "Right there, see her? She's the cute one." Claire's mom squinted in that direction, then realized that Joseph was joking. She slapped his shoulder, laughing. James managed to crack a smile. Amy gave up her futile search and turned her attention to Joseph. "Claire tells me you are a successful insurance broker. How did you get into that line of work?" James kept looking straight ahead, probably listening, but not wanting to look interested.

"I joined the marines right out of high school, and after my four years of service, I went to work at Jensen & Jensen because they were willing to hire a young man without a college degree. The firm has been good to me, and I really enjoy what I do."

"Do you plan on going to college to get your degree?"

"Originally, my plan was to take advantage of the GI Bill, but I've been learning on the job, as they say, and it has been working out pretty well. Before the ceremony starts, I want to take a minute to tell both of you something." He waited for James to look his way. "Your daughter is an amazing young woman. I know you love her and want what's best for her. I want you to know that I am continually amazed by Claire and feel fortunate to be her friend. I'm honored to have this chance to meet you and be with you today."

James nodded his way, and Amy said, "Well, that's about the sweetest thing I've ever heard. Did you rehearse that?"

"No. I wasn't sure what I would say. I just knew I wanted to say something nice about Claire."

"Claire tells me that you won't be able to join us for dinner after the ceremony. "No, unfortunately I've had a business trip planned for weeks, and I can't put it off."

Chapter Six

⟢⟡⟡⟡⟢

T HE NEXT DAY, JAMES MCKINLEY HAD JUST PUSHED THE CRUISE CON-
trol button on his Mercedes AMG-S Class. He settled back in his seat
while his favorite playlist was tuned in perfectly for the five-hour drive back
to Pasadena after Claire's graduation ceremony and celebration.

Amy turned the music off and said, "What do you think about Claire's
new friend?"

James said, "Which one?"

"Joseph, her new boyfriend!"

"He seemed all right. He must really like Claire to sit through a two-hour
ceremony like that and then wait for her with flowers in hand."

"I don't know. He seemed a little too cool. We don't know one thing
about his family. Does he seem ethnic?

"I don't even know what that means. He can't be all bad if he drives an
R8."

"Well, I have no idea what *that* means. The Hahn's were especially distant
at the dinner party. I'm sure they are furious at us because Claire broke it off
with Hugh. What was Claire thinking? Hugh is mad about her. He's from
such a nice family. Why would she want to give that up? It doesn't make
sense. This Joseph fellow hasn't even gone to college, and he has no plans
to get an education. How is he going to support her?"

James said, "It sounds like he's doing very well."

"Yes, but how do we know that? That's what he told Claire. She thinks
his family is from the East Coast somewhere, and she doesn't even know

where. I can just see them running back to his family, and then we'll never get to see our grandchildren. James, you have to do something about this."

"About what? They barely know each other, and you already have them living in Manhattan, married, with children."

"You have to find out who this guy is. It's early in their relationship. If there are skeletons in his closet, Claire should know about them now. Promise me you'll put one of your investigators on it."

"Okay, dear. I'll figure something out."

"Promise?"

"Yes, dear. You know I always do everything you say." James turned the music back on.

Chapter Seven

⟶∗✦∗⟵

THE NEXT DAY JOSEPH WALKED OUT THE FRONT DOOR OF THE FOUR Seasons hotel in Buenos Aires, Argentina, into the crisp morning air. The front entrance of the hotel was high enough for him to see between multistory buildings and industrial-sized cranes in the distance to what looked like the ocean, except the water was a murky brown color. Not the picture postcard view he was hoping for. He was on his way to check out the Ricoleta Cemetery, where his research suggested it would be the best place to kill his next target. He had assumed the research for this hit was good, but he still came down a day early to get a feel for the place.

Keeping in character, he limped down the sidewalk on the narrow, tree-lined residential street. *This neighborhood is elegant.* There were small, very neat restaurants across the street. *I may have dinner at one of them tonight.* The Four Seasons hotel was just seven blocks from the cemetery, and the target's house was on the way there. He slowly walked past the house. *It really does look like a fortress. And there are outdoor cameras everywhere, just as the notes said.* His research described the security of the home as outdated. The key to the front door was also used to activate and deactivate the alarm system. The target was known as a hermit who had no domestic cleaning or meal services. He was a man in his forties, of average build.

Joseph walked on, and a block later he noticed a man that fit the target's description crossing the street carrying a grocery bag. Joseph followed him and noted his movements and mannerisms. If this was the target, he was an odd-looking man, mostly because of how he dressed. His pants and shirt were black, and he wore a dark gray sports coat even though it was very

39

warm. His black, narrow-brimmed fedora was pulled down on his head. The front brim of the hat almost rested on top of his black, wraparound sunglasses. His brisk pace contrasted with his short strides. His head was down, and his shoulders were hunched.

Joseph confirmed the target's identification by following him back to his house. He noticed how the target opened the gate and rushed past the gardener working in the yard. The target used a key to open the front door and enter his house.

Joseph felt lucky to have made the visual contact and turned his attention to the grand entrance of the Ricoleta Cemetery, which was just a couple of blocks away. He had read up on the cemetery during the long plane ride down and learned it was a famous international tourist attraction that was laid out like a small city. When he walked under the arched entrance, he noticed street signs on the lanes to help visitors locate political figures and celebrity's crypt. Large marble mausoleums that looked like small homes lined stone-paved lanes. Each of the tombs was unique in its size and architecture. *This place has an eerie beauty to it. Some of these towering mausoleums look big enough to have a large room or rooms inside.* He wound his way through the labyrinth of the cemetery's lanes and alleys, noting the unique sculptures and Masonic symbols at the entrances to many of the tombs. A few of the crypts were in complete disrepair. As the generations passed, absentee owners abandoned their family's property and heritage. The abandoned mausoleums could not be sold without the family's consent, and there were laws prohibiting eminent domain. The derelict properties gave the cemetery some additional mystery and character. *I can see how a person could spend hours in here walking around and taking in all the sights.* There were expert-led tourist groups around every corner.

There's the target's family crypt. Their mausoleum was large but unremarkable. *I'm sure they purchased the space from an Argentinian family decades ago.* He knew that the target came here every Monday at about this time of day. The research laid out a plan where he could wait in the alleyway across the lane behind one of the other tombs. When the target unlocked the door to his family's mausoleum, he would let him have it with two shots to the head. Their plan was an excellent one for killing the target, but it was a terrible plan for him. There were tourists everywhere, and it was broad daylight. He would have to come up with another plan.

Joseph strolled past the front entrance of his target's mausoleum to get a good look at the lock on the door. *Not an easy one, but if I had enough time … I could enter the crypt tonight, lock the door from the inside, and then wait for the target to walk into his own tomb. I'll take a few pictures for proof of death, and then disappear. Easy.* He walked on and looked around for cameras. There were a few. He'd have to figure out a way to get past them.

⸺◦◦⸺

That night Joseph had an excellent steak dinner and found a nightclub where a pair of professional tango dancers put on a sultry display of perfectly synchronized movements. *I wish Claire could be with me to see this dance. Maybe tango dance lessons are in our future. I bet she'd get a kick out of the suggestion.*

⸺◦◦⸺

At 4:00 a.m. the next morning Joseph picked the lock on the target's mausoleum and entered the tomb. Faint light from the moon seeped through two of the stained glass windows. The light allowed him to see the layout. Beyond a small foyer was a large room. The first thing that caught his eye was a long amber-colored bench on one side of the room. Above the bench were cluttered bookshelves made of the same tawny-colored stone. Across the room from the bench were two neatly upholstered high-backed brown leather armchairs. Behind the chairs were floor-to-ceiling bookshelves filled with hardback books. At the back of the room was a white marble mantle resting on amber columns five feet from the floor. On the mantle were three polished marble vases. *Those had to be the target's family urns.* On each side of the mantle were four bronze caskets. They looked brand new. *I would have expected decaying wooden coffins.*

An opulent chandelier hung from the ceiling. *This place looks like a nice den or study in someone's house.* The hazy glow of the soft light, the caskets, and the urns slightly disturbed him, even though he didn't believe in any of that religious mumbo jumbo.

Joseph felt good about his plan. He set his watch for 8:30 a.m., took off his jacket to use as a pillow, and lay down on the long bench. *The target should be coming for a visit around 9:00.* Thoughts raced through his mind as he lay there waiting.

According to the research notes, the target was a descendant of a German family. The target's grandfather escaped from Germany before the Allies rolled in, and he lived undetected in the same house where the target lived now. Twenty years before, the grandfather was in Switzerland when Interpol caught up with him. Nobody knew what happened to the target's parents or siblings, but they were all long gone.

The research detailed how the target had been funding neo-Nazi attacks against western targets in Europe. The authorities also discovered how this Nazi took his extreme hatred one step further by funding Islamic radical's terrorist actions.

How the target kept his wealth hidden all these years was unclear, but that would come to an end in a couple of hours when the "Last Nazi" would suddenly contract lead poisoning.

This one is a head-scratcher, he thought. *Why was my family sanctioned for this contract? I've accepted several contracts over the last three years to take out some very bad men. It has been good money, and since I created my second identity with the second condo, the risks have been low. This hit seems different, as though their new business plan is to accept higher-pay international kills while I take all the risk. After I get back, I'm going to have a talk with my uncle about this arrangement and about how to get out of the business. Then I'll get to see Claire again. Can't wait. She is something else. Maybe taking her on a vacation at an exotic place like this would be the best way to get close to her. Whatever it takes, whenever it happens, it will be worth the wait.*

The lock on the door made a sound—*click, click, click* —as its tumblers turned. Daylight poured into the room. I was tucked behind the doorway of the entrance to the big room. The amber color in the stone floor came to life when the bright, natural light touched its surface. It almost took my breath away; the translucent, amber stone floor looked three-dimensional. The target flipped a light switch, and that's when I did lose my breath. The entire room was covered with amber stone, gold flake, and mirrors. I had never been so surprised or so awestruck by such sheer beauty. I heard the target place something on the floor, take off his coat, and lay his keys on a table in the entryway. He should walk right past me, and he did.

"Freeze!" I said. He stopped. "Do not move a muscle." *I did not want to see his face or engage in a conversation.* "Nod your head if you understand." He nodded. "Take off your shirt." The target waited a couple of seconds, then began the process.

He said, "I'll double—I'll give you ten times what they're paying you."

"Shut up." *He knows why I'm here; he was expecting this. I didn't want to hear his voice. I didn't care about him.* He tossed his shirt onto the bench. "Now your shoes and pants." The target stood motionless. I waited, but he didn't move. I wanted to get his clothes off him now. It would be much easier for me later. "You need to understand that I'm here as a warning, and I'll lay this out for you nice and slow. The people who hired me have certain demands. One of the demands is they want you to walk home in your underwear. I don't know why, and I don't care, but one way or another those pants are coming off." The target processed the new information and toed the heel of his shoes off. He pushed his shoes to the side, loosened his belt, dropped his pants, and tossed them on top of his shirt.

"Good job. Now listen closely to the other demands." I lifted the end of the silencer to a few feet from the back of his head. The red-and-white circles of a target appeared. I squeezed the trigger. The target fell forward onto the floor. I snatched a plastic bag from a small metal trash can and quickly pulled the bag over his head. Then I tied it off around his neck. For some reason, I wanted to protect the beautiful floor from his blood.

I wanted to see what was going on outside the crypt. But, I had no reason to feel I was in danger. The muffled sound of the silenced gun couldn't penetrate the walls of this palace.

I sat down on one of the nice leather chairs to think a minute. The beauty of the room trumped the bad vibes of what I had done and the dead body lying across the room. *Where did this material come from? How did they construct this place?* I looked up at the ceiling. The entire room was made of the amber stone.

I had to refocus. The soft chair and the sights around me were peaceful and calming. *The target must have come here every week just to hang out for the very reason that I find it comforting.*

His clothes fit me pretty well. I gathered up my clothes and went back to the entryway, retrieved the briefcase that he had brought with him. *My clothes and disguise should fit in there.* Inside the briefcase was a hardback book, a homemade sandwich in a plastic bag, a can of Coke, and some cleaning supplies. *No wonder it looks so spotless in here. The dude took some pride in his refuge.*

My clothes were a tight fit, so I had to open the case again to shuffle my shoes around. *What's that?* Inside a pocket in the lining of the briefcase was a small key. *A key? What the …?* I went back into the amber room and scanned the walls and bookshelves. I spotted a lock in plain sight above the long bench. The key fit the lock. *STOP!* I screamed to myself. *That's too easy. It's a trap.* My thumb and index finger had a firm hold on the key, ready to turn it. *Step away. It would be stupid to turn that key. It was too easy. I'm not stupid.*

I looked around the room again, moved some of the books, slid one of the coffins forward, and dropped to my hands and knees to examine the base of the bench. *"Where would I hide something?"* I looked up, and there it was, screaming at me, wanting to be found. *The family urns.* I stood next to the urn that was in the middle of the mantle, went with my gut instinct, and pushed the vase over. A lock was there. The key fit. I covered my face and turned the key. There was a quick hydraulic swooshing sound below the long mantle. Three steps back were all I needed to see a wall of gold bars stacked from the floor up to the bottom of the mantle and extending the entire length of the mantle. I counted thirty bars high by thirty bars across. Nine hundred bars. There were five bars gone from the top row. I backed into the leather chair. My gaze on the gleaming gold bars turned into a blissful trance.

I googled *gold bar* on my phone. Each bar was four hundred ounces, or twenty-five pounds. Four hundred ounces times $1,800 an ounce equaled $720,000. The value of each bar was close to three-quarters of a million dollars! Nine hundred bars times $720,000 equaled $648,000,000!

Now what do I do? I slid one of the bars off the top row to hold the power of almost three-quarters of a million dollars in the palm of my hand. It was heavy. Heavy in weight, *heavy as a potential burden.* There was a Nazi swastika stamped on the top of the bar. I took out another bar and held it in my other hand. *I should take at least ten of these with me.* I slid one bar after another from the pile. *Wait. That would be two hundred and fifty pounds. I couldn't carry that much weight back to the hotel. I should at least take two.*

STOP! I screamed to myself again. *Don't be stupid. Leave the gold. You don't need it, and it's a dumb way to get caught. Don't be stupid.* When I lifted a bar to slide it back into place, I saw more bars stacked the same way behind the gold bars in the front. *Come on! How many rows are there? I don't care. Not right now anyway.* The vault closed with the same ease as when I had opened it. I replaced the urn and dropped into the soft leather chair. *Now what?*

I've been in here long enough. I need to come up with a good plan to get the gold out. But first I had to finish my job. I needed proof of death and needed to do something with the body if I ever wanted to come back here again.

<hr />

Joseph dragged the body to the entryway, where the walls and floor were made of ceramic tile and frame construction. He didn't want to give the viewer of the pictures any hint of the amber stone inside the mausoleum. He used some of the cleaning products to wipe the target's face clean and then propped him in the corner to take several pictures with his phone. He took a chance and opened one of the coffins. His hunch was correct. The coffin was just as clean and new on the inside as it was on the outside. Because the target's relatives had been cremated, Joseph assumed the coffins were empty. He lifted the dead body into the coffin, put the soiled cleaning supplies in there to give him some company, and closed the coffin. He slid the coffin back into place and walked around, admiring his work.

After he opened the door to the outside world, Joseph tucked his rubber gloves into his front pocket. He locked the door with one of the target's keys as he held the briefcase with his other hand. He used the same short steps and hunched shoulders that he noticed from the target the day before. He walked out of the cemetery and back to the target's house. Things went well, so he took a chance by going directly into the target's house. He waved at the gardener the same way he had seen the target wave. The key that opened the front door also deactivated the alarm. He found no evidence of life in the house as he went from room to room. The house was just like the crypt, exceptionally well decorated, clean, and tidy.

He sat down on one of the kitchen table chairs and lowered an open hand. He could still feel the weight of that gold bar pressing him down—pressing him where he didn't want to go. Then he opened the briefcase and looked at the two gold bars that he had taken. An uncontrollable urge to take the gold was too strong for him to fight. The power of it and the greed tricked him into rationalizing a reason to take the gold—*a stupid reason.* Sunlight that streamed through the kitchen window illuminated the bars. A sparkle from the gold caught Joseph's eye. *Now what?*

Chapter Eight

"HELLO. THIS IS REED JACKSON FROM THE AGENCY RETURNING YOUR call. What can I do for you, Mr. McKinley?

James McKinley replied, "Thank you, Mr. Jackson, for getting back to me so promptly. Your firm came highly recommended by our San Francisco office. I'm a partner in the law firm Fields, Busch, Hutton, and Hanssen in Los Angeles."

"Yes, I know the firm. We've done some work for you in the past."

"Mr. Jackson, I need your expertise for a personal matter. Our twenty-two-year-old daughter has recently begun a relationship with a young man that we met for the first time a few days ago. My wife and I are concerned and want to flush out any potential issues early in their relationship. I'm asking you to do a thorough investigation into this man and his family."

"We can get started right away. How deep do you want us to go?"

"Deep. You may have to allocate some of your resources to the East Coast. We believe his family lives there. I'll send your retainer now, and you can let me know whenever your expenses cross the ten thousand dollar threshold. I'll email you everything we know, which isn't much."

"Sounds good, Mr. McKinley. I'll be in touch."

Chapter Nine

JOSEPH UNWRAPPED A NEW BURNER PHONE, TOSSED THE WRAPPING INTO a garbage can, and sat down on a park bench. It had been a week since he came back from his Buenos Aires trip, and he had some extra time between appointments that afternoon. He punched in a phone number, let it ring twice and then hung up. He waited a minute, dialed the same number, let it ring four times and hung up. A few minutes later Joseph's phone rang. Joseph said, "Uncle Geno, it's Tony."

"Tony? It's been a while. The last time I saw you, you were an eighteen-year-old punk kid. You had just ratted on the Rossi family when the feds dragged you outta that courtroom. Now I hear you're a big shot livin' the sunny California life. Why are you callin' me? You gotta problem?"

Just hearing his squeaky voice took me back to my days on the streets.

He went on, "What can I do for you, big shot? You in some kinda trouble?"

Joseph said, "I have to talk to you about that last job and the info I just got on the next one. Those are way beyond our agreement and my expertise."

Geno said, "You did okay. You got a knack for this kinda work. Things have changed around here, and we have to change with them. We're all in this together, kid."

Joseph thought, *This is where I have to go for it."* Geno, we agreed after my dad went in that I would turn state's evidence against our enemies and then be out. That was your idea. You took Dad's place, and I got rid of all your enemies. I've helped you out with jobs in the U.S. over the years, and that's been good business for both of us. But, going to Buenos Aires last week and now you have another one for me in Europe already next week?

That's too much, Geno. I have the feds keeping tabs on me, and I have a regular job out here."

Geno said, "That's all true, but as I already told ya, things have changed here. The protection costs for your father at Souza have increased. I'm payin' a lotta money to keep him alive in there. Your mother is set up in that nice house, and I allowed your sister to have a way out. You know your sister should be takin' care of one of my soldiers, and you also know all that could change. We need you to stay engaged."

Joseph didn't respond. There had always been an unwritten rule: If one of the bosses went in, he and his family would be taken care of. *Geno was suggesting that his support would stop if I got out. Would he really do that?*

Geno said, "There's no getting out, Tony. Know why? You can't ever get out, 'cause guys like you make too much money for guys like me."

There was another period of silence. *I couldn't come up with a rebuttal. Silence was better than making a mistake.*

"Look, Tony, the paydays for these new hits are just too good. We have a contractor who's payin' us in advance with clean money. You're gonna have to figure this out, 'cause they're gonna keep coming. You're paid very well, and that will continue. You will continue. Capisce?"

Don't say a word unless you have something to say. Let him open a door.

"Don't go screwin' up a good thing here. We'll slow down the pace. I know you want to spend some time with that pretty red-headed peach".

There it was. He's out in front of me.

"The Bruzzelli boys tell me she's about as ripe as they come."

You touch her and I'll use my skills on you.

"I just deposited your cut for that Nazi in your Swiss bank account. Your next job pays quite a bit more. That's some serious cash for a punk kid who use ta shine my shoes. Quit your whinin', take care of your family, and lap up every drop a that fine ripe peach."

Geno hung up.

I didn't see that coming. Those fuckers have been watching me, anticipating my move. Geno was smarter than I gave him credit for. He's got me by the balls. Claire is in play now. I messed up. I should have listened to my old man. He told me not to trust Geno. He told me he could do the hard time on his own. Geno's squeaky voice reminded me of the promises he made to me. It reminded me of what Dad said, and it took me back to my life on the streets.

I can't imagine living that life now. That all seemed like a long time ago. Thinking of those days felt like an old movie that I had watched years ago, a movie that I barely remember. But this wasn't an old movie. I turned into a ruthless gangster a second after I witnessed Geno put a bullet in a man's head and then drag a young girl into the back room. I was sixteen years old, and that girl was my cousin. Her older brother was tied to a chair. The Bruzzelli crew surrounded us. Sean was my friend, and he was forced to listen to the sounds of his sister's terror while some random dude who didn't do what he was told bled out on the wood plank floor. The Bruzzelli crew waited for me to make a move, a move that would have opened the door to their psycho-pathic violence.

Sean was eighteen years old. He had said no to Geno, because he wanted to get out and go to college. Looking back now, it was probably never about college. Geno had his eye on Sean's pretty sister, and he created a way to justify his actions. That incident changed my life. I changed from a boy getting in trouble to a man who had witnessed the brutal side of street life that I would come to know well.

Sean and his sister were from my mother's side of the family. They were Irish, and they had no protection. I was half Irish. With Dad as the head of the family, we were protected. But with Dad in Souza, Mama and Isla were vulnerable.

My Dad was in Souza for killing my grandpa, his father. None of it made sense. He didn't even fight the charge or sentence. I loved him. I idolized him. He pulled me forward; he always led me down the right path. Then it all changed. How could that happen?

I can't get out. I'll have to keep feeding the beast. But if I see one of those Bruzzelli men around Claire, they will be gone. This will have to be my life going forward unless I figure a way out.

I'd have to take them all out. Three bosses and at least twelve captains, all at the same time. Not possible. I'd have to get them all at the same place. Not possible. I could do the bosses in one day, then the captains the next day. Not possible. Geno's got me by the balls.

I'll bide my time, do the next hit, keep an eye out for the Bruzzelli thugs, and protect Claire.

Chapter Ten

L ATER THAT SAME DAY, REED JACKSON CALLED JAMES MCKINLEY. "GOOD afternoon, Mr. McKinley. I wanted to touch base with you regarding your daughter's friend Joseph Johnson. I'll send the complete report of what we have so far, but I wanted to give you the highlights on the phone."

"Okay. Go ahead."

"Everything Claire has told you about Joseph has checked out. He is very successful at what he does. He's the top salesman in the firm. He owns a luxury condo in one the hottest real estate projects in San Francisco. He was in the U.S. Marine Corps and was part of their elite Raider special forces unit. The unit is similar to the SEALS unit within the U.S. Navy. He was a decorated hero who had the respect of the soldiers in his unit and his commanding officers. All indications are, Joseph Johnson is an exceptional young man. He has an arrangement with a café in town to feed homeless men on a regular basis. He attends a veteran's support group, where he takes the lead, supporting vets who are in trouble or need help. He rarely drinks alcohol, and he works out at a boxing club where he's considered the toughest man in the club.

"I've been in this business for over fifteen years, and when you dig into anyone's life like we have his, you always find something. It's when a person thinks that no one is watching, that's when you find out what kind of person they are. I have to admit that I have a soft spot for someone who went through elite training and then distinguished himself with great valor on the battlefield like he has. But to put a twenty-five-year-old man under a magnifying glass like we have him, it's amazing that we haven't found one chink in his armor.

"That said, we have not been able to find one piece of information about him before he joined the Marine Corps and nothing about his family."

Mr. McKinley said, "I'm sure you have exhausted the list of your contacts."

"Yes, we have. This is very unusual. I have strong contacts in the FBI and the CIA, and they were no help."

"That's interesting. What's your gut feeling?"

"The only other time I've run into this was with a witness protection situation. But this guy is so young. He would have had to go into the program when he was eighteen years old. That would be very unusual."

"Is that in your report?"

"No, sir. That is pure speculation."

"Good. I don't want to get my wife upset."

"We'll keep after it and figure it out. Just give us some more time. I have a couple of my men following him. That may give us some direction. Before I let you go, I wanted to add that he seems to be a real gentleman. From what we have witnessed, he is very respectful toward your daughter."

"That's good to hear. Let's end our conversation there."

Chapter Eleven

I DOWNSHIFTED THE R8 AND CAME TO A SLOW STOP IN FRONT OF CLAIRE'S apartment. She was on the balcony with two of her friends. I'm sure they wanted to get a good look at me. It's the way. *I'll give them a show.*

I pretended that I didn't see them, jumped out of the car, and hustled around the front of the car onto the apartment's front walkway. I stopped and looked up at the three girls on the small balcony. "Have you girls seen my beautiful girlfriend?" The girls giggled. "Claire, is that you? Are you ready for our adventure?"

"Hi, Joseph. I'll be right down."

I could tell by her big smile that I had made her happy. I yelled up to her friends on the balcony, "If we had more room, you two could come with us."

One of the girls yelled back, "Have a good time. Maybe we'll see you when you get back."

Claire bounced down the steps. *My beautiful reward. What a sight.* I reached for her hand as she approached with her dazzling smile. "Hi, baby. You look fabulous. Are you ready to taste some wine?"

Claire had arranged this daytrip down to Paso Robles to visit a few wineries. We had been spending more and more time together, but this was the first time we'd planned a whole day together. I had offered to book a night in one of the quaint boutique hotels, but Claire wasn't game. Claire had the whole day planned. *I'll be a good boy and make it fun for her.*

She said, "I am," and she stepped in for a kiss. *That was nice, but I wasn't sure if that was meant for me or for her friends watching.* She waved to her friends as we pulled away.

The top was down, and her hair was flying all over the place. She dug something out of her purse and twisted it in her hair. Then she smiled at me. *I had to admit that I was falling for her.*

Claire glanced down at her phone and said, "Traffic looks light. We should be right on time for our first tasting.

I said, "Remind me again what our plans are for today."

Claire smiled at me. "Well, I'm glad you asked. We have an eleven o'clock tasting at Niner Wine Estates. They have a grove of large, mature oak trees that form a heart on the hillside of their estate. Our private wine tasting is right in the middle of those trees. After the tasting we'll have lunch at their award-winning restaurant."

She scrolled down on her phone and said, "Then we have a hosted tour in the vineyards before a private tasting on the patio of the Tobin Family Winery. According to the reviews I read, the place is beautiful, and they're making some world-class wines. Then, if we have time, we could visit a really cool small operation, Hoage Vineyards. Terry Hoage was a professional football player. He and his wife have settled in Paso and have been creating some spectacular wines. Or we could leave early and take the long way home for a dinner in Monterey."

"That all sounds really good. Thanks for putting all this together."

We pulled up at a stoplight before the exit on to the 101. I flipped the toggle switch that closed the convertible top. The top latched just as the light turned green. The engine behind us growled as we picked up speed on the ramp. There wasn't much traffic when I eased into one of the middle lanes. I reached for Claire's hand. I felt that she was waiting. *It was a good feeling. Holding hands with her meant something.*

She squeezed my hand, and we locked gazes with big smiles.

———❊———

Men from The Agency followed Joseph and Claire. One of the men, Cochise, called his boss, Reed Jackson. "We're on them, boss. Geronimo is in front of them, and I'm behind. Plus the GPS we attached to his Audi is working fine."

Reed Jackson said, "Okay, let me know when you figure out what they're up to."

———⋖○⋗———

A few hours later, Cochise called Jackson. "Boss, I thought I better let you know they finished their lunch at Niner, and it looks like they're heading up to the Tobin compound."

Jackson said, "Are you kidding me? What are the odds of that? Keep your eyes on them."

———⋖○⋗———

"They're walking around the Tobin Winery like regular tourists," Cochise said to Jackson.

"Boss, Max is here. He stopped Joseph when he walked past him. They are talking. I'm far away, but it looks like they're old friends, hugging and laughing. Joseph introduced Max to Claire."

Jackson said, "Max doesn't have any white friends on this side of the Atlantic. You have to get closer and see what's going on there."

Cochise walked toward the group when Armando and Anna pulled up in Juan's old pickup, with Mandy in the bed of the truck. "Max, Joseph, and Claire jumped into the back of Juan's old pickup with Mandy. Armando, Anna, and baby Bella are in the front. It looks like they're heading down that dirt road to the lake."

"No way. You better double time it down there and keep your eyes on him."

"I'm on it."

Chapter Twelve

JACKSON CALLED JAMES MCKINLEY FROM HIS OFFICE THE NEXT DAY. "Sorry to call you on a Sunday, Mr. McKinley, but we had a fortunate breakthrough yesterday that I wanted to report right away."

"Good. Go ahead."

"My men followed Claire and Joseph down to Paso Robles yesterday. They had a day of wine tasting. At one of the wineries, a young man who is a friend of mine and I know well recognized and approached Joseph. I was able to talk with my friend later, and it turns out that Joseph Johnson grew up in Boston, where he went to a Catholic school with my friend. Joseph's name back then was Tony Cairo.

"I've been able to do some limited research. It looks like his family has mob connections in the Boston area. I'll get back to my contacts at the FBI with this new information tomorrow."

"So, it looks like your hunch may have been correct. Maybe Joseph is in the witness protection program."

"That does seem to be where this is leading. I'll be able to dig deep tomorrow and get back to you."

"That all sounds good, Mr. Jackson. Thank you. I'm glad you called me today."

Chapter Thirteen

I WALKED FIFTY FEET BEHIND THEM. THE TARGET LOOKED WEALTHY. HIS bride was probably a third his age. There were two bodyguards with them. The guards were intentionally visible, a rude spectacle for the tourist-filled streets of Paris. It was like they wanted to draw attention to themselves, spoiling for a confrontation. The bodyguards looked exceptionally fit and professional. *They must be fresh out of the military, or maybe they were GRU, and the target was more connected than I had figured. If they were GRU, there had to be more soldiers around. Probably behind me, watching me.*

I veered off the sidewalk, walked between some outdoor tables, and looked at a menu at the entrance of a small cafe. I used the window's reflective glass to monitor what passed behind me. Nothing. Then I saw myself in my disguise and didn't recognize myself. *Who am I?* Not the time to deliberate that question. *Focus! Pay attention!*

There was no activity of interest in the reflection. I turned and engaged the hostess so I could get a better view of the scene. I spotted a guy across the street following my target. *I was right. Had to be GRU.* I pulled a map out of my back pocket and looked up at the street sign as I walked back into the natural flow of traffic on the sidewalk. The target couple hadn't gone far. I kept walking. They walked down steps that were on the side of one of the Seine River bridges. I walked past the steps and on to the bridge. There were hundreds of tourists milling around on both sides of the bridge, peering at the sights of Paris. I slipped into a spot between sightseers and watched the couple, their four bodyguards, and some other tourists embark on one of the dinner river cruise boats. *I have to get on that boat.*

61

Using my phone to google the business name displayed on the side of the cruise boat, I found an online reservation option. *Table for one. Yes, I'm in.* I had a few minutes to spare. I took some touristy-looking pictures with my phone. It would have been better if I were part of a group. They'd be looking for someone who was alone. No choice. *Just don't call attention to yourself. Play it cool.*

I boarded the boat. *Do not look for them. Do not look at them.* The Russian bodyguards were professionals. They would spot me in an instant. A young man dressed as a waiter led me to the back of the boat, where he showed me my place for dinner. It was on one side of the boat, close to the bar. My seat was bar-height and faced out, toward the city. There were other singles on both sides of me. *I probably walked right past the couple to get back here.* I took a few pictures with my phone, then looked down at the tourist map. That same young man brought me an unexpected glass of white wine.

I kept my focus outside the boat when we started our cruise and acted like a typical tourist taking pictures, but I had my phone in video mode, reversed. As I pretended to take pictures, I recorded what was going on behind me. The video showed them sitting at a table of four, with the other two bodyguards right behind me. *Play it cool.*

Dinnertime came and went. The waiter cleared my place setting. There was some kind of activity behind me. I turned around slightly to accept another glass of wine and saw the couple walking my way. Most of the crowd were walking with them to the back of the boat, probably to have an after-dinner drink. The back of the boat was a better place for seeing the sights. We passed the fire-ravaged Notre Dame Cathedral. I heard some oohs and ahs.

The couple stood right behind me. I heard them talking, but I couldn't understand a word they said. I did hear the words *Auvers* and *Van Gough* several times. Van Gough was a famous painter, but what was Auvers? I had my phone on video again to record the Notre Dame ruins. The video would pick up their Russian conversation, and I would translate their words later tonight. The rest of the cruise was subdued. The sights of Paris from the cruise boat were spectacular. *I wished Claire was with me and we were on a normal vacation. This is all pretty cool.*

There was time to take in the sights as I thought about why I was here. Why I was on this boat. I wanted to readdress the question *Who am I?*

I had agreed to help my family. The money was good. This Russian guy must be a politician or one of the Russian oligarchs. This hit was a dangerous one. I bet the mission had been turned down by smarter people than Geno. There was limited research for me this time. The only things I knew: *The couple was on their honeymoon, and they're staying at the Paris Ritz. My instructions were to take out the groom but leave the bride alone. The payday for this one was quite a bit more than usual, but so were the risks. And I don't even need the money.*

The next day my driver stopped right in the middle of the small village of Auvers. The streets were empty. I gave him an extra twenty euros and asked, "This place is deserted. Where is everyone?"

"Today is Victory in Europe Day. It's a national holiday. Everything will be closed today. "

"But I wanted to visit the Van Gough spots."

The driver pointed across the street and said, "Right there is the house he lived in. It looks like it's open."

"Okay, thanks. I'll meet you back here at two."

Earlier that morning I had walked a few blocks to the Paris Opera House and hired an English-speaking driver out of the taxi line to drive me thirty-five miles north of Paris to Auvers.

Based on the words I had heard from the honeymooners last night on the dinner cruise, I knew they had plans to walk around Auvers and see where Van Gough lived, where he spent time with the doctor who treated him, and where he painted some of his most famous works. I didn't know what day they planned to go there, but that day's plan for me was to do some recon and pick out a place in the small town where I could take out the Russian. I had changed my disguise to that of an old man with gray hair and a flat tweed cap on my head. Thick, black-framed glasses, a cane, and a cardigan sweater rounded out my look for the day.

I paid the cashier in the gift shop ten euros to walk up the narrow staircase of the old house where Van Gough had rented a room. I guess I was curious to see the bedroom where he had died. *Where the demons in his head and his days on this earth ended. I would have no opportunity to do the hit there. Not enough room.* The bedroom was eerily small.

I was the only customer in the downstairs gift shop. The cashier, who spoke English well enough to suggested I walk a few blocks down the street to the doctor's house and then walk back this way, go past the shop and up the hill to the Church of Auvers. "Both of the sites are closed today," she told me, "but they're popular stops when the tourists are in town."

What am I going to do here until 2:00? I asked her. "Where's a coffee shop or café?"

"There's nothing open today. I'm surprised they made me open."

I let her keep the few euros of change from the little book I bought and walked back out to the street. The doctor's house was just a few blocks away. The street was narrow, and the houses were close to street. *Not enough room here. The four bodyguards will be with them, and I have no help. I don't even have a car. I have to rely on a cab driver for my getaway. Way too much risk here.*

There was nothing unique about the doctor's house. I walked up the driveway to the small backyard, which had a steep incline leading to the rest of the property. The back slope was covered with thick brush. *Nothing good here.* I'd never get a shot off and escape, even with the silencer on the gun. The only good thing was that I didn't see any cameras here or at the gift shop.

I headed back toward the gift shop on the other side of the street so I could get a better view of the layout. *There they are!* A large black SUV dropped the five of them off in front of the Van Gough home/gift shop. Two of the bodyguards went in first, followed by the couple. One bodyguard walked away and the other drove the SUV away. I shuffled along with my head down. *Glad I changed my disguise.*

I sat on a bench to think. *I bet they didn't know about the holiday either. I bet they'll pay the ten euros to look at the bedroom, and the cashier will give them the same suggestions she gave me.*

I tottered up the hill to the church a few blocks away. *The church was pretty cool; I had seen the famous painting "Church at Auvers."* The front doors were locked. I walked around to the back of the church. *Good. No cameras here either.* There was a back door. I easily picked the lock, walked into a small room on one side of the alter, and gazed into the large, empty nave. The church was filled with soft sunlight, which filtered through the stained-glass windows onto wooden pews, maybe thirty rows deep.

I thought, *I'll unlock the front doors. They might walk in here to check out this place. I'd be completely hidden in here. I could get a shot off and exit through the back door. If the shot wasn't there, I could just let it go and wait for a better opportunity.*

The front doors unlocked easily. I even left one of the doors open, inviting the target into the famous church and into his own funeral. If they were on my same schedule, they would be done looking at the doctor's house by now and heading this way. I called my cab driver. "Looks like I'll be finishing up here soon. Can you pick me up at the gift shop in twenty minutes?"

"Yeah, no problem. I'm just hanging out at a park."

"Good. See you soon."

I considered everything that could go wrong with this plan. *If the shot's not there, just walk away. Too many things could go wrong. I have to walk away from my uncle. He'll keep putting me out there until I get caught or killed, and he won't give one shit either way. I don't even need the money. I have my own life now. Claire. They'll never let me go.* I remembered my uncle's words. *"Guys like you can never get out because you make too much money for guys like me." Claire would be the first one they'd come for.*

Bright sunlight poured in when the front door of the church opened. Two bodyguards lumbered in. I had a perfect spot, tucked under a table in the sacristy, behind some robes hanging on a rack. With the sacristy's door open, I could see about two-thirds of the inside of the church. The guards walked up and down the aisles, checking under every pew. They looked behind the alter, and one of them glanced into the room where I was hiding. Then the guards left the church, and the couple came in. They were by themselves. *This is good.*

The young lady had a somber look on her face as she walked up the aisle. She picked out a pew and slid across the slick wooden seat. She leaned forward and knelt. Her eyes were closed as she clasped her hands. Her husband walked around looking at the stained glass windows. I leveled the gun on the brace of the table legs. The end of the silencer nosed through the hanging robes. A red-and-white target appear on the man's head. I squeezed the trigger. The man quietly collapsed onto the stone floor. The young lady remained in prayer, oblivious to what had happened behind her. I picked up the shell casing and eased out the back door. *The other two bodyguards had to be around here somewhere.* I wanted to run away, down the back alley, but I played it cool. I kept my head down and shuffled down the hill. I never saw a bad sight or heard a bad sound. *Keep it slow, play your part. They might be watching.*

The first few minutes in the backseat of my cab were intense. My heart raced, and I worried the SUV would show up behind us. After we turned on to the highway, my heart rate slowed. I couldn't believe it had gone that smoothly. *That was luck, dumb luck. Do not ever think it was anything else.*

The driver dropped me off at the Eiffel Tower. I told him, "I'm meeting my family here. We're going to go up to the top of the tower." I gave him another extra twenty euros and said, "*Merci beaucoup. Au revoir.*"

I was able to change my airline ticket, and I left Paris two days earlier than planned. When I got home, I parked the SUV in the south parking spot and took the south elevators up to the condo, where I shed my clothes and disguise. I opened and closed the secret panel from the closet into my dojo and went for the bookcase door; back to my other life. But I couldn't open that door; I wasn't ready to be that man. I plopped down on the floor, exhausted. I looked around the small room, noticed my killing weapons, and asked the question, *Who am I?*

It was four o'clock in the afternoon. I wanted to call the office. I wanted to call Claire. I wanted to see Claire, but I didn't move. I had to turn myself back on, back to me. I had to turn off the killer that I had been the last few days. Turn it off. Turn it on. I thought about the Russian who I had killed and I couldn't care less. *Why? Who am I? Am I a cold-blooded killer with no remorse? Or am I the nice guy who's falling for the beautiful girl. Am I capable of affection? Is it love, or is it lust? Shouldn't I feel a little bad for the guy, his new bride, or his family? Nothing.*

I googled the definition of psychopath on my phone. (1. Someone affected with a personality disorder marked by aggressive, violent, antisocial thought and behavior and a lack of remorse or empathy) *Hmm. The no remorse could be because of my time on the streets or the military training I went through. All that made me a killer, created a dead zone in my brain. Sniper training had taught me to hit the target, not a person. I had been trained to place the red-and-white target circles over the target's head. It was just a target. Hit the target. Take the kill shot from a thousand yards away and snuff out a man who deserved the bullet. He was just a target.*

I did feel a little regret. But if I hadn't pulled the trigger, someone else would have. The dude probably deserved what he got. Maybe I saved his young bride from years of abuse. I don't feel like I'm violent or aggressive. I care about Mama, Isla, and Claire. Is Claire just a conquest? Can I get the perfect girl?

I sat on the floor in my underwear and pondered those questions for a while. Then I stood to return to my other life. *Turn it off, turn it on.*

Chapter Fourteen

⊰◈◈◈⊱

COCHISE TO JACKSON: "HI, BOSS. I WAS ABLE TO GET INTO THE NORTH side garage of Joseph's condo. His Audi is here, parked right where it should be."

Jackson said, "So we're assuming that he dropped Claire off four days ago from their Paso Robles trip and he hasn't come out of his condo for four days? Something isn't adding up here."

"I know. His vehicle is still tagged. It hasn't moved. I wish we could just ask Claire. She's been carrying on as usual."

"I'm calling our friend Kent at the CIA back. I haven't told him about what we found out about Tony Cairo yet. There's more to this story. Keep your eyes open and stay in contact with Apache and Chirica. They're assigned to Claire."

Chapter Fifteen

JOSEPH WAS IN DISGUISE. HE SAT ON A PARK BENCH, ATE HIS LUNCH, AND watched Claire and her sorority sisters playing touch football. Claire and her friends had volunteered to play a touch football game against another sorority as a fundraiser for the local children's hospital. Joseph left Paris a few days earlier than originally planned and kept his travel plans to himself. He wanted to take the opportunity to let Claire carry on with her normal activities and at the same time keep an eye out for the Bruzzelli boys. Geno and his crew would have assumed that Joseph was still in Paris.

Claire was more athletic than the rest of the girls and at the same time more feminine. *What a sight. This is pretty cool, getting a chance to see Claire with her friends.*

Apache to Jackson: "Not much going on here, boss. The girls are playing football in the park. This is the kind of surveillance I don't mind doing one bit."

"Okay, keep your eyes open. Is Chirica set up?"

"Yes, sir, just like we drew up. He has a great spot on the edge of the timber where he can see the entire park. There are some kids skateboarding, some playing Frisbee, and a few families out for a stroll. There is an older, hippy-looking guy sitting by himself on a park bench. He's drinking a big soda and getting an eye full of the young ladies."

"Sounds good. Call if you see something interesting."

Even though it was hard to take his eyes off Claire, Joseph scanned the rest of the park. *Not a lot of activity.* That was when three cars showed up near the girls. The vehicles drove over the curb and stopped on the park lawn. A bunch of college boys swarmed out of the vehicles. Hugh was one of them. *This will be interesting.* One of the boys ran into the middle of the group of girls and took their football. He threw it to his friends, who had split up. They played keep-away with the girls. It looked as if it was all in good fun. Hugh made a beeline for Claire. She talked with him briefly, then tried to walk away. He grabbed her arm and jerked her back. Joseph stood, prepared to bolt across the field. Claire broke away and ran to the cluster of girls.

Wait a minute. Two men walked together on the bike path that bordered the park. *I know those guys. Vince and Albert Bruzzelli. They're not here on vacation.* They sat on a bench together, gawking at the girls. Joseph couldn't let that stand.

He limped toward the two men. *There's no way the Bruzzellis could recognize me. I'm going to make them pay.*

Joseph stepped in front of them and said, "What are you perverts doing here watching those girls? You don't belong here."

Albert said, "On your way, old man, before we lay you out."

Joseph threw his drink in Vince's face and then took off toward the edge of the park, where the timber and trails were. He limped along just fast enough to keep ahead of the two men chasing him.

———◦———

Chirica to Jackson: "The guy ran just fast enough to stay ahead of those two guys chasing him. When he got them into the woods, he beat the living shit out them. That guy has had some serious training, boss. He hit them in all the weak spots, could have easily killed them with his combination of punches and kicks. He was as quick and as strong as any man I've ever seen. Maybe fifteen seconds passed before they were out cold. Then he just left them there and limped back out of the timber, the same way he went in."

Jackson to Apache: "You got eyes on him?"

"Yeah, I have him. He's limping down the lane like nothing happened."

Jackson said, "Okay, Apache, you follow him. Chirica, you go have a look at the men he beat up. If they're still down, grab their wallets. Let's find out who they are. Then I want you to stay on Claire."

––––⊸◦⊶––––

I haven't had that much fun in a long time, Joseph thought. *Those guys will be in the hospital for weeks, and then they'll go home with their tail between their legs. Plus, there's no way they can put this on me. I'm still in Paris.* Joseph got into his SUV and drove away. *I wish Sean could have seen what I did to those two.*

––––⊸◦⊶––––

"Yeah, boss, I'm still on him. There's enough traffic clogging up the streets to keep up with him." Apache kept up the pace, but had to catch his breath before he spoke again. "But I'm running out of gas."

"Stay with him. You got his plate number?"

"Yeah." Apache had to sprint through an intersection and nearly got hit by a car. A few minutes later he said, "Boss, he's pulling into the south parking ramp of Joseph's building."

"Try to get in there."

After a minute Apache said, "He's gone. The garage door closed before I could get down the ramp."

"That's okay. Good job. We'll sort it out later."

––––⊸◦⊶––––

Later that day, Reed Jackson sat behind the small metal desk in his office, typing away on his computer. Standing around him was most of his crew. Cochise said, "You know, boss, you're gonna have to get a bigger office someday." Renegade said, "I've never been in here with more than two of us. This must be important."

Jackson kept typing as though he was alone in the room. The men stood at attention, knowing that their squad leader wasn't in the mood for anything but business.

Jackson finally stopped typing. He looked up at his men and said, "Gentlemen, I have a story for you. Earlier today, Apache and Chirica saw an old-looking hippie limp away from two men who were chasing him. He led them into the timber on the edge of the park and proceeded to beat the holy hell out of them. Chirica surmised that the hippie had some combat training. Apache double-timed it through the downtown streets and followed the guy to the south parking ramp of Joseph Johnson's condominium building.

Chirica lifted the beaten men's wallets, and after a little digging, we found out that they're from Naples, Italy, and have mob ties there and to Joseph's uncle back in Boston. More on that in a minute.

"A couple hours ago I got off the phone with our good friend Gorman Kent at the CIA, who you men know well and could be standing right here with us today." They nodded in agreement.

Jackson said, "Kent dug deep into the new information I gave him regarding Joseph Johnson, aka Tony Cairo. I told him what we found out from my contact in the FBI, that Tony had turned state's evidence against part of the Boston mob and went into the witness protection program as Joseph Johnson. He joined the marines and came out of its elite Raider unit to the life he leads now. Hell, he could be here with us right now. That story on its own could end there, but Kent gave me this.

"The current administration in the White House has made a decision to change the way they battle the world's problem dictators and other bad characters. In the past, if a dictator got out of line, the United States would slap sanctions on their country to cripple their economy. That method has finally been identified as a complete failure. The crippled economy just made things really bad for its citizens, who then blamed the United States. That method also created a vacuum of power, where Russia, China, or groups like the Taliban or Isis could come in to gain a foothold.

"Their new operation, called Operation Queen Bee, is designed to find and neutralize the queen bee instead of starving the worker bees, hoping the worker bees would choose a different queen. The unwritten law of not targeting heads of state is gone. Kent told me the CIA has structured the operation so that America has complete deniability. There would never be any trace of the assassinations linking back to our government, because they have found a way to hire a specialist to do the wet work.

"The CIA hired the Boston mafia, headed by Joseph's uncle, to execute strategic assassinations here in the States over the last several years. The last hit in the U.S. was a Saudi bombmaker right here in San Francisco several weeks ago. After that hit, the CIA wanted to test their capabilities with an international assignment, so they gave the Boston mob another assignment in Buenos Aires and then an unusually difficult assignment in Paris just a few days ago. The target in Paris was a Russian oligarch who was responsible for funneling money and weapons into Syria and Afghanistan for the purpose of killing Americans soldiers. The Russian was well protected, but somehow this assassin found a way to take him out with no repercussions. The hit in Argentina went off just as perfectly. The CIA doesn't know who the assassin is and doesn't want to know. They pay the mob and stay completely anonymous. The assassin's kills have all been perfect. There was no evidence left at either scene that led anywhere. The CIA got what they wanted. The civilized world got what it needs.

"I have good reason to believe that the assassin is none other than our very own Joseph Johnson, and the old hippy that Chirica and Apache watched beat up the mobsters from Naples is also Joseph Johnson. Somehow Joseph moves from the north side to the south side of the condominium building and changes his disguise. Joseph must have taken offense with those guys watching Claire. It's obvious Joseph's uncle and his contacts are a threat to Claire, and that's why Joseph took such drastic measures. Maybe he's looking for a way out or had a disagreement with the mob bosses."

Jackson looked down at the top of his desk. Eventually, he looked back up at his men and said, "This presents us with a dilemma. We were hired to give a report on Joseph Johnson. One option is to give an accurate report and walk away. We have completed the job. Another option is to use this information as an opportunity, an opportunity to engage Joseph and offer to partner with him. This partnership would mean that we would do the recon work for him and then support him with what he does best. We could be the contact for the CIA instead of his mob family.

"Joseph's father is in a federal penitentiary, and Joseph's uncle has taken his father's place as head of the Boston syndicate. Uncle Geno has brought in some bad characters from Naples, Italy. Two of those men from Naples just took the severe beating from Joseph. We have to assume this disagreement between Joseph and the Bruzzelli men will only intensify. You know damn well that if they find out Joseph was responsible for their beating, there will be acts of revenge. Joseph and Claire are not safe with Uncle Geno in the picture. We would have to find a way to take out Joseph's mob family and their associates and then replace them as the contact point for the CIA hits.

"There are a lot of moving parts here. But I think we should consider this because it's good money, and we would be helping our government fight wars the way we know they should be fought. We could keep thousands of U.S. soldiers safe by getting to the bad queen bee before multiple hives are destroyed."

Jackson looked at the faces of his men. He already knew the answer, but wanted agreement from his troops. He said, "So what do you men think? I want this to be a group decision."

Cochise and Renegade were the leaders of the group. They looked at each other and smiled. Cochise said, "You mean we could go back to using our training, Boss? You know we all want to be part of this." The rest of the men smiled in agreement.

Jackson said, "Good to hear. Kent gave me the intel for Joseph's next job. It's just a couple of weeks from now. I have the details. We'll be able to observe his method of operation before we bring him into our tribe.

Chapter F

Coach Mortti and Coach Ricci ran up to me after the game. Mortti said, "Great game, Brando! You came through again. We want to go over the film with you after you shower up."

"Sorry, Coach. I'm on my way out of town right now. I don't even have time to shower. My train leaves soon. I gotta go right now." I didn't give them a chance to respond. After every game they always wanted to review the game. It was a waste of time.

There were a lot of nice people standing around, slapping me on the back and saying great game as I left the futbol complex. They really got excited about the school's team. They were all good people, but they cared about the win way more than I did.

Gina ran through the gate and caught up with me in the parking lot. "Great game, Brando. Let's celebrate."

"Thank you. But remember, I have to catch the five o'clock train. The game went longer than it should have."

"Do you have to go tonight? There's a train in the morning."

"I do have to leave right now. There's a problem at the winery."

Lia walked into the conversation. "What's going on?"

I said, "Pascal called and said there's a problem with the contract grape pickers. They're not coming, and we have to get the grapes off the vine this weekend. All that rain we got a few days ago plumped up our grapes. They have to be picked right away, and I have to catch the train right now."

I didn't think I was yelling, but the girls looked upset. Lia looked at Gina and then back at me. "We'll go with you and help. Come on, I'll drive." Lia grabbed my hand and Gina's. We ran to her car.

We had been on the road for a couple of hours. Gina and Lia talked the whole time about school stuff and what they were missing at the Friday night party. I called Mama and told her what was going on so she wouldn't worry.

Gina broke off the chitchat with Lia and asked, "What happened with the grape pickers Pascal thought were coming?"

"We had that rain, and then it's been so hot the last few days. The grapes all over Montalcino plumped up at the same time. Their brix level, the amount of sugar in the grapes, is close to getting too high. All the big growers have contracts with the pickers before we can use them. They're not letting any of them go to pick our vineyard."

Gina said, "Lia's making good time. We should be there in about an hour. We can get some supper and crash early so we're ready to pick grapes first thing in the morning."

I said, "No, we'll be picking grapes right away when we get there. It's best to pick grapes after it cools down. We'll be picking all night. We need to get you guys some gloves."

We were still in the vineyard at three o'clock in the morning. Our five-man crew consisted of Lia, Gina, Pascal, his mule, and me. We cut bunch after bunch of grapes off the vines and filled wicker baskets with them. Pascal loaded our baskets onto a cart. He and the mule transported them to the winery. Pascal dumped the grapes into the crusher and then poured the juice and skins into large fermentation tanks. By the time he finished that work, we had filled enough baskets for him to do it all over again. The moonlight was just bright enough for us to see well enough to work. The girls worked hard, and we made some great progress.

Pascal pulled the cart next to our baskets and called us over. He said, "The mule needs a break. No more picking tonight. Help me load these baskets."

We rode on the back of the wagon to the winery. When we got there, Pascal was busy with the grapes. He said, "Give the mule some water and feed him. Then lead him to his stall. I put a couple of blankets in the loft for you. You're going to have to share. That's all I have."

I used a pitchfork to gather and spread some loose straw into a makeshift bed. Lia said, "That's our bed?"

I laid one of the blankets on the straw. Gina plopped down and pulled me with her. "Come on. I'm exhausted. This will be fine."

The three of us laid next to each other, and we used the other blanket to keep the cool breeze off of us. Our bed was in front of the large, wide-open sliding doors of the loft. Through the open barn doors was a crystal-clear sky filled with the brightest stars we'd ever seen. The moon was part of our big picture.

Gina used one of my arms as a pillow, and Lia used my other arm. Gina was right. We were exhausted, but we took a moment to view the beautiful sky. Lia said, "This turned out to be a great bed, Brando." She kissed my cheek.

Gina said, "How did we do tonight, boss?"

"Great. It couldn't have been better. Thank you."

She said, "It was a lot of fun." She kissed my other cheek.

⚬

I woke to the crowing of a rooster and the sun peeking through the trees. The girls and I were tangled up in bed. They were still asleep. I eased out of our bed and stepped down the wooden ladder to check on the mule. He looked content. Outside the barn, Pascal stood on top of the fermentation tanks, stirring the juice inside the tanks with a big rake.

"Good morning, Pascal. How did we do last night?"

"If we can do half this much tonight, we'll be caught up. These grapes will make some great wine. We got them off the vine just in time."

I said, "I think we can get another night out of the girls. They really came through for us."

"They sure did."

"Shouldn't there be a lid on those tanks?"

"Not for a couple more days. The land around us naturally produces yeast. You can't see it, but it floats all around us in the air. The yeast will find its way onto the grape juice in these vats and start the fermentation process. Our homegrown natural yeast is one of the many reasons our wine is so good."

The girls slept until noon while I helped Pascal clean more tanks and prepare for the night's harvest. When the girls came out of the barn together, Gina said, "You look pretty silly in your futbol uniform, Brando." They laughed.

I smiled and said, "I'm sure I do. Come up here and look at the juice from the grapes we picked last night."

I gave them a brief tutorial about winemaking before Pascal yelled for us to get down. He had lunch set up under a big shade tree on his old picnic table. The table was set with bread, cheese, and salami. He picked some lettuce, tomatoes, cucumbers, and olives from his garden and made a salad for us too.

Gina said, "Thank you, Pascal. This is by far the best-tasting food I've ever had."

"I have to agree," Lia said. "I'm so hungry."

After lunch, Pascal cleared the table and said, "Why don't you take them down to the creek? It's warm enough to go for a swim. You guys should rest this afternoon before we hit it again tonight."

<hr>

It wasn't long before the three of us were splashing in the cool water of the wide stream. There were pockets of deep pools in parts of the stream where we could duck under water. We splashed, yelled, floated, threw rocks, and had a great time.

On a grassy part of the bank next to the water we caught warm rays from the bright sun. We were in the same position that we had been in the night before in the loft, lying next to one another. Most of our clothes hung from tree branches behind us, drying in the sun.

Gina looked straight up at the blue sky, then turned to me and said, "I want to stay here forever."

Lia said, "Why don't we? This place is beautiful. I can't imagine going back to Naples or back to school. Nothing will be the same again. Why didn't you bring us here months ago?"

"Good question. My fault. I wouldn't change a thing."

<hr />

It was after ten o'clock that night when Pascal and his mule pulled up next to our baskets. "This is the last load. Our tanks are full," he yelled down the rows of grape vines to us.

An hour later we sat around the picnic table again, eating one of Pascal's gourmet, farm-to-table meals. There was a big bonfire blazing close by, and he had turned on some sparkly lights that dangled from branches of the trees scattered around his yard.

We drank plenty of Pascal's wine and listened to him tell stories about his farm. Lia put some music on her phone, and she and Gina danced by the bonfire. They pulled Pascal up and made him dance with them. Eventually, Pascal turned in, and so did we.

I wasn't sure if it was the wine we drank or the closeness we had felt down at the creek, but there seemed to be a shared anticipation about what would happen between the three of us the rest of the night.

The stars and the moon were in the same place they were the night before, right out the wide-open loft doors. We were on our straw bed, gazing at the beautiful sights of the night sky. Lia and Gina were at my side. We lay in the splendor of the scent of the fresh straw, the cool night breeze, and the warm thoughts we had for one another.

Chapter Sixteen

⇒◦◦◦⇐

JOSEPH WHISPERED TO CLAIRE, "HI, BABY. WHY DID YOU WAKE UP SO early?"

Claire whispered back, "I'm too sore to sleep. Not sure I'll be able to walk after what you put me through. I guess I need to get in better shape. Mt. Diablo's seven-mile trail was more than I bargained for. I never would have guessed hiking could be so strenuous."

Joseph whispered, "Are you going to be ready for today's adventure?"

"Yes, I am. I'll be ready in an hour. I'm all packed and ready to go."

"Great. I'll be over to pick you up."

Chapter Seventeen

CLAIRE STOOD IN FRONT OF JOSEPH. THEY WERE WAITING IN LINE TO check in at The Bellagio Hotel and Casino in Las Vegas. The flight over was quick. Joseph hoped their room was ready. He was ready, and he thought Claire was, too. They hadn't been able to keep their hands off each other the last few weeks, but they still hadn't sealed the deal. The line didn't move.

Claire backed into Joseph. He could tell it was intentional. He put his hands on her hips, hoping no one around them noticed their intimacy. She led his hands around to the flat of her stomach and then up to paradise. Joseph took the opportunity to explore her gift. She turned her head and whispered, "Let's not go straight to the pool."

Joseph whispered, "The fuse is burning, baby."

The next day we stood next to each other along with a couple hundred other people, waiting ... I put my hand on the curve of Claire's lower back, then slid my hand to the top of her hip and pulled her close. She relaxed into the side of my body. She felt good. She looked up and smiled at me.

Yesterday and last night were amazing. Joseph was a true gentleman. I could tell he was dying to take me. I was ready to give it all to him. It was worth the wait. I noticed the music for the first time. The Sinatra song, "Fly Me to the Moon" was perfect for this setting. He put his hand on my lower back. Just that touch got me going. He moved his hand to my side and pulled me close. If his hand went any lower, I'd have to lead him back to the room. I looked up at him and smiled. Just to think … I could have lived my whole life with Hugh and never once felt that sensation of passion. All Joseph had to do was touch me.

Joseph said, "Tell me more about Giada. Why do you want to go to her restaurant?"

"She's a celebrity chef. She has her own TV show, she's Italian, and she's very pretty. You would like her. Her restaurant is close by, and you have to feed me, Joseph. After supper, let's turn in early and have some more fun."

"That's an excellent plan. You always come up with the best ideas. Last night was spectacular, but so was this morning, and this afternoon after our time at the pool. As a matter of fact, I'm about ready to explode right now. You are, too. I felt your shudder."

I thought, *He does have my number.* I looked at him with a big smile and said, "The fuse is burning." Joseph smiled. I said, "You're going to have to wait until after supper to get your dessert." He laughed again and pulled me close. There was a period of silence while we listened to the music and waited. *You know things are right when silence feels good.*

Joseph said, "Remember, I have an appointment at the high-stakes table tonight."

"Tell me what's up with that again."

"I was lucky a few times in the past, and instead of cashing in my chips, I keep them in a safety deposit box at the casino. That way I don't have to pay taxes on my winnings and, more importantly, we get that massive suite for free.

Claire said, "You're on a solo mission for that adventure. Midnight is when I go to sleep. Plus, I would excite you too much. You need to focus all your attention on the game."

The sound of the music increased, and the fountains in front of The Bellagio began to dance with the music. *That was very cool.*

⸺◦◦⸺

I lay in bed watching her sleep. *She is so beautiful. I never want to be without her. I guess that settles the question of "Who am I?" I'm a whipped man who will be forced to let her go if I can't figure out an exit plan. I can't let anything bad happen to her.*

I kissed her cheek, got dressed, and left the room with my rack of one-hundred, thousand-dollar chips.

On the casino floor I waved to one of the hosts. She hurried over and I said, "I need to put these back in my safety deposit box for now."

She led me to the vault, turned her key in box numbered 24601, and I did the same. She slid out the box and left the room. I pulled out a gun and a silencer, put the rack of chips into the box, locked it, and called through the curtain, "I'm ready to put this away."

I slid into the back of the taxi and said, "Sapphire Gentleman's Club." Traffic was light. Hopefully, this would be a quick in and out. The intel for this job seemed good. Tonight's mark was the strong-arm dictator of a South American country who was taking money from the cartels with one hand and from the U.S. to fight the cartels with the other hand. He killed any political dissenter and allowed gangs to rule the streets, forcing its citizens to flee the country. Once a month he came to Las Vegas to act like the big shot that he wasn't. He was a true "whale" in the eyes of all the casinos. They all fought for his business because he lost millions on each trip.

The plan tonight was for an unidentified accomplice, probably a waitress, to slip a powerful laxative into the target's drink at twelve-thirty. The effects of the drug would take about ten minutes to deliver its unpleasant effects. The target would be forced to go to the men's room with great haste. I would be waiting.

I arrived at the club at 12:15. The target and his entourage were upstairs. There were two muscle-bound goons standing guard at the roped-off stairs that led to the balcony. I could have shelled out a few hundred to gain access, but didn't want the attention. There had to be an employee-only back stairs. I found it and slid past the hurrying waitresses without commotion. My intel said no cameras, and I didn't see any. It was 12:25 when I sat down. I gave a dancer a hundred-dollar bill and asked her to dance for me. "Don't touch me," I said. The last thing I needed was stripper perfume or sparkles on me when I crawled back into bed with my beautiful reward.

The target squirmed in his seat. I waved the stripper away and went to the men's room. There were men coming and going. Too many. I wasn't sure if this was going to work out how I had planned it. There was no way I could get a shot off unobtrusively, even with the silencer. I went to the sink and washed my hands. I pulled out a wad of paper towels, put them under the water, and worked them into a ball.

The target burst into the bathroom and dived into a stall. I followed him in and loudly said, "Hi, Daddy. I've been waiting for you." *That should clear things out.* He was in a hurry to get to his business when I surprised him with a quick uppercut just under his sternum. He gasped for breath. I shoved the wad of wet paper towels into his mouth. Then I covered his nose with my hand. He shit himself. In a few seconds his body went limp from lack of oxygen.

A scuffle began outside his stall, but then, just as fast, silence. *Are they waiting for me?* I pulled the wad of paper towels out of his mouth and slid under the barrier into the next stall. I threw open the door with my gun at my side. No one there. I tossed the ball into the trash and tucked the pistol under my coat just as two men came in to do their business. I walked down the back stairs, strolled out the front door, and slid into a cab that was waiting in the taxi line. I was in that bathroom for only a couple of minutes. *South America and the rest of the world would be a better place without that whale making waves. I couldn't care less that he had shit his pants with his last breath.*

⸺∘⸺

Twenty minutes later I placed a hundred thousand dollars' worth of chips on the blackjack table. I said to the smart-looking dealer, "Color me up, please." I was the only player at the table. She was exceptionally attractive, with plenty of natural cleavage on display. A girl like that would make it pretty easy to stay at the table a long time. She gathered my bumblebees and replaced them with twenty, five-thousand-dollar chips. I put four of them in play.

She flipped over the six of spades for me and a face card for herself. My second card was the five of clubs, and hers went down. I put four more chips

86

on the line to double down my bet. She turned over a face card for me and paid me forty grand. I let it ride.

I won the next hand and left all the chips on the table. The pretty dealer called over the pit boss. He counted the $160,000 and nodded to her to let it play. She dealt me a blackjack, counted out $192,000, and set it beside my $160,000 bet. I moved the two-thousand dollar chips off to the side and then added the $60,000 that was left from my original rack to the winnings. That stack added up to $410,000. I said, "Can I get a rack for these?"

While she stacked the chips the pretty girl said, "Do you want to play with me … a little longer?"

I said, "That's a fine invitation, but I know way too much about math to keep playing this game tonight."

She smiled and said, "Can I lead you back to your deposit box, Mr. Johnson?" as she pushed the rack across the table with eighty-two, five-thousand-dollar chips in it.

"No thanks. I'll take care of that in the morning." I slid the two one-thousand-dollar chips across the table with a broad smile of my own." She winked at me and said, "Thank you."

That was dumb luck, I told myself. Do not think it was anything more. One-thirty in the morning. Not a bad night's work if you add the $250,000 that will be deposited in my Swiss account for the hit. Not bad at all.

Now I was going to crawl into bed with the most beautiful creature on Earth.

Chapter Eighteen

⟶◈◈◈⟵

A FEW DAYS HAD PASSED SINCE WE WERE IN LAS VEGAS, AND I WANTED
to get in a good, hard workout. I went to the gym for my weekly bag
work and hopefully to find a sparring partner. The place was a little less
crowded than usual. That was good for getting a bag but not so good for
getting in the ring.

"Hi, Ray."

"Hey, Joseph."

"Any chance for me to get in the ring today?"

He pointed to a man working out by himself and said, "Yeah, we got
some fresh blood in here today."

I said, "Set it up if you can. Give me about ten minutes."

The man across the room looked fit, and the bag he was working was
taking some punishment. *This one will be different.* Normally, I got the
young punks who want to box but don't want to train. This guy was big,
but I thought I could wear him down pretty easily.

The bucket boys laced us up. Ray stepped between us and said, "Three
three-minute rounds, men. This is a gentleman's workout, so no cheap shots
or low blows. Get in a good workout and walk away friends."

That was good advice. No reason to hurt the guy. Two two-by-fours
smacked together, and the clock started. We danced around each other and
threw a few jabs to get loosened up. *The dude has some spring in his step and
a few good moves.* Bam! An invisible jab came out of nowhere and caught me
square on the nose. I shook it off and moved away. I stepped back in with one
of my patented one-two combinations. He blocked them before they were

89

halfway to him. I stepped back in and threw a quick uppercut. *Not really a gentleman's play.* He slapped that away and proceeded to bat me around like a cat playing with a mouse. He was twice as quick and twice as strong as me. The bell for the end of round one saved me from further humiliation.

I dropped onto my stool, feeling out of gas already. He walked to his corner and stood there like he was waiting for an elevator. Round two was even worse. He could have killed me out there, but he just kept slapping me around. I got in one lucky shot to his midsection, but it felt like I hit the side of a rhinoceros. Mercifully, the bell for round two sounded, and I stumbled to my stool. He walked to his corner, stood there, and waited for another three minutes of domination.

The bell rang, and I stood up with my hands in the air and said, "I give. You got too much for me."

He said, "No problem. Thanks for the workout."

We touched gloves and turned away. Ray looked at me, laughing, and said, "You didn't see that coming, didja?" He laughed again. *I bet if I got him in the octagon where I could use my feet, it would be a different story.* That's when I heard the familiar loud thud of a forceful strike into a heavy bag. That man was working the heavy bag with his feet. He struck higher and with more force than I'd ever seen. *I guess I better stay away from him altogether.*

After my workout, I showered and was heading out when he stopped me and asked, "Did you do some training with the Marine Raiders? I know a man, Brian McAreavy, from that unit. We ran some ops together when he was just coming in. He's a friend of mine."

"Yeah, he was my C.O. in the Special Operations training program. One of the good ones."

"I need to talk to you. You got time for a beer?"

"I'd like to, but I don't have time today. And those days are far behind me." The big man grabbed my shoulder as I turned away. He looked down at me with a menacing glare and said, "You and I need to talk right now. You follow?" Those words and that look gave me no choice. I had to get out in front of this. I said, "No problem. A cold beer sounds good. There's a little place across the street."

He paid the bartender and swaggered back to our table. It was early afternoon, and along with a stale beer smell and a few neon beer signs, we were the only patrons in the place. He slid my pint across the table and tilted his glass at me. He said, "My name is Reed Jackson, and you and I have something in common. We both care about Claire." He stopped, and so did my heart. I didn't say a word.

He went on, "And you, my friend, haven't been doing a very good job. You have been careless." He took a swig of beer.

Who is this guy?

"Taking her to Vegas with you must have been a lot of fun, but you got lucky there. My men saved your ass in that bathroom debacle." He took another drink. "How do you think this is going to end?" He looked deep into my eyes. He knew I didn't have an answer.

He said, "I'll tell you how this is going to go. You have two options. Option number one is to break it off with Claire and never see her again. That might save her if you continue to do what they say."

How much does this guy know?

"Choice two is a little more complicated, but I have to tell you, if you say no to choice two, you'll be forced to take option one. Do you want to hear about option two, or do you just want to walk away now?"

He was slapping me around right now, just as he had done in the ring. "Let's hear what you have."

"In the simplest terms, option two involves me as your partner. First, we take out your uncle, his soldiers, and anyone else that has control over you. I will be your contact for these international hits, and we will work together. You can continue to work your insurance man gig, keep your second identity as the overweight hippy with a limp, and go on with your life as a witness-protected mobster." He stopped and waited for my reaction.

Who is this guy? There was no point in trying to dodge him or lie. So I decided to ask him a question that I didn't know the answer to. "Who is sanctioning these international hits, as you call them?"

"The CIA. The U.S. government has changed their strategy as to how to deal with rogue nations and their leaders. No more playing Mr. Nice Guy by slapping sanctions on the working people and sending our men in to fight their wars. All while the dictators continue to line their pockets. This new policy is why I'm offering to partner with you. The men you took out were bad men who deserved what they got. We can do some real good here and save American lives.

"My team and I would work with the CIA to gather the intel, then work with you to complete the mission. You have proven yourself to be a capable asset. But you need better training, and you need help. You've been lucky up to now, and you know it.

"We have to start in Boston. The Bruzzelli men you beat up in the park, or men just like them, are going to keep coming. You have to know that the whole crew is a bunch of scumbags who don't deserve another breath of life. My team is made up of myself and twelve men just like me. You should consider it a privilege that we're asking you to work with us.

"It's your choice, Tony. You can be one of the good guys and work with us or say good-bye to Claire McKinley and continue to live under your uncle's thumb."

I sat there dumbfounded. I hadn't touched my beer. I was too upset. My mind raced. Somehow, he knew everything—*everything*. He waited for me to react, but I couldn't come up—. "You are a hundred percent right about everything, Mr. Jackson." That came out of my mouth while I was still trying to figure out what to say. "I have been lucky, and I never should have taken Claire with me to Vegas. Sitting here with you may be the best thing that's ever happened to me. What is your interest in Claire?"

"Her father hired me to check you out."

Half talking to myself and half talking to Mr. Jackson, I said, "I can't blame the guy. Have you told him everything?"

"No. The last time I talked with him, I told him everything I knew at that time, which included your family ties in Boston and that you were possibly in the witness protection program. Nothing about your ongoing work with your family."

I said, "I think you can tell that you've caught me completely off guard, just like you did in the ring. I don't know what to say other than I want to stay with Claire and it would be an honor to work with you and your team. So now what?"

"First of all, you have to come clean with Claire. Tell her everything. You'll have a couple days to get that done before I update her father. I'll tell him that you work with the CIA on matters of national security. That's the minimum you'll have to tell Claire, but if I were you, I would tell her everything.

"Next, we will develop a plan to get your Uncle Geno and his lackeys out of your life for good. I have some ideas about how to do that, but that's something we'll work on together. After we have those two things taken care of, you can live a somewhat normal life until we get the next assignment

"That all sounds good, Mr. Jackson. I— we—can do this. I want to say that I'm sorry about taking Claire to Veg—".

"No need for that, Joseph. Claire is a very special young lady that could unintentionally cloud anyone's logical thought process. The main thing now is that we go forward." Jackson pushed a button on his phone.

A few seconds later, the front door of the small neighborhood bar opened, and a group of men who looked mean and strong walked in. They came straight to us.

Jackson said, "Stand up, Joseph. Say hello to your new family."

Chapter Nineteen

CLAIRE FELT THE SMOOTH TEXTURE OF THE PICNIC BLANKET SPREAD on a patch of soft, green grass. The blue horizon of the Pacific Ocean offered a cool breeze that climbed the slope past large boulders that bordered the edge of Lands End Trail. Flocks of gulls soared below them with the sun's rays reflecting off their white wings, which created a sharp contrast to the blues of the ocean. Joseph was on his knees pulling cheese, crackers, wine, and wine glasses out of his backpack. Claire said, "This is wonderful, but you seem to have more on your mind than a picnic."

Joseph looked up and smiled. "You know me well. I have a story to tell you." Joseph spread the cheese and crackers out on their blanket. "The story is about how I grew up, and it's about things in my life that you need to know."

Claire said, "This sounds serious."

Joseph twisted the corkscrew into the top of the wine bottle and used the hinged tool to lever out the cork. "It is serious, but it's something I have to do." The release of the cork created the expected *pop* sound.

"Okay, pour me some wine and tell me your story," Claire said with a smile.

"You already know that I grew up in Boston, that my father was head of the crime syndicate there, and I was part of that world. His brother, Geno, took over as the head of the Boston mafia when my father went to prison. Geno came up with a plan where I would turn state's evidence and testify against some of our enemies. After that I would go into the witness protection program. His plan would get rid of his enemies and let me get out of the business. His commitment to our deal was to ensure protection for my father while he was in prison, to leave my sister alone, and to make sure my mother was taken care of. After I testified, I joined the marines under my new identity, Joseph Johnson, and later I moved here to start a new life."

Claire said, "I already know all that, and don't care. You told us all when we ran into your friend from Boston, Max Tobin, at the Tobin Family Winery. There's more? I want to hear it all."

"When I was in the Marines, I was part of an elite fighting group that taught me unique skills. In Afghanistan I used those skills against our enemies and received multiple medals for valor. After my tour of duty, I left the marines and moved here. I hoped my past would stay behind me forever. That turned out to be a foolish thought. My uncle threatened to hurt my father, mama, and sister, Isla, if I didn't use my training to make money for him. Had enough?"

Even though Claire was afraid of what would come next, she said, "Go on."

"The U.S. government has changed the way they deal with international problems. The CIA now eliminates men who commit brutal crimes against humanity in order to spare all the citizens in that country from suffering years of hardship and violence. To maintain complete anonymity, the CIA hires my uncle, and he sanctions me to assassinate these criminals. The CIA doesn't know who I am, but technically, I work for them."

Claire said, "So what kind of skills are you talking about?"

"Skills I learned in the marine's special forces Raider unit. I'll give you more details about that later, but let me keep going. Within the last week another group has entered the picture. Your father hired a man named Reed Jackson, who owns a local private security company, to look into my background. Jackson and his team of ex-Navy SEALS checked me out, and now they want to be part of these CIA missions. Jackson has offered to develop a plan that will take out my uncle and his crew. His plan will protect Mama, Isla, and you. Jackson will replace my uncle as the go-between for the CIA and me. And he will assist me when these missions come up by doing the initial reconnaissance work." Joseph stopped and looked into her eyes and waited for a response.

"My father! He hired someone to check you out?"

"He did. In his world that's the smart thing to do. Your parents love you and want what they think is best for you. I understand. In the end it's been the best thing that could have happened for us. Reed Jackson looked deep into my past and decided to work with me. He sees this as an opportunity to save American lives and make our world a better place."

Claire looked at the vast horizon. She wasn't sure what to think. She'd never felt threatened by the assassin sitting next to her; she felt the opposite. She wondered how Joseph could be the kind of person who could kill someone. "How many people have you killed? And how often are you hired to do this?"

"In the war I killed many people. Since then, there have been a handful of bad men whose number was called. The jobs come at random times. I never know when. But going forward and partnering with Jackson are patriotic and humane reasons to continue. Jackson sees our partnership as a way to save American soldiers." Joseph looked down at the blanket between them and remained silent.

Claire sorted out the information in her mind. After a brief time, she said, "This all sounds really dangerous."

Joseph said, "Yes, it is. But with Jackson's help and getting Geno out of my life, the level of danger will be greatly reduced. Jackson, his team, and I can do some real good. There are evil people in this world who need to be held accountable for their crimes."

Claire processed what she was told, then said, "I want to know a lot more, and I want to help."

Joseph looked dumbfounded. "You can help by understanding. There isn't a scenario where we put you in any kind of danger. That's why we have to get Geno out of the picture. You are not safe with him around."

"Why doesn't the CIA just hire you?"

"The CIA requires that extra level of deniability. There can't be a trail that ends with the U.S. government outed as the originator of these hits. I'm meeting with Jackson tomorrow to develop a plan for Geno and the crew he's gotten into bed with from Naples, Italy."

Claire said, "Pour me some more wine and tell me about these bad-ass skills you have."

Joseph straightened as though he was on high alert. He gathered up their picnic supplies and said, "Something's not right. There are people coming our way from different angles. We have to move."

Claire looked around, but didn't see anything.

He said, "Stay right behind me, behind this shoulder."

Claire followed Joseph back down the trail. *These same pine trees that looked so pretty on the way up now looked sinister, like they were hiding something.*

Hugh stepped from the pines and on to the trail in front of them. He approached them and said, "Isn't this a pretty picture? I guess I haven't made it clear. Claire is mine."

Claire said, "Are you crazy, Hugh? I'm not yours."

From both sides and from behind, five of Hugh's friends walked out of the woods, all of them holding a baseball bat. They surrounded Joseph and Claire.

Hugh said, "Step away from him, Claire. This is going to get ugly."

Joseph said, "What's your plan here, sport?"

Hugh walked forward, then stopped directly in front of them. He held a club of some kind. He said to Joseph, "This is going to end with you on your knees begging for mercy. You're about to get a lesson that you will never forget. And Claire will witness what a true pussy you are."

From behind, Stu pushed Joseph. Hugh grabbed Claire's arm, jerked her away from Joseph, then pushed her to the ground.

—◦—

Later that evening in Claire's apartment.

"Claire! Stu is hurt really bad," Jenn said. "He might not be able to play. What if he loses his scholarship? All those guys are beat up really bad!"

"Jenn, he and half the football teamed jumped us in the park. Look at my bruises where Hugh hurt me. Those guys planned to beat up Joseph. He was just protecting himself and me."

"I saw him drop you off, and he didn't look injured at all. Stu told me that Joseph started it. Ever since you started hanging out with him, everything has been wrong. Claire, you're ruining everything. Now Stu, Hugh, and the other players can barely walk. You're telling me that one guy did that without even getting a scratch?"

"Those guys snuck up on us when we were having a picnic. I was there, Jenn. They had baseball bats, and they planned to beat up Joseph. He didn't start anything. He's not hurt because he has skills that I hope you'll never have to see.

"It's about time you see Stu and Hugh for what they are. I'm not going to let them ruin my life. You can do whatever you want, but if you believe Stu's version of what happened, then you deserve everything you're going to get." Claire whirled around, stomped into her bedroom, and slammed the door shut behind her.

She called Joseph. "Can you come and get me? I want to stay with you tonight."

"I'll be there in fifteen minutes."

Chapter Twenty

———◦◦◦———

ON THE PLANE RIDE TO BOSTON THE NEXT DAY THERE WAS PAPERWORK neatly stacked on the tray table in front of Joseph, but his concentration was on the meeting he had with Reed Jackson earlier that day. He told Jackson that he needed to go back to Boston to get a better understanding of what was going on there. Jackson had asked, "What do we want to accomplish? What's the mission?"

Joseph said, "The end result has to be more than just taking out Geno and the Bruzzelli group. There needs to be someone to fill that void. There are competing gangs that would take over our neighborhood the minute it's no longer protected. That wouldn't be good for families who live there."

Jackson said, "The Boston police have a good reputation. They wouldn't turn a blind eye."

"You're right. The police force is excellent. But their hands are tied. They have to wait for a crime to be committed before they can step in. In the real world that doesn't work. You have to hit your enemies before they have a chance to strike, especially on your own turf. Just as important, the threat of retaliation needs to be worse than the original crime. If there isn't someone to take Geno's place, there would be a massacre in that neighborhood."

Joseph told Jackson about his past relationship with his cousin Sean and how he thought Sean had moved up in the ranks. He told Jackson that they both had the same distain for the Bruzzelli crew, and he knew he could trust Sean.

They talked about his family and the mob structure. Jackson asked a series of very specific questions, then said, "Number one, you need to talk with your father. Even though he's in Souza, he'll be able to give you some good advice. I have a contact who works at a law firm in Boston. I'll arrange it so he picks you up tomorrow morning. You'll be in disguise and accompany this attorney as his associate. We'll set up the meeting with your father. Research the dress code that's mandatory for attorneys, and be prepared for a dog that sniffs out contraband. The guards and inmates will think the visit is just part of a typical prisoner's appeal request.

"Number two, schedule a meeting with your cousin Sean. He'll be able to bring you up to speed on what's going on there. Meet him in a public place where one of his mob associates won't accidentally stumble onto you. A meeting on the Harvard campus would work. Get what you can out of Sean, then head straight to the airport and get out of there. We'll meet again here, the day after tomorrow for a briefing."

Jackson's plan sounded simple enough, but Joseph felt uneasy about it. He felt anxious about seeing his old life resurrected, no longer just a memory from a bad movie. But Jackson's plan was sound. Get in, get the intel, and get out, then create the perfect plan for taking down Geno's organization. Jackson was a true professional. His method of operation was the way an elite leader would think. *Trust Jackson. Trust the plan.*

Chapter Twenty-One

THE NEXT MORNING JOSEPH WALKED OUT OF THE LOBBY OF THE HOTEL where he had stayed the night before, wearing the fat suit from his hippy disguise and a salt-and- pepper wig. The dress code at the prison prohibited wearing a hat. The sport coat looked good enough; he carried a briefcase and wore glasses.

Outside the front entrance of his hotel, he waited for his pickup.

A late-model Camry pulled up at the curb with the passenger-side window down. The driver beckoned to him.

He approached the car and looked inside. The driver was a young lady about his age wearing black, horn-rimmed glasses. Her tight skirt was hiked up high on her thighs. Her legs looked good. She looked good.

Joseph said, "Souza Correctional Center?"

"Hop in. Let's get this over with." She looked pissed about something.

They drove in uncomfortable silence for several blocks through slow traffic. Then Joseph said, "I guess you drew the short straw."

"You could say that," she responded in a monotone voice with her gaze aimed straight ahead.

Joseph said, "Sorry. This will be a quick visit. Thanks for helping out." She didn't respond. Joseph looked at his phone. They were forty-five minutes from their destination. *This is going to be a long ride.*

They drove for forty minutes before Joseph broke the silence again. "Shouldn't we go over a few details before we get there?"

She pulled a folder out from the side of her seat and said, "There's a business card and identification for you. Let me do the talking when we get there. I've been instructed to sit with you while you have your conversation. I've brought some paperwork that we'll leave with your father that includes a brief I prepared for his appeal. I was up past two o'clock this morning creating that bogus brief."

That's why she's pissed. "Again, thank you. I assume my father and I have attorney/client protection?"

"Yes, you do."

It was clear she had never been to Souza before. She had a hard time finding the place, and she wouldn't ask for help. There was a line of people waiting at the visitor's entrance. They were a motley group that looked like they should be on the other side of the bars. Joseph followed the girl's long legs to the back of the line. She looked uncomfortable in such close quarters with the hard-looking citizens. There was a separate entrance off to the side. A small sign on the door that said "Court" and another word Joseph couldn't make out. He left his partner and approached the door, talked to a uniformed officer, and then waved her over.

They went through the screening process, which was fairly invasive for a young lady wearing a short skirt. She showed no emotion. There was some yelling behind them. A man from the long line was trying to push his way through the "Court" entrance. Two uniformed officers hustled to the door and settled the dispute. She seemed upset by all the commotion. Joseph put his hand on her back and guided her through another big door. The noise of the door clanging shut behind them startled her.

Joseph said, "We'll make this fast and then get out of here." He hoped that would calm her down.

The room they entered next was filled with round tables and groups of people. There were criers, there were yellers, there were lovers, and there were kids running around. Joseph's father swaggered across the room and joined them at one of the tables in the middle of the chaos. Joseph kept his head down and let the lady do the talking. Joseph's father said, "What's this all about?"

She replied, "Good morning, Mr. Cairo. I'm Traci Lorenz, and I'm your new attorney." She opened a folder and turned it toward him so he could read the contents. Joseph raised his head to get a good look at his father.

Their gazes met. Joseph's father looked down at the paperwork again and said in a low, hushed voice, "What the fuck are you doin' here? I told you a long time ago to stay away from me. I did that for you."

"Did what for me?"

"Look, Tony, I don't want you anywhere around here. You could make things worse for me and your mother and sister.

Joseph said, "I came here because Geno is putting the squeeze on me with threats of stopping your protection in here and not taking care of Mama."

"That son of a bitch hasn't done one thing for me. I've had to make alliances with some serious criminals with money I don't have just to keep myself and a coupla guys from my crew alive. You can bet that'll cost me dearly if I ever get out of this place. If I do get out of here, the first thing I'm gonna do is find Geno and beat that little motherfucker to a pulp right in fronta those Bruzzelli turds he's brought in."

Joseph said, "I'm going to take Geno and the Bruzzelli crew out, but I need your advice. Who do you have that could step in until you get out of here?"

"You're gonna take them out?" Joseph's father laughed. "The vendetta between the Cairos and Bruzzellis goes back hundreds of years. We finally got away from them when your grandpa came here as a young man. Then Geno brought them back in. Even if you could get rid of the Bruzzellis in Boston, you'd have to deal with Naples. There are hundreds of those cockroaches over there just waitin' to take out a Cairo."

"Just humor me," Joseph said. "If they're gone, do we have someone who could take Geno's place?"

"With those guys gone, it would be back to the old crew. There are still plenty of soldiers out there who want to get things back the way they were. Those guys from Naples are runnin' that meth shit in our neighborhood. They're killin' our own. I heard the Bruzzellis now work with a Chechen group that kidnaps underage girls from Europe, gets 'em hooked on smack, and then turns them into whores. It won't be long before they start takin' the girls from our neighborhood. They're squeezin' everyone there by overcharging for protection. Everyone wants them gone."

"Where does Sean fit in? Could he take over until we get you out of here?"

"He'd be the best candidate. He's runnin' the construction sites and the docks. He's kept all the unions working with us, and he's made himself untouchable because of his connections.

"You gotta be crazy if you think you can take all those guys out. Like I said, this feud goes back generations, and there's more to it than I know. It's not something anyone can change. Those guys are ruthless, evil men. And Tony, I'm never getting out of here."

Joseph wanted to bring up his grandpa to know what happened there. He'd never talked to his father about what went down. He asked, "How did Grandpa get away?"

"Look, Tony, it's hard for me talk about him, and there are some things I don't know about our family. If you want to find out about the Cairo-Bruzzelli feud—" A guard walked behind Joseph's father. He stopped talking, slowly looked around the room, and waited for the guard to move away. Joseph's father grabbed the attorney's pen and tore off a piece of the last page of the brief. He wrote *Find Luca De Luca* on the piece of paper, then pushed the note across the table to Joseph.

Joseph's father waited until he thought it was safe to talk again. He pointed at the note and said, "He's a Cairo, and he knew your grandpa a long time ago. The last I heard he was livin' back up in the caves where our family started. To find him you'd have to start at one of the Cairo shoe stores scattered around Naples."

Joseph's father lowered his head. Joseph understood that to mean he was done talking about the subject. Joseph asked, "What can I do right now to help you?"

"I need money. Five large would square me with the gangs in here. Ten would change my life and the lives of the other guys from my crew."

"I'll deposit twenty grand in your account later today. Anything else? What's going on with Mama and Isla?"

"I don't know. I don't want them anywhere near this place or around Geno. I haven't talked with them in months." He shook his head. "You're takin' a big risk comin' here." Joseph's father picked up the file and turned the pages. He looked at Traci Lorenz and said, "So when can we start the process?" Then much louder, "When can you get my court date?"

She was prepared to handle the ruse. "Mr. Cairo, we're working on a different angle for your defense. We hope to be in front of a judge sometime next month."

He opened the file again. He pointed to a section on one of the pages and pushed the papers back to her. She read that page and the next one and said, "We'll be in touch, Mr. Cairo."

She left the file with him and stood to leave. Joseph folded the note his father wrote and put it into his coat pocket. All eyes in the room were fixed on her legs as they walked to the visiting room door.

Getting out of that place was no picnic either. Eventually, the last door closed behind them, and fresh air filled their lungs. Joseph said, "You were great in there. Let's hope neither one of us ever sees the inside of that place again."

She still looked a little shaken. She grabbed Joseph's arm to keep her balance and handed him the keys. "Will you drive us back?" After a few steps she said, "Man, you've got your hands full. I hope you know what you're doing."

Joseph didn't answer. He opened the door on the passenger side of the car for her.

They stopped on the way back to get some gas. Joseph took the opportunity to shed his fat suit and take the wig off. He tossed them onto the backseat and topped off the tank. When he returned to the driver's seat, the lady lawyer looked surprised. She said, "Wow, you clean up well."

Joseph smiled.

She was way more talkative during the rest of their ride, even flirty. At one point she said, "So how long are you going to be in town?"

Joseph said, "I'm heading to the airport today, after one very quick stop."

"Too bad," she said with a smile.

⸺◦⸺

Joseph accepted her business card before he waved good-bye. He walked under the arched entrance to Harvard's campus. He was a little late, but thought, *With the traffic around this place, no one could be on time for anything.*

Sean sat on a bench next to the Charles Sumner statue. Joseph strolled around Harvard Yard, looking for anything out of place. Students came and went everywhere. The scene made Joseph think of a time in his life that he had missed, a time when he could have been roaming around as a student in a place like this.

The only thing that looked out of place was Sean. He looked like a hardened fifty-year-old man, not the fresh-faced, curly haired, redhead he knew just a few years before. The site of Sean's transformation was unsettling.

Joseph sat on the bench next to him and said, "Hey, big brother. How's it hanging?"

Sean turned and flashed a smile that Joseph remembered well. "What are you doing back here? It's great to see you, but you're in deep shit, Tony."

"What are you talking about?"

"Those two men you beat up are back in Naples recovering. They're pretty sure it was you that put the hurt on them. What happened?"

Joseph cringed. Deep down he thought they may have put it together. His change of plans for leaving Paris early wasn't a strong enough alibi. "Geno is threatening me and everyone I know. I can't let it stand. A couple of those Bruzzellis, the ones who used to push us around, were eyeballing my girlfriend. That's taking it a step too far."

"They push everyone around. You gotta get used to that. What were you thinking?"

"Sean, I'm going to take Geno and that crew out. Dad and I are hoping you can step in. But I need you to tell me you can."

"Really?" Sean said with a sarcastic tone. "Look, Tony, the old crew would love to get Geno and those Naples fucks off our backs. But you'd have to get them and a couple other bosses who Geno keeps feeding the profits. There's some bad shit going on here that you never would have thought we'd be involved in. That bad shit is feeding the beast, though."

Joseph said, "I'm part of a good crew. We can do it. Do you have enough backing to take over?"

"Yeah, with some help. I'd get the backing, especially with your father's blessing.

"The once-a-month Sunday meeting is this week, and I heard the name Lochlann Lynch. All the bosses will be there, along with all the Bruzzellis.

Geno doesn't take any chances being alone. You're going to have to figure out a way to handle what comes at you from Naples. They'll be coming for you, probably for me too if I'm running things here."

"That's good info, Sean. I'll take this back and let you know what we come up with. How are Mama and Isla? Do you ever see them around?"

"Your mom's doing okay. She moved back to Providence, hangs out with my mom, and works the second shift at the tannery. She's in the front row at church on Sundays, of course. Geno does nothing to help her. She turned down his advances a long time ago. She's just as pretty as ever though, and her smile is still the best thing ever seen on the Hill. The beautiful Isla lives upstate, and from what I hear, she has a nice family and is doing well. We're all glad to see her out. They're both pretty hurt by what your father did, though. That changed everything around here. Have you ever figured out what happened there?"

"Nah, Dad won't talk about it. Thanks, Sean. This is great help. We're going to do this." Joseph slapped Sean on the shoulder and stood up to leave.

He walked back under the arched entrance and looked for a cab. He didn't go far before the tan Camry pulled alongside him, and the window slid down. Traci Lorenz waved at him and said, "Hop in. I'll give you a ride to the airport. You'll never get a cab here."

Joseph slid into the passenger seat. "Thank you again. We have to stop by the hotel. My bag is in the coat check there."

She wasn't wearing her glasses and had put on some makeup. "No problem. I have the rest of the day and night free." She gave him a wicked smile. Besides, you left your disguise in the backseat."

Joseph turned around, and sure enough, he'd forgotten his supplies.

The ride to the airport went quickly. Joseph was aware of some provocative chemistry floating around in the car, but his mind was on the West Coast. She was a fine young lady and no doubt would be a lot of fun. A few months before, he would have charmed her skirt off and taken the red-eye back. But Claire was the real deal, his deal.

Chapter Twenty-Two

THE NEXT MORNING, JOSEPH WHISPERED TO CLAIRE, "I'M GLAD YOU decided to stay here the last few days. It's nice waking up next to you. I could get used to this."

Claire snuggled close. Their faces were almost touching. She said, "Thanks for letting me crash here. I'm done with that whole college life drama scene. Somehow I think that same group will be replaying the same scenes over and over for decades." She pulled him even closer and gave him a sweet smile. "I can think of a lot of better things to do."

A little later they were in the kitchen when Joseph said, "You know, this is the first time I've actually had breakfast here."

Claire asked, "Have you thought more about what you're going to tell Jackson about the Boston trip?"

Joseph walked around, tiding up the kitchen. "I'll tell him everything I told you. It will be interesting to see what he comes up with. I wouldn't be surprised if I have to leave today because of what Sean told me regarding the meeting scheduled for this Sunday. The last time I talked to Jackson he mentioned that I would be part of a crew that would go in early to set up the scene."

"What do you mean, set up the scene?"

Joseph walked over to the table and lifted his sport coat off the back of a chair to put it away. "I don't know for sure because he hasn't finalized the plan for the mission, but the bottom line is to free us from those gangsters."

Joseph wanted to change the subject. He didn't want Claire thinking about the carnage that would happen at the Sunday meeting. He said, "Jackson is an interesting dude. I hope you get a chance to meet him. What does your dad say about him?"

"My dad? Not much. He doesn't say much about anything. Oh, they want me to come home for a while."

While Claire was talking, Joseph noticed something in the sport coat's pocket. It was Traci Lorenz's business card and a folded piece of paper. He unfolded the paper and saw his father's handwriting: *Find Luca De Luca*. His attention turned back to Claire as he put the note and card into his wallet.

Claire said, "Now they're trying to talk me into taking an intern position at my dad's law firm. I might go for a visit, but I don't want to work at his firm."

Joseph hung the coat over the seatback and sat down. He grabbed Claire as she walked past and pulled her into his lap. "You're not going to forget about me, are you?" He stood up with Claire cradled in his arms.

She smiled and said, "Never!" Joseph took a few steps toward the bedroom with Claire's arms around his neck. Claire looked into his eyes and said, "I never thought I could be this happy."

Chapter Twenty-Three

A WHITE, UNMARKED BOX TRUCK RUMBLED EAST ON INTERSTATE 80, past Lovelock, Nevada. Joseph and Cochise sat in the cab. The back of the truck was filled with old furniture and clothes. Behind a false wall were their weapons, surveillance equipment, and the supplies needed to eliminate Geno and the gangsters from the old country. If they were stopped by the police, their story was that Joseph was on his way back to college and his uncle was making the trip with him.

Joseph studied the Maps app on his phone. He said to Cochise, "We've gone 340 miles in five hours. If we keep up this pace, the next three thousand miles will take another forty-three hours. So it will take us three days to get there if we drive sixteen hours a day." Cochise didn't respond. He just shook his head. Joseph sensed that he wasn't thrilled about this road trip. He asked, "So why did you volunteer for this one?"

"I didn't volunteer. Jackson makes those decisions. We all learned a long time ago to trust Jackson. Following his orders has saved us many times."

"I know this is a big sacrifice for you guys to help me clean up this mess." Cochise nodded. Joseph waited for him to say something. The wind, the tires, and the shaking of the cab were the only sounds. Another hour passed in silence. Joseph felt a growing tension in the cab.

Joseph asked, "Do you want to take the next exit to fill up and change drivers?"

Cochise looked at the gas gauge. "We'll keep going. The less stops, the better."

"Okay, good call, but this is going to be a really long ride if you don't loosen up a bit and let me off the hook. I feel bad about involving you in my family affairs, but I'm doing what Jackson told me to do."

Cochise kept looking straight ahead with no expression on his face. Eventually, he said, "Look, this isn't about you or me. Jackson sees a much bigger picture. A picture of saving the world. He sees working with you as an opportunity to accomplish all the things we tried to do on the battlefield. He believes in you and is clearly willing to take care of you like he would one of the crew. We believe Jackson sees your partnership as a mentor and protégé relationship. You are about twenty-five years younger than we are. Jackson's vison of saving the world by working with the CIA will need a new leader someday.

"The thing is ..." Cochise looked at Joseph. "We don't know you. Jackson must see something in you that he sees in himself. I'm sure you're a good man, and we all trust Jackson's instincts, but having you with us is taking a huge risk, and it's a major financial burden on all of us. This mission will cost us tens of thousands of dollars. And if we get past this mission, I understand we're taking our show on the road to Naples, Italy. That mission will require full SEAL equipment that could cost hundreds of thousands of dollars. I bet you haven't thought about that."

"You're right, I haven't. I'm glad you said something. Number one, I'll pay for this mission, and I'll figure out a way to pay for the Naples operation. Number two, I won't let you guys down."

Joseph rolled down the window a bit to let the tension blow out of the cab. He pulled his phone out to shoot Claire a quick text. *I miss you like crazy already.*

They traveled east on Interstate 80 until midnight.

———⊙———

The sun was rising the next morning as they rolled east across the plains of Nebraska. There were no mountains, hills, or even trees to block the sun's piercing bright rays. Joseph looked at his phone for the hundredth time since he sent the text to Claire the night before. Still no reply. He sent another text. *Good morning baby. Did you miss me last night?*

A few minutes later, Joseph's phone vibrated. The text from Claire said, "I moved back home. We decided that I should concentrate on my schooling.

I'm going to intern at my dad's law firm for a year, then go to law school. Good luck with your trip to Boston. I can't be part of that life. I'm sorry. I was mistaken."

Joseph turned the phone away. He let out a big sigh and then looked at the text again, hoping he'd read it wrong the first time. The text read the same way. Joseph felt stunned. He had to talk to her. He called Claire. The call went straight to her voicemail. "Please call me." Joseph put his phone in one of the cupholders on the dash. He leaned forward and put his face in his hands.

Several hours of silence passed before Cochise said, "This is going to be a really long ride if you don't tell me what's bothering you. It had something to do with that text, didn't it?"

Joseph shook his head as he gazed through the windshield at the flat, empty landscape. He said, "Claire broke it off with me."

"Oh, man, that's a tough one. I'm sorry. I thought you guys really had it going on."

"So did I. So did I." Joseph remembered thinking early on, *She doesn't belong in my world, and I don't belong in hers. Maybe this is for the better. She deserves a better man. Except that I'm doing all this to protect her. I guess this is the best way to protect her. I have to let her go. I bet her parents changed her mind. She moved home. That says it all.*

Joseph took his turn behind the wheel and drove for hours in a daze. *She can't forget about us. She can't just shut it off. If she can, she's not who I thought she was. It's better to find that out now. She can get on with her life, and I can get on with mine.*

Cochise said, "I just noticed that sign said Iowa City, forty-five miles. Iowa City is a great college town. We deserve a break. Let's cruise in there for dinner on the campus somewhere and watch girls in their summer clothes walk by."

Joseph wasn't in the mood. "Sounds good for another time. Let's press on."

Cochise laughed. "That was a test. You passed."

Joseph grinned, but he wasn't in the mood for clever banter, either.

Cochise said, "You got to let it go. It's nothing you said, did, didn't say, or didn't do. Guys like us aren't meant for girls like Claire. Don't beat yourself up. Let it go. I saw Jackson go through the same thing twenty years ago with a girl just like Claire. Jackson was a good-looking guy back then, too, but that didn't matter. Some people just aren't meant for this kind of life. It's not their fault. It's just the way it is. He spent twenty years living down in a hole until he met Deshi, Mandy's mom. She's a sweet lady who was able to pull him out of that hole. Don't start digging yours now."

"Thanks. That's good advice."

Chapter Twenty-Four

⸻◈◈◈⸻

CLAIRE WALKED OUT OF HER BEDROOM FOR HER FIRST DAY OF WORK at her father's law firm. Her mother was waiting. She said, "You look so beautiful. No one will be able to take their eyes off of you."

"Mom, I'm going to work. I don't want anyone's eyes on me."

"The sooner you meet someone else, the sooner you'll forget about … him. Maybe you and Hugh can start over now that he's out of the picture."

"Let's go, Dad! Claire yelled. Then she said to her mom as she walked out the door, "That's never going to happen."

⸻◈⸻

As they passed the outskirts of Cleveland, Joseph checked his phone and said to Cochise, "Looks like we'll get to Boston in about nine hours. What's our plan when we get there?"

"We're going to lay low tonight. Then first thing in the morning we'll go to the cemetery and find the Lochlann Lynch headstone. Jackson has it located for us on a Google maps app. Then we'll set up the surveillance equipment and set the ropes."

"I noticed we have some state-of-the-art surveillance gear."

"Yeah, Jackson wants the full monty for this one. We'll set up the audio and video from different angles. Jackson will want to know what's happening at all times. Do you have any training with that gear?"

"Yes. I know all the equipment that we packed. What does 'set the ropes' mean?"

"That cemetery is full of mature trees. Jackson has a tree assigned to each one of us where we'll be perched, waiting for the meeting to begin. When it's close to go time, Jackson will give us the order to slide down. He wants us all on the ground when the shooting starts. We'll each be assigned three or four targets. It should be all over in seconds. Then we'll put all the corpses in this truck and burn everything at a discrete location to destroy the evidence. If all goes well, we'll be able to fly back to Frisco with the rest of the crew."

"Tell me about the ropes."

"You and I will secure one end of a rope to a branch of a tree, close to the trunk of the tree. We'll cut the rope to length, then tack a Velcro strip on the tree so the other end of the rope to stays in place. We'll tie a thin piece of twine on that end so that when each of us finds our tree, we just tug on the twine, and the rope will fall down."

Cochise added, "Tomorrow morning we'll get an early start and should have the scene set up by nine o'clock at the latest. The rest of the crew will arrive in the afternoon and meet us at the hotel. Jackson will get an update from us, then brief the team again on the plan. Jackson will have two other contingency plans to go over with us as well. I haven't heard what he's cooked up for those yet."

"Sounds good."

"The only thing that could go wrong with this mission is if you got some bad intel from your cousin. We don't know if they changed the headstone or rescheduled the meeting. How good is your intel?"

"That's a good question. I don't know any more than I told Jackson. But these guys are all idiots. I don't expect any surprises. Maybe I didn't make it clear to Claire how bad these men are. Maybe she freaked out about us coming here to kill these guys."

"Let it go, Joseph. Thoughts like that are how you start digging your hole."

Joseph didn't answer. He knew Cochise was right.

⸻ ⊰∘⊱ ⸻

Claire and fifteen other interns sat around a large oval conference table. The room had floor-to-ceiling windows on one side of the room that looked into the lobby and open office space. Opposite that wall were floor-to-ceiling windows that looked outside to a parklike setting with a fountain off to one side and beautiful shades of green in the lawn, plants, and trees on the other side.

Each intern had a box lunch in front of them and an empty glass. Pitchers of water were scattered about the table. The interns' morning had been hosted by three people from HR. It was mostly mundane corporate speak about compliance issues and the core values of the firm. The interns had been led to the conference room and told to wait for a few of the managers. There was uncertainty among the group as to when they should open their lunch box and eat. The interns didn't talk much to one another. Claire felt that they were all intimidated by their surroundings and by the thought of what the managers would say.

There were five other girls in the room. The six girls sat together at one end of the table. Two of them acted like they knew each other. Claire listened to the small-talk conversations around her, but didn't engage.

The door opened, and five men in their mid-thirties walked in and stood at one end of the room. One of them said, "Welcome, interns! It wasn't that long ago that the five of us were sitting where you are right now, wondering how this is all going to work. So please relax and go ahead and have some lunch if you want to."

Two of the male interns opened their box. A different manager took center stage. "Interns are at the bottom of the food chain," he said. "There are several steps before you get to our level and several steps above us to become a partner. The partners run the show here, and they only care about one thing. It's not defending an innocent client or helping protect a business from a lawsuit. The partners care about making money. They pay us very well and task us with that result. If we don't produce, we are gone. If we do produce, someday we will be asked to be a partner."

That man stepped back, and another man took his place. He motioned to the men standing with him and said in a deep voice, "We are respectful associates, but make no mistake, we are in fierce competition with each other. When we look at you, we only want to use you, use whatever talents you have to help us produce more. We don't want to be your friends, so don't be offended when we tell you to do something. Just get it done."

He rejoined the other managers, and another man stepped forward and said, "So how do you make everyone happy? Billable hours. Billable hours are all you are to us. We don't give a shit about your family life, your love life, or even if you are alive. The only thing we care about is how many billable hours you can give us. To score billable hours, you need to be asked by one of us to help with a case. You will all be given an initial opportunity, and then, depending on how you deliver, you'll be asked to help with other cases. You could be working for three or four managers at any one time, depending on their case load and if you are asked. If you are not asked for your help and do not produce billable hours, you won't work for the firm." He stepped back, and the last manager stepped forward.

He spoke in a much softer tone, almost amiable. "Each of you have different assets that can help us. You need to find what those assets are and deliver."

Claire noticed the men were looking at the females in the room with that last statement. Two of the females smiled. He went on, "It's all about a team effort here. If you work well with the team, and the team delivers the goods, so to speak, you will be rewarded with future assignments. Keep in mind that these nice people sitting here with you are your competition. All you have to do is demonstrate your best asset, log as many hours as you can, and be a team player. It's that simple."

As the managers filed out of the room, leaving the interns to their lunch, one of the managers said, "HR will be back in to give you your assignments for tomorrow. Yes, tomorrow. Interns work Saturdays and Sundays."

———⊙———

Joseph and Cochise secured the truck, checked into the hotel, and met at the hotel restaurant for a late supper. A waitress brought them pints of cold beer and then took their order of burgers and fries from the menu.

Cochise said, "This will be the best meal we've had in a few days."

"Yeah, the only meal."

"How do you feel about tomorrow and Sunday? Are you up for all this?"

Joseph said, "For sure. We'll set up the surveillance gear, and then it's just a waiting game. I have no second thoughts about watching my uncle fall face first onto a grave. He dug that grave when he turned his back on my family and when he brought in the Bruzzelli group."

Joseph's phone was on the table. He looked at it and then at Cochise. "Do you think I should call her?"

"No! If it's not meant to be, you can't force it. Besides, you need to forget about her for a few days and get your game face on."

"You're right. She's made her choice."

"I'll offer you something my pop told me. He said don't marry a ten, because you'll never make her happy. Marry a seven and make her feel like a ten. You'll both be happy for a long time. Maybe you should stay here a few days after the mission and spend some time with that hot attorney who gave you a ride to see your father."

Joseph smiled, but didn't reply. After a while he said, "The last words she said to me were 'I never thought I could be this happy.'" Joseph didn't expect a response from Cochise, but it was nice to say those words out loud.

———⊙———

That evening Geno sat with Mateo Bruzzelli, the head of the Bruzzelli group in Boston. Mateo's cousin and two of his nephews were at the same table. The white table-clothed table held two bottles of Sangiovese red wine, three baskets of bread, and five big plates of pasta with sausage. The men devoured everything within reach.

Their table was in the back of the restaurant. The kitchen was right behind them, with the chef and line cooks visible through a picture window. Servers rushed to and from the kitchen next to them. Geno's cloth napkin felt smooth but crisp. The twelve-year-old bottle of Casanova di Neri Brunello di Montalcino's finish was long and strong; it complimented the sweet, spicy flavor of the homemade sausage. Clatter from the kitchen competed with the Italian music crooning through the speakers in the wall, but it was the smell of garlic, bread, and tomatoes from the kitchen that ruled the senses.

Geno filled his wine glass and topped off Mateo's. He set the empty bottle down and yelled to one of the waiters, "Grab us another bottle of the same Brunello." The waiter stopped what he was doing and jogged up to the bar.

He asked Mateo, "What do you think of this sausage? I told you it was the best in Boston."

"You may be right about that," Mateo replied as he shoved a large wad of pasta into his already full mouth. "Look, Geno," Mateo said, chewing with his mouth open. "This is a nice place, and you're a stand-up guy, but you know we're here for a reason."

"Yeah, I figured something was up."

Mateo wiped the tomato sauce off his mouth and chin with a white cloth napkin and took three big gulps from his wine glass. He set the glass down, looked at Geno and said, "At the Sunday meeting in a coupla days, you're gonna make the two other bosses an offer. You'll say that you'll let 'em walk away from their businesses." He took another drink of wine and waved his stained napkin at the other men at the table. "We been givin' 'em a cut of our profits, and they do nothing for it. We wash their hands, but we're washing our own face with just one hand. That's over, Geno. You're gonna make them the offer, but it don't matter what they say. They're all gonna take one to the head right there. This is straight from the top. There ain't nothin' you can do about it except join them."

Geno didn't flinch. He said, "I knew it was just a matter a time. I agree, they been pullin' from our well too long."

"Mateo said, "There's a coupla other issues that concern the boss in Naples. Number one, he wants the Chechen foster girls' program up and runnin' soon. Where are you with that?"

"We got the director of the Boston Foster Care program locked in and a list of the foster girls who just graduated from high school. We got two warehouses set up in different locations and a doctor in place. But the contact for the doctor is one of the bosses who's gonna take one in the head on Sunday."

Mateo said, "No problem. On Sunday, get that information from him before you make the offer. Number two is also directly from Naples. They're takin' the lead in evenin' the score with your nephew. You had to know that wasn't gonna go away."

"Those guys wanna take out our best earner?"

"Not take him out, but he hasta pay. Every day they see two men limpin' around the compound back in Naples with their faces smashed in. Like I said, it's not gonna go away."

"Look, I know you're gonna do whatever you want, but Tony is different than anyone you know. He won't take it without hittin' back."

"We'll see about that."

All the men at the table laughed at Geno.

Chapter Twenty-Five

INSIDE THE BRUZZELLI COMPOUND OUTSIDE NAPLES, ITALY, THERE WERE twenty-five well-dressed men in the boardroom. Eight men sat around the oval the table with their eyes on a man at the head of the table. His white hair was combed straight back, tight against his scalp. His face was a smooth, tanned brown. His extra-white teeth looked unnatural. The sixteen remaining men stood at attention a few steps away from the table with their back to the wall. The walls of the oval room were a dark walnut. There were amber-shaded sconces equally spaced around the room that emitted a soft light. Two crystal chandeliers above the large conference table focused their brighter white light on the table and on the seated men.

The chairman of the board, Dante Bruzzelli, focused his attention on the meeting agenda in front of him. Some of his notes were scratched in the margins. Half of the bullet points were crossed off. He looked at one of the seated men and asked, "Where are we with phase three of the port expansion?"

The man answered, "We're back on schedule. The extra euros we threw at the politicians paid off. The permits are all in place, and construction has started again. The extra capacity will allow us to double our imports and triple our exports. Your commitment to enhance our shipping options will give us a tremendous upside going forward."

"Good to hear. Keep on top of that." Dante looked at another man. "What's happening in Boston? I want the Chechen plan of taking the foster girls up and running. Finding some American girls and trading them for girls the Chechens have will save us a lot of money, and both groups of girls are less likely to run away because they won't have their passport and won't know the language. We'll train the Boston girls here and send the girls we get from the Chechen's over there."

Ciro said, "I talked to Mateo this morning. Everything is on track there. They should have a roundup in the next few days. Tomorrow we're taking out all the mob there except the Cairo group. It's going to be a bloody mess, but once we get Boston set up, we'll be able to concentrate some of our resources on New York City. One more thing that's connected to the Cairo group but located in San Francisco is the man who messed up Vince and Alberto. He's the trigger man that's been doing the high-paying international hits."

Dante said, "Even the top earners have to fall in line. Make him pay." Dante paused to think, then said, "Is he a Cairo?"

"Yeah. He's Vincenso's grandson."

"Ah, I remember him now. We forced his father to take the fall for killing his grandfather, Vincenso, so we could put Geno in place." Dante smiled as he leaned back in his chair, then said. "How good was that idea? This couldn't be more perfect, another Cairo under my thumb. I wish Papa were alive to witness this.

"Leave his family and friends out of this one. I want him to feel the pain. But don't hurt him too bad. We want his skills intact. I understand he's got a pretty face. Mess that up good." Dante looked directly at Ciro and said, "I want you to take responsibility for this one. If you want to include Mateo, that's up to you. But it's on you. Understand?"

Dante turned to another man. "Did we get the weapons and explosives from that last shipment from Russia?"

"Yes. They came into our port late last night. We have the weapons loaded on our smaller boats and will run them to our Croatia partners up at Dubrovnik later tonight. They should be in the Syrians' hands within a week."

"Was that heroin shipment from Afghanistan as much as they promised?"

"Again, yes. That's headed straight to Boston hidden in a shipment of wine and olive oil. The Cairo group has a man who controls the unions at the docks there. We can move whatever we want through that port."

Dante said, "That's the last item on the agenda, gentlemen. Anything I missed?" Dante waited a moment, then turned around to get a nod from his consigliere. He said, "I'll see you men here on Monday." He turned back to Ciro and said, "Give me an update Sunday, after the Boston massacre. And, on the return trip from the shipment to Boston, load the new girls that they rounded up on the ship." Dante smiled and said, "We'll bring them back here and get their training started right away." He snickered, and the rest of the men in the room followed his lead.

Chapter Twenty-Six

———⟨⟩———

THE NEXT MORNING JACKSON WAS IN BOSTON IN THE BACK OF THE BOX truck, which was parked next to the entrance of the cemetery. He checked the video monitors and audio equipment. His men from the Agency had been perched in their assigned trees that surrounded the Lochlann Lynch headstone for the last thirty minutes. It was half an hour before the ten o'clock Sunday meeting. Jackson didn't expect any vehicles to roll in until a few minutes before ten o'clock. The video feeds worked well. *Joseph and Cochise did a nice job with the setup.* He tested the audio. "Renegade, come in."

"Loud and clear, boss. But I want to let you know that I can't see much from my position. The leaves are thick. I can only see directly below me."

Apache added, "Apache here, boss. Same problem."

Jackson responded, "No problem. You guys don't need to see anything from your vantage point. I'll let you know when to descend. Double-check the camo blanket under your feet. No one ever looks up, but we brought them along for a reason."

Jackson heard a clicking signal come in. "Identify yourself," Jackson said.

He heard six deliberate clicks.

"Outlaw, do you have company?" One click sounded. Jackson checked the monitors. Nothing. He asked, "Civilian or bogie?" Two taps sounded. "Got him. He's directly below you. Be alert, men. We have company. I have two others. The three of them are carrying micro barrel automatic weapons."

Jackson's thoughts raced. *Were they expecting us? Is this a trap?* He wanted to get out of the truck and look around, but heard multiple warning signal clicks come through. "I hear you guys loud and clear." Jackson picked up the activity on the monitors. The three bogies worked their way across the lane, separated, and hid behind gravestones. Jackson said to his crew, "Men, I have three bogies just south of the lane closest to Lochlann Lynch. They're packing AKs. This could get ugly. Keep calm and silent. The more I see, the more it looks like an ambush setup. Maybe one of the bosses has gone rogue."

Two big Lincoln SUVs entered the cemetery and drove straight to the meeting site. Eight men got out. Four of the men stayed with the vehicles, and the other four walked on the green lawn, up a slight incline to the Lochlann Lynch headstone. Two Suburbans and two Escalades pulled in behind the Lincolns. Men got out of those vehicles and went through the same exercise.

Twelve mobsters stood around the headstone. Jackson whispered to his men, "It looks like everyone is in place. I have good sight and sound. Stand down until we figure out what's going on here."

The surveillance setup was so good that Jackson saw and heard the introductions and pleasantries like he was watching a movie. One of the bosses said, "Geno, we agreed to keep that meth shit outta our neighborhoods, but there's some bad shit goin' on south of Fifty-Sixth Street that tells me otherwise."

Geno answered, "Not our guys, Remi. That's your turf down there. You clean it up. Don't come whinin' to me if the Honduras gangs are moving in on you."

Remi said, "Really? Okay, remember this conversation. We'll grab one of the runners and make him talk. They look like our boys. When we prove the obvious, you're gonna have to give us our cut and guarantee that shit won't go north of Fifty-Sixth."

Another boss said, "We have the same concern about how you're runnin' those young girls from Europe. We don't want that filth in our neighborhoods, so don't even think about taking any of our local girls."

Geno said, "I understand your concerns. You men have been in on these changes from the beginning and have taken your share. All I've seen is an open hand from both of you. By the way, do you have that doctor lined up?"

"Yeah, he's lined up."

"What do you have on him?"

"He was easy. He walked away the first time. The next day he found the family dog hangin' from a tree in their back yard. That should be enough, but the dumb shit loves his family and doesn't want to see them floatin' in the harbor. We got him."

"Who is it? And how do we get him when we need him? asked Geno.

The boss nodded to one of his men and said, "I thought you'd ask." His associate gave Geno a piece of paper.

Geno glanced at the paper and then looked at Mateo Bruzzelli.

Geno said, "Look, this business is getting' away from you guys. We been carryin' the full load too long. We wanna make you an offer." He looked at Mateo, then at the worried looks on the other men's faces. "The offer is to let you walk away from this before it's too late." Geno and Mateo yanked a handgun from their coat and shot both bosses in the head. The soldiers who were hiding behind the gravestones charged the unprepared men waiting by the vehicles, with their AKs on full automatic. The Bruzzellis with Geno filled the six other men at the headstone with lead before they had a chance to respond. It was over in a few seconds. The Bruzzellis emptied their magazines into the dead men as they walked past them on the way to their vehicles. The two Escalades raced away.

Jackson had seen it all. *I could block the entrance with this truck, and then we could take them all out right now, but I have enough on them here to get what I wanted.* Jackson said to his men, "Mission aborted. Get down, get our equipment, and get out." In an instant his thirteen men dropped from their tree, bagged the surveillance gear, and ran in different directions to their pickup points.

Jackson drove the box truck away, feeling like he had dodged a bullet.

Chapter G

MAMA HAD NEVER BEEN OUT OF NAPLES. THE BEAUTY OF THE TUSCAN countryside was amazing as the quiet train sped along the smooth tracks. She wasn't content looking out just one side of the train. She turned her head back and forth, not wanting to miss a thing beyond the windows of both sides of the train.

We were on our way to pick up my winery partner, Pascal Barone, then on to France to see a French oak barrel manufacturer. We wanted to begin customizing our future new wine barrels. In the past we'd bought whatever barrels were available. The decision to make this trip was a big one for us and for our business.

The farther we raced away from Naples, the younger Mama looked. She was only in her mid-thirties, and she was a good-looking woman. In Scampia she intentionally tried to look as plain as possible to avoid problems. Today she wore her good blue dress with white shoes and a white belt, and she carried a matching white purse. Her hair was up, and she wore a touch of makeup on her lips and cheeks.

She was in a daze as we passed the vineyards and olive orchards on the sunlit Tuscan hills. I'd never seen her in that light. She looked like a little girl who was lost in her thoughts. She was someone's little girl, but whose? She never talked with me about her family. I could tell it hurt her when I brought up the subject. There had to be a horrible story hidden behind her sweet, pretty face. Living alone in Scampia, and with me having Bruzzelli for a last name, had to be part of the story. She told me who my father was, but said, "He never wanted anything to do with us." She went further, with an unusual fury. "And we never, ever want anything to do with him."

While her eyes were focused on the beautiful vista, a slight smile came to her lips, probably from one of her private thoughts. I wanted her to have those pleasant thoughts more often. *New goal: Get Mama out of Scampia. Figure out a way.*

"I still can't believe we're going to France," she said. "This seems like a dream, Brando. Thanks for letting me tag along. What's Pascal Barone like? We're getting close to the station."

⸺◦⸺

Pascal had papers scattered on the tabletop between his seat and the seat where Mama and I sat. He was dressed up, too. He had shaved and cut his hair. I never before realized that he was a good-looking man, a little older than Mama. He was all business, all the time. He said, "it says here their oak stave mill is right on their property. That's a pretty good setup for a

130

family-owned, boutique cooperage. I think we'll be okay with twenty-four-month air-dried staves. The thirty-six month option costs quite a bit more, and our bold Sangiovise grapes need the stronger oak influence. I'm not really sure what to do about the barrel toasting yet. I guess that's another thing we'll talk to them about."

Mama asked, "Why don't you buy barrels from Italian oak trees?"

Pascal responded, "The oak varieties from France have a much tighter grain in the wood, which gives the wine a smoother finish." Then to me he said, "The more we learn about the different cooperage options the more I see why you wanted to make this trip."

I said, "I know you hate to take time away from the vineyard, but it'll be good to establish a personal relationship with the cooperage."

Pascal lifted his gaze from the pages in front of him for the first time. He looked at me, smiled, and said, "Think about how far we've come since that day you wiped blood off my face at that highway rest stop."

"Look! The Alps!" Mama cried, pointing out the window. The sharp, snow-capped peaks of the Alps filled the windows on both sides of the train. They were breathtaking. Pascal looked down at his papers again.

"I can't believe we're going to ride through them," Mama said in her dreamy state.

Chapter Twenty-Seven

TEN DAYS HAD PASSED SINCE THE BOSTON MASSACRE. EVEN THOUGH IT was after ten o'clock, Joseph remembered that it was still early in the night by college kids' standards. The bar was only half full. Music boomed through large speakers scattered around the space. Nick was busy behind the bar of Joseph's old watering hole in Palo Alto. Joseph was glad to see Nick was still working there.

Joseph eased into his usual spot at one end of the bar. Nick looked up and saw him. Nick turned the water off and dried his hands with a bar towel as he sauntered over to him. Nick said, "Well, well. Look who decided to show."

"Hi, Nick. It's been a while."

"It's good to see you, my man." Nick said, then reached across the bar for a fist bump.

"Have I missed anything? It looks like you have things under control here."

"The summer crowd is a little different, but I'm sure you'll see some of the usual suspects come rolling in here soon. Are you sticking around for a while?" Nick backed away when a guy at the other end of the bar called to him.

"Yeah. Get him taken care of, and then we'll catch up."

At the same time, in a restaurant in downtown Los Angeles, Claire sat at a candle-lit table with one of the managers. She said, "What are we doing here? That was a great dinner, and this place is really nice, but I thought this was going to be a working dinner."

He said, "This is what I call research. I need to get a better understanding of who I'm working with."

Claire cringed inside, but was able to flash a flirty smile. "You do, do you? So … are we on the clock?"

"Yes. These are billable hours for you. We'll stay on the clock all night if you want to come over to my place after we're done here."

Nick came back to Joseph and said, "Are you back in the game? Can I count on some of your scraps tonight?"

Joseph smiled. "I wouldn't count on anything crazy tonight."

Joseph felt his phone buzz. He was surprised to see a text message from Claire: R U THERE?

What does she want? He texted back: YES

Claire: CAN U TALK

Joseph: YES

Claire: DO U WANT TO TALK

Joseph thought about what to say, then texted, IS THIS THE GIRL THAT DUMPED ME

Claire: I'M SORRY! DO U MISS ME

Joseph: YES

After a long pause, Claire texted, WELL SAY SOMETHING

Joseph: I'M MADLY IN LOVE WITH YOU

Claire: WILL YOU COME GET ME AT MY PARENT'S

Joseph: ON MY WAY

"Gotta run, Nick. See you next time."

Chapter Twenty-Eight

⟫⟩◈◈◈⟨⟪

A WEEK LATER, JOSEPH WALKED OUT THE FRONT DOOR OF THE FOUR Seasons hotel in Buenos Aires, where he experienced the same disappointment he felt the last time he was there. His expectation of seeing the blue ocean was again dispelled by the sight of the water's dull, brown color he saw between the buildings. Claire held his hand as they walked down the steps. Joseph said, "I know you don't want to hear this again, but what's most critical to our mission's success?"

"Follow the plan and do what you tell me to do. I don't mind you asking. I know how important this is, and I know that my one week of training isn't enough for me to think on my own."

Joseph squeezed her hand as they got to the bottom of the steps and turned left. He glanced right and left as they crossed the street. He said, "That's good. Now tell me again. What are the four steps of our mission?"

Claire answered, "Step number one, 'Is It Safe?' Step number two, 'Extraction.' Number three, 'Logistics.' And number four, 'Escape.'"

"Perfect, Double-O-Ten; you are a natural spy, and that semester you spent studying in Spain will be a big help. I'll let you talk with the gardener if we get the chance. Every time I attempt to speak Spanish, I automatically start speaking Italian. I'd be a dead giveaway. It's best if I just keep my mouth shut. The last time I was here I gave him a note and some cash. We'll find out in a minute if it worked."

They walked along the tree-lined sidewalk in the ritzy Ricoleta neighborhood. Joseph said, "Is It Safe? officially starts now. Up here on our left is the Nazi's house." They nonchalantly walked past it just like the tourists

135

and locals walking around the neighborhood. The grounds looked as if the gardener had been doing his job.

Joseph tipped his head toward the street opposite them and said, "We'll have our lunch over there where we can see what's going on around the house." Small, upscale restaurants dotted that side of the street. "The cemetery is just a few blocks from here."

Claire asked, "What exactly are we looking for?"

"Anything or anyone who looks out of place. We have to be sure that it's safe."

"Claire said, "So now is the time. You have to tell me the whole story."

"A couple months ago I had an assignment here. The target's grandfather was part of the German Reich before and during World War Two. From what I've been able to figure out, the grandfather was responsible for overseeing the treasury department of the German government. Buenos Aires was a popular destination for the Nazi leaders. Many of them had second homes here, and some of them fled to Argentina when Germany lost the war. The target's grandfather bought the house we just passed and a large mausoleum in the cemetery. He transformed the mausoleum into a remarkable place. The interior floor, walls, and ceiling are made of amber stone. I found out that the Germans stole the amber stone, gold leaf, and mirrors from Catherine's Palace in St. Petersburg, Russia during World War Two. At the time, the Amber Room was considered the eighth wonder of the world. The location of the contents of the Amber Room was a mystery until most of it was recovered in 1979. I found the gold bars hidden in the crypt by pure luck. I have the key to the mausoleum and a key to a secret vault where the treasure waits for us."

Claire asked, "What are we going to do with the amber stone?"

"We're just going to look at it. We're going for the gold bars in the secret vault as a way to pay for the expense of taking out the Bruzzelli group in Naples. The cost of that mission could be as much as a million dollars. But ever since I saw the amber room, I wanted you to see it, too. It's remarkable."

Claire said, "It all sounds unreal. I want to see the amber room, but still don't understand specifically what we're looking for."

Joseph said, "There's a possibility that someone knows about the treasure in there, but can't access the crypt and doesn't know where the gold is hidden. There is also a possibility there are lethal booby traps set in the crypt for someone to come for the gold and make a mistake trying to locate it. These people may be watching and waiting for the man I killed to carry the gold out into the open. It's all very unlikely, but we want to be sure that it's safe."

"I get it. We'll see if there are people watching the crypt as we act like tourists today. If it looks clear today, then tomorrow we'll execute The Decoy part of the safe mission."

"Exactly. We'll blend in with one of the guided tour groups and pretend to be in love and on vacation as we look for bad characters."

"That's one thing I can do well." Claire grabbed Joseph's arm as they walked under the arched entrance and into the famous Ricoleta cemetery.

Chapter Twenty-Nine

━━◦◉◦━━

THE NEXT DAY'S EARLY MORNING SUN CREATED LONG SHADOWS THAT crossed the narrow lanes of the Ricoleta cemetery. Claire used her cane as she shuffled through the thinning fog on one of the gray cobblestone lanes. She wore a small hat on top of a gray wig. Her hunched posture complemented the dress and demeanor of an older lady carrying flowers to one of her ancestor's resting place. She turned a corner and looked in both directions, then spoke into her collar. "Still nothing."

"Good. Go to the crypt I showed you yesterday. I'll walk past you in a couple of minutes."

Claire placed her flowers at the door of a random crypt. She stepped back, clasped her hands, and bowed her head as if in prayer. She peeked right and left and listened for any activity around her. Nothing. But Joseph had told her, *It's what you can't see that is important.* She heard the Nazi's mausoleum door clang shut.

In the same hunched posture, she tottered to a bench near the front entrance of the cemetery. There she had a good vantage point where she could survey the path that she had just left and several other places around her. She opened her purse and looked inside. The neighborhood was waking up, the fog had lifted, and there was more activity around her. She looked up from her purse to survey scene. Nothing was out of place. She spoke into her collar, "All clear," then turned her attention back to her purse.

A few minutes later Joseph walked past her on the other side of the lane. She barely recognized him in his Nazi black suit, hat, and glasses. Joseph took short, quick steps with his head out in front of the rest of his body.

139

Claire waited for a while, then walked about a block behind Joseph on the opposite side of the street, where she could monitor everything around him. Joseph turned onto the sidewalk of the Nazi's house. No one followed him. She turned to her left and walked away from the house.

She stumbled over a crack in the sidewalk. She regained her balance quickly, but thought her cover might have been blown because of how fast she had reacted. She stopped and pretended to catch her breath. Now all the faces around her looked suspicious to her. *Stay calm. Stay in character. Trust the plan,* she said to herself as she shuffled along.

A couple of hours later she walked out of a small market with a bag of groceries and with renewed confidence. She had changed her disguise back at the hotel to that of a slightly overweight middle-aged woman. Her dark-brown hair fell onto a dull, dark gray sweatshirt. *Joseph better be on that front porch where I can see him.* The gardener was working near the front entrance. *I didn't expect to see him.* She waved at Joseph, the Nazi, and opened the front gate. The gardener was on all fours, spreading mulch under the bushes. Claire stopped, spoke to him in Spanish, and gave him a bright smile. "Hello, my name is Lola. I am Mr. Helms's girlfriend. He told me that you are the one responsible for keeping this place looking so good. Thank you. What's your name?"

The gardener calmly stood up, took off his hat, and said slowly, "My name is Augy. Nice to meet you."

Claire looked up at Joseph and said, "Herman, doesn't the yard look wonderful?"

Joseph waved back in agreement.

Claire said, "Augy, wait right here. We have something for you." She ran up to Joseph, who gave her an envelope filled with fifty American one-hundred-dollar bills. They figured that with the current exchange rate on the black market for American dollars, it would be at least two years of Augy's salary. Claire handed the envelope to Augy and said, "Here you are. We appreciate your help. Have you had any problems?"

"No, miss. Everything has gone well."

"Has anyone asked about Mr. Helms?"

"No, miss. I don't think he has many friends. I'm glad to see him with you."

Claire said, "We'll be going back and forth from here to my home in Switzerland several times over the next few months, so you may not see us again for weeks. Is that okay?"

Augy looked into the envelope and beamed at her. "Yes, miss. That isn't a problem. I'll look after everything. Do you want me to continue to put all the mail on the dining room table?"

"Yes, that is perfect."

"Miss?"

"Yes, Augy, what is it?"

"I think it would be a good idea if my wife came with me at least once a week to dust and look over the inside of the house." He lifted the envelope and said, "This is enough to cover her labor."

"That is a good idea. Please ask her to help. Thank you for the suggestion."

Claire climbed the steps to the front porch and took Joseph's outstretched hand. They walked through the front door. Claire asked, "How did that go?"

"Perfecto," said Joseph. "We'll hang out here for a while. I'll finish putting the cameras in position. You finish going through the mail to see if there are more bills to be paid. Then we'll go across the street for dinner. After dinner we'll come back, then sneak out the back door and go to the Four Seasons. We'll monitor what's going on in the house from our room at the Four Seasons."

Claire asked, "If we don't see anything, will that end The Decoy and the Is It Safe? parts?"

"Yes, it will."

⸻○⸻

The next morning Joseph left the Four Seasons early to take a morning run. The empty streets allowed him to maintain a steady pace and gave him a chance to let his mind race. *What could go wrong? How do I keep Claire safe?* The crisp morning air helped clear his lungs and mind.

The morning sun was still low when Joseph snuck through the back door of the Nazi's house. He called to Claire, "How are you doing?"

"I was just on my way over to meet you at the house."

Joseph said, "I decided to make a change to the plan. Instead of you helping me carry the gold out, I'm going to make two trips, and you're going to be in the old lady character keeping an eye out."

"Then I won't get to see the amber room."

"That's right, but this is much safer for you." Joseph expected some pushback and was prepared to remind Claire not to question his judgement.

"Okay. I can be on the bench in thirty minutes."

Joseph said, "Perfect. I'll be in the crypt by then and should be ready to come out. I'll have three bars in the backpack and two in the briefcase. That's one hundred and twenty-five pounds. I should be able to manage that for the seven blocks. If you see anything unusual, call me."

"Got it."

⚬

The door to the mausoleum creaked as Joseph pushed it opened. He shut and locked it. He flipped on the lights and smelled the air, anticipating a foul smell from the Nazi's remains. Nothing. *Glad they bought the premium model casket.*

The room looked just as amazing as it had yesterday and when he was there weeks before. He turned the key in the lock under the urn. The hydraulics in the hidden vault worked perfectly. The gold seemed to have an internal light. The breathtaking glow tugged at Joseph's senses.

He lifted five bars off the stack and placed them on the bench. He couldn't resist looking behind the second row of bars to see if there was a third one. He took the bars off quickly. There was a third stack but not a fourth one. He locked the vault back up, loaded the gold into the backpack and briefcase, and then called Claire. "Anything?"

"Nothing."

"Okay. Go to that outdoor café we picked out. I should walk past it in five or six minutes."

⚬

Joseph walked past the café on the sidewalk across the street. Claire sat at an outdoor table with a good view of the activity around her. It was a beautiful day. Her place on the café's patio was comfortable, and the coffee was delicious.

A few minutes passed before she caught the waitress's attention. "I'll have another cup of coffee and a croissant." She sipped her coffee and watched the people on the sidewalk and on the street. She studied the faces and tried to look past their expressionless gaze to see if there was a culprit lurking inside. Joseph was relying on her instincts to keep him safe. *What should I look for?* Joseph had told her, *you'll know it when you see it. Look for a person who's trying too hard to fit in or someone who you have seen before. Anyone who looks questionable is a warning.*

Joseph walked past her in the opposite direction on his return trip to the crypt. *I should be on the bench by the entrance so I can keep my eye on what's going on near the mausoleum. What if someone is waiting there for him? I'll call in a few minutes and ask if I should change location.* The few minutes came and went. Claire didn't call him. *If he wanted me on the bench, he would have said so. I'm sure he's thought that through.* She waited on high alert looking for danger. She remembered Joseph thinking that he would be most vulnerable on the sidewalk when he walked back to the house because a van could pull up alongside him and force him into the vehicle. *Look for a van or someone waiting to give a signal.*

Claire sipped her coffee and took another bite of the croissant. She glanced at her watch. Seven minutes had passed. She figured that it would be five minutes before she saw Joseph again. Traffic on the street had picked up. She tried to see and interpret everything around her without standing out from the crowd.

Joseph suddenly appeared. He was on her side of the street this time. He looked as if he was laboring a little because of the weight of the gold. Claire looked away from him and looked around. Nothing caught her eye. Joseph walked through the front gate and up to the house. *He made it!*

She didn't want it to appear that she was in a hurry, but wanted to get back with Joseph. Claire finished her coffee, left most of the pastry and enough pesos for her snack. When she stood up, she felt that something was wrong. Something was out of place. She sat down, looked into her big purse, and then looked up. An older lady stood on the sidewalk, staring at her. The lady said, "I'm sorry, I thought you were someone else."

Claire smiled a crooked smile, showing no teeth, as they had practiced. In a low voice she said, "It's okay. I get that all the time."

The lady walked on, and Claire's heartbeat slowed. When she stood again to leave, Joseph's voice came through her earpiece. "Sit back down and order another cup. I need to follow her. I'll get back to you." Claire sat down, got the waitress's attention, and felt her heart racing again. *Joseph has been watching me from the house. He doesn't believe in coincidences. This is just a precaution. I'm glad I smiled my smile and lowered my voice. Joseph would be proud of his student.*

A couple of hours later, Claire joined Joseph in the Nazi's house. She said, "This spy stuff is nerve-racking."

Joseph pulled her close and said, "You did great, Double-O-Ten. There is definitely tension when you're in the theater, but we just knocked Extraction off our list."

"Where's the gold? I want to see it."

"It's on the floor in that closet." Joseph pointed into the dining room.

Claire picked up one of the bars and said, "It's really heavy." She noticed the Nazi swastika stamped into the top of the bar and said, "Heavy to hold and heavy to think where it came from."

Joseph said, "I know. I have a plan for that, too. But right now, we're on to Logistics.

Chapter Thirty

———◦◦◦———

THE NEXT MORNING CLAIRE AND JOSEPH WAITED ON THE FRONT PORCH of the Nazi's house. Joseph was dressed as the Nazi, and Claire was in her disguise as his girlfriend. An SUV with *Carmelo Wine Region Tours* written on the side of the vehicle pulled up to the bottom of the steps. The driver was on time and professionally dressed for his chauffer duties. A young lady got out of the passenger-side door just as Joseph and Claire stepped off the last step. In Spanish Claire said, "You must be Marie. I'm Lola, and this is Herman. We're ready for our big day."

Marie said, "Nice to meet you. It's a beautiful day to visit some of the very best boutique wineries in the Carmelo Wine District."

The driver walked around the back of the vehicle and opened the passenger-side back door. Claire and Joseph climbed into the backseat.

As the SUV pulled away, Claire waved good-bye to Augy. Marie said, "Our first stop is an hour's ride from here; that gives me enough time to explain to you how the Malbec grape was introduced to Argentina and why the vineyards here are some of the best in the world.

———◦———

Six hours later Joseph and the driver carried the last two cases of wine into the Nazi's house while Claire settled the fee and tip for the tour with Marie.

Joseph and Claire stood in front of the twelve cases of wine they had purchased. Claire asked, "So how is this supposed to work?"

Joseph took off his hat, glasses, and coat. He walked up to Claire and began to remove her disguise. He said, "I can only tell my beautiful girlfriend, Claire, this plan. I've seen enough of Lola today." He unbuttoned her jacket as he talked. "The story starts with the Cheshire catlike smile of Hans Brekman. He is my private banker for an account I have with a bank in Lucerne, Switzerland. He is responsible for keeping me happy so the bank can take their seven percent cut of the money that goes in and out of my account. That seven percent fee changes dirty money into clean money with the snap of a finger and a big, toothy grin from Hans. He has legal and illegal connections all over the world. He is an odd combination of ruthless and goofball. He always has that smile on his face while he assures me that nothing will ever go wrong, but if it does, it will never get back to me."

Claire said, "Okay, I get the picture. Go on."

"Each case of wine has twelve bottles and weighs fifty pounds. We are going to take six bottles out of each case and replace them with one of the gold bars that weighs twenty-five pounds. Then we'll seal the box back up and put on this shipping label." Joseph reached for the UPS shipping labels.

"The UPS truck will be here in …" Joseph looked at his watch … "forty-five minutes to pick up these twelve cases of wine. The boxes will be delivered to Hans in Lucerne. He will sell the gold and deposit the proceeds into my account, less the bank's seven percent. Twelve bars times four hundred ounces per bar times eighteen hundred dollars per ounce … That's over eight and a half million dollars. The bank will take about six hundred thousand off the top, and the rest is ours. That's more than enough to fund the Naples mission and get the Bruzzellis off our back. I told Hans that he could keep the wine for himself. I'm sure his smile grew even bigger when he heard those words."

"That's an excellent display of fine logistics, Joseph. But you only brought back ten bars."

"There are two gold bars already here from my first trip. I say we open one of these fine bottles and get to work."

⸻◦◦◦⸻

Later that evening in the candlelit Four Seasons' Elena restaurant, Claire said, "This is about the coolest place I've ever been in. I love the way they let us pick out our own steak."

"I agree. The vibe in here is unique. It's a perfect place to celebrate the end of Logistics and the beginning of Escape." Joseph waved the waiter over, and they placed their order.

"So ... how does this restaurant compare with the place you were when you decided that being an attorney wasn't for you?"

Clair answered, "It doesn't compare. And neither does the company. It only took me a few days to realize that everything about that business is probably just as corrupt as what you escaped in Boston. I could have played the game, but all I could think about was you and getting out of that corporate jungle. Tell me more about the Boston mission."

"Jackson created a good plan, but as I told you we had to change that plan because of the ambush we witnessed. I'm not sure what we're doing next. Jackson will come up with something. I talked to him this morning. He gave me a report on three men from Naples who showed up in San Francisco a few days ago."

"How did he find them?"

"Jackson has contacts in the CIA, and he found out that the Bruzzelli group had been put on the CIA's watch list years ago. One of Jackson's contacts told him the Bruzzelli men were heading to Frisco.

"The three men from Naples' problems mysteriously started as soon as they left the San Francisco airport. The car they rented had flat tires, their luggage was stolen from their motel rooms, and they got into a fight where they lost their IDs and money. Jackson and his men had fun making their lives miserable without them knowing what was going on. They're now on their way back to Naples with no luggage, identification, or money. With the CIA's help we will be able keep tabs on everything they do."

Claire said, "Change of subject. I haven't had a chance to tell you. When we were on our break ..." She stopped, smiled, and went on, "I went up to the Tobin Winery and hung out with Mandy, Anna, and Sophie."

"Really? How did that come about?"

"Mandy called and asked us to come up. I told her you were out of town, and she insisted that I come anyway. So I did, and I had a blast with them."

"Did you tell them anything about us?"

"No, just that you were out of town."

"What was Max like? We went to the same Catholic school together. I thought he was a little strange. I was probably his best friend, but he didn't fit into my world. As we got older, he went the athletic route, and I went down the gangster path. The poor guy didn't have any family. He was totally alone all the time."

"He's great. The whole family seems so happy and in love. Baby Bella stole the show, though. It's hard to take your eyes off that one."

The waiter arrived with their meal, and at the same time the sommelier presented the cork from one of Argentina's finest Malbec bottles of wine to Joseph for his approval. Joseph tasted a small amount of wine and nodded to the sommelier. He poured half a glass for Claire.

Joseph asked, "Would you please put a bottle of your best brut champagne on ice for us? We'll ask you to open the bottle after we finish our dinner."

"Right away, sir," the sommelier said, then walked away.

Claire said, "You know what happens when I drink champagne."

"Yes, I do. I can already hear the zipper sliding down the back of your dress."

Claire smiled. Her hair was up. She wore a matching set of emerald earrings and an emerald necklace that Joseph had bought at one of the neighborhood high-end jewelry stores there. He surprised her with the jewelry just before they came down for dinner. The color of the stones matched her eyes and paired perfectly with her auburn hair and porcelain complexion. Joseph moved his eyebrows up and down and said, "We can sleep in tomorrow."

Claire answered, "Not sure how much sleeping we'll be doing."

Joseph grinned. "The driver picks us up at noon for the start of the Escape phase. We'll spend a few nights down in Patagonia on a red stag hunt and then fly home from the small airport there. Have you ever been on a red stag hunt in Patagonia before?"

Claire laughed. "No, I haven't. What's that all about? I assume you've done as much hunting as I have—none."

"A good friend told me about this bucket-list experience. The area is beautiful, and you don't have to shoot anything. We'll get in some good hikes and spend some alone time in a really cool resort-type property.

"Our driver for the start of Escape will drop us off with the identities that we used to check into this hotel at a resort about halfway to the hunting lodge. That driver will think we're staying where he dropped us off. A guide from the hunting lodge will pick us up, and we'll use our real identity at the lodge. No way anyone could trace our movements or follow us without being noticed in that remote area."

An hour later the restaurant was packed. Claire sat on the same side of the table as Joseph, almost in his lap. Everyone looked their way with the sound of the cork erupting from the bottle of one of France's finest. Claire smiled and winked. She whispered into Joseph's ear, "The fuse is burning."

Chapter H

MORE THAN THREE YEARS HAD PASSED SINCE I TALKED TO VITO ABOUT how I wanted to invest in the winery by buying a few new oak barrels.

I had a big office in the Vomero Bank and Trust, with staff and a six-figure income. I didn't go back to school after my second year there. Lia and Gina were gone. Futbol and my studies seemed like a waste of time. I lied about my age and got a job at a small bank as a teller and lived in an apartment that Vito owned. I worked at that bank for a year and learned the business.

Vito got me forged university credentials, which I used to secure a position at a different bank—the biggest bank in Vomero. It wasn't long before I was promoted and then given the title of vice president and a plush office. Not bad for a nineteen-year-old kid. I had inside knowledge of what was going on all over Naples, and I gave that valuable information to Vito. It was a good setup for me and a great one for Vito.

My last heist was a big one. I learned the armored truck routine for the main bank, where my office was located. After some good planning, a dry run, and then the execution, I was able to swap bags filled with magazines for bags filled with euros on one of our biggest cash days.

It's a long story, but it worked perfectly. No one got hurt. No one got blamed. The loss was insured. I gave Vito two hundred and eighty thousand euros. He gave me back twenty-eight thousand. I added that to the two hundred and fifty thousand I held back.

That heist was a big deal to me because it meant Vito would continue to let me work by myself for a long time. And I used my share to buy a small vineyard that bordered my wine partner's operation.

The only downside of my life was Vito was on his way to pick me up. It had been over three years since I invested in those new French oak barrels with Pascal. The wine from those barrels had just been sold, and it turned out to be very good. We made some serious money. I was proud of how my investment had paid off. I had to tell Vito that morning how much money we made, and I knew he would take at least half of my profit.

That wasn't all. Lia and Gina were home from university. They had come to my apartment the night before. We went out for a late dinner and then returned to my place. They stayed with me. We were together like that nearly every weekend. What would Vito think if he knew about Gina, Lia, and me? What would he do? The three of us didn't know what to think. Our shared intimacy seemed natural and beautiful to us. Vito and the rest of society could never understand the situation. How could they when we couldn't?

I waited outside the bank until Vito's Bentley rounded the corner. He wanted me to go with him to the Bruzzelli's headquarters at their shipping port south of Naples. It was an honor to be invited, but I didn't want any part of that group. I wanted to live on the far side of that world.

Chapter I

THE BOARDROOM OF THE BRUZZELLI COMPOUND WAS THE CENTERPIECE of their port south of Naples. The room was full of men, all dressed like gangsters. Chairman Dante Bruzzelli sat at the head of the conference table. The eight other men at the table gazed at him in silence. I was one of twenty men standing at attention behind them.

The meeting had gone on for over an hour. I just wanted to get out of there, get back to work, back to Lia and Gina.

Dante said, "Gimme an update on the latest Afghan shipment."

One of his men said, "It's being offloaded on the docks in Boston. There will be five smaller box trucks there for distribution in New York. We wanted to spread out the risk by using the smaller trucks. But we gotta move forward with establishing our own distribution system in New York City. That's where the real money is."

Dante responded, "Patience, my friend, patience. We'll get there, but we're not ready yet."

Dante shuffled the stack of papers in front of him. He said, "That takes care of the items that needed our attention today." He looked at Ciro and said, "Where are we with that pretty-faced Cairo punk in San Francisco?"

Ciro said, "I contacted our friends in Sicily, and they suggested we sanction the one and only Natalia for this job. She's taking her two bodyguards with her for backup. I didn't want to take any chances with this one. She should be making contact with him soon."

"How much is this gonna cost us?"

"Her services are not cheap."

"Have you ever seen her?"

"I have not, and I don't want to, because the only people who have seen her are dead. Word is, she has a unique beauty that no man can resist, and she only comes out at night. They say she's from a rural area in the Valencia region of Spain. The Cairo kid will be on his knees begging her to cut up his pretty face for just a little taste."

Dante laughed. "Maybe we should ask her to record that scene for us."

Everyone in the room laughed. I didn't see the humor. Dante's attention turned to another man. Dante said, "Who do we have drivin' in this year's Targa Florio?"

"Vito is driving his Ferrari again, but we haven't heard back from Sicily yet, and the race is in two weeks."

I could only see the back of Vito's head, but I was sure he had a proud look on his face. Maybe he'll take me with him.

"Do you think they're done gettin' their ass kicked year after year?"

"Maybe. Remember last year when their driver wrecked and hurt some spectators? Maybe they're having trouble setting up our private race this year."

Dante said, "Shake the branches of that tree and find out what's goin' on. Offer to help them set it up. That's a great time. I don't wanna miss it."

Dante stacked his papers in a neat pile and looked around the room to find one of the men standing against the wall. When he found the man he was looking for, he said, "What's on the menu for tonight's dinner?"

"Chef got in several nice lambs this morning, and his sous chef got back late last night from Alba, up in Piedmont. He bought an eight hundred and thirty-six-gram white truffle at the auction. On the way back, he stopped in northern Campania and picked up some fresh buffalo mozzarella from that creamery you like. That's the one we made an offer to last year."

Dante said, "That sounds good. Tell chef to marinate and grill a few lollipop chops for me. Ask him to roast our red potatoes with plenty of garlic. I'd like the mozzarella on some bruschetta along with some very thin slices off that truffle. Grab a case of Nero d'Avola from the cellar as a reminder of our friends from Sicily.

"It's a nice day out there today. Set up our lunch on the veranda and take one of the new girls to my bedroom. Have her cleaned up and ready for my afternoon siesta." Dante looked at another man and asked, "What's our entertainment tonight?"

We have those dancers from Rome you wanted, for two nights."

"Excellent. Oh, one more thing. He motioned to one of the men standing at the back of the room, right next to me, and said, "My wife told me there are some gypsy kids hangin' around the school and marketplace in our neighborhood. Take those two guys next to you up there and run those mutts outta there." He pointed to me and another man.

What were the odds for that happening? I'm getting pulled into something that I want no part of.

"Make it clear to them. Don't ever come back." He looked at the men sitting around the table. "Did you hear any of this from your wives?"

One of the men said, "Yeah, she said something about the marketplace. But, to tell you the truth, I wasn't listening to a word she said." The men in the room broke up with laughter.

I hooked Vito on the way out the door and said, "I have all kinds of appointments scheduled the next few days at the bank. Can you ask them to get someone else?"

Vito just laughed. "There's nothin' we can do. He pointed directly at you. There are no substitutions when you been called out. Just figure it out, keep your head down, and do what you're told. I never shoulda brought you to this meeting, but we can't change it now."

Chapter Thirty-One

J OSEPH OPENED THE DOOR TO REED JACKSON'S MODEST OFFICE. JACKSON waved him in and said, "Hi, Joseph. Have a seat. How was your trip to Argentina?"

"Everything went really well. We had a blast."

Jackson said, "Good to hear. I wanted to bring you up to speed on what we've found out about the Bruzzelli operation in Naples. I asked Renegade to send a report on what he and Apache learned in the five days they've been on recon there. His report is brief, so I'll read it aloud."

Jackson pulled up the document on his computer screen and said, "Apache has been responsible for the sea, and I've taken the land. He has been going out with charter fishermen to see what the Bruzzelli compound looks like from the water. They have an active little port with boats coming and going there day and night. He's seen their boats meet large ships several miles offshore and then come directly back. He wants to get close enough to see what's going on. But he can't get the fishing boat captains to take him close to the port because "*nessun pesce li.*" No fish there.

"The compound behind the marina is shaped like an upside-down V that rises from the port up a hill. He said that the base, or the top of the upside-down V, was dark at night over the weekend. During the week, it's all lit up and has a lot of activity.

"They don't seem to have much security around their port. It looks like they operate as though they have complete immunity.

"He hasn't been able to get a rental boat that he'd be able to take out by himself. Language is a big problem for both of us here. This Naples area isn't like Rome where people speak a little English. No one speaks English here. He found out that he could rent a pleasure boat on the small island of Capri. Capri is a resort area for the rich and famous. It's about fifteen miles from here, and there are shuttles going back and forth every day.

"I've rented a motorcycle but can't get close to the compound to see what's going on inside the gates. It looks like they work two shifts every day including weekends. Workers enter the compound at seven in the morning, and a new shift comes in at three in the afternoon. The second shift works until eleven. From eleven until seven in the morning, the place is shut down.

"Last Friday I saw a parade of very expensive luxury cars leave the compound after lunch. The same group came back to the compound Monday morning. I suspect the executives stay at the compound during the week, then go home on the weekends.

"Naples is pretty cool. It's not geared to the tourist trade. It's just Italians living their lives. We've had some great meals here, but as I said before, the language is a real problem.

"It would be nice if we could get eyes inside the compound. With our joint intel, Apache and I assume the Bruzzelli executives sleep and have their offices up the hill, in the base of the V of the compound. Maybe there are offices where we could plant some bugs. We'd have to get an interpreter, though. Maybe there are blueprints of the compound on file in public records.

"Our plan next week includes Apache getting to Capri to rent a boat so he can get closer to the compound during the day, and we'll try to see what's going on there at night. I'm going to pick out one of those executive cars when they leave Friday afternoon and follow it to see where it's going. Then this weekend I'm going to try to get into the compound at night and on foot.

"Tell Joseph we've noticed several shoe stores around here that are named Cairo Scarpa. They look like high-end stores."

Joseph smiled and said, "This op is turning out to be much bigger than I expected."

Jackson said, "I've been in touch with my contact at the CIA to get a nod from them regarding our plans for the Bruzzellis. The CIA and Interpol have had the Bruzzelli group in their sights for a couple years. They've given us the green light to do what we have to do."

Joseph said, "Before we get going on that, I wanted to give you this." Joseph handed Jackson a check made out to "The Agency" for $100,000. "That's to cover the expenses for the Boston op." Then Joseph gave Jackson a piece of paper and said, "These are the account number and the security code for access to a Swiss bank account that I set up for your use. Also, notice my personal banker's name and private phone number. I've instructed him to comply with your requests just as he would my own. There's two million dollars in that account that we can use to fund the Naples op. There's more if we need it. I want you to spare no expense for supplies or whatever the men need."

Jackson looked stunned. Then he smiled and said, Thank you. Very much appreciated. This will give us more options. I'll tell all my men about your commitment."

Joseph said, "One more thing before we get going. That money …" Joseph pointed to the note "… is a small part of a big story that includes a secret treasure. If things work out with us working together, I'll bring you in on the secret, and we'll work together to monetize the treasure. There's enough there to fund everything we would ever want to do."

Jackson said, "That all sounds interesting, but let's take care of this Bruzzelli business first. Based on Renegade's report, I've determined the next step. You and I will go over there and put a fresh set of eyes on the op. You don't speak Italian by any chance?"

"I do. I grew up speaking Italian as my first language."

"Great! That will help us a lot. Make arrangements with your office and tell Claire you'll be gone for several days. I'll get us on a plane tomorrow or the next day. Is there anything I should know? Any concerns you have? I need to know everything."

Joseph shook his head in a slow, thoughtful way and said, "I guess there are a couple things. I don't feel comfortable leaving Claire here by herself and I got a call from an associate at the office about something that wasn't normal. A lady who is a movie star, model type, wants to meet me at a condo she's buying this afternoon. She said that she wants to work only with me, even though they told her that I work only with business insurance."

Jackson leaned back in his chair. After a moment he said, "That does seem odd. With Claire, I have an idea about that. Give me what you have about the mystery lady. I'll run her through Kent, my CIA contact."

Chapter Thirty-Two

J OSEPH PUSHED THE BUTTON LABELED THIRTY-THREE AND WATCHED THE elevator doors close in front of him. He reviewed what his friends at the office said and what Jackson found out from his CIA contact. *They said she was a knockout who was dressed to kill. They said that she wanted to work only with me and had made an appointment to meet me at a luxury condominium not far from my place that she was buying. She wanted my expertise on how to insure the property. Nothing about the story seemed right.*

Using his CIA connections, Jackson discovered that the woman had arrived at the San Francisco International airport with two men from Spain. *We assumed right away she was an assassin hired by the Bruzzelli group.* Jackson laid out a plan that started with his men keeping the two men from Spain away from the meeting site at the condo. I was to engage the lady to find out what I could about the Bruzzelli group. Jackson had said, "A perfect outcome for this op is to get what you can out of this femme fatale regarding how the Bruzzellis run their operation. Any intel you can get from her will help our Naples operation. Use your skills to turn her. Make her want to help you."

When the elevator doors opened, Joseph felt confident he could accomplish what Jackson wanted without getting himself killed.

Joseph knocked twice on the door and heard, "Come in, it's open."

When Joseph opened the door, he saw a tall woman looking out the floor-to-ceiling windows. She had dark-brown, shoulder-length hair, a flawless hourglass shape, and long, thin legs. She wore a tight black skirt and exceptionally high stilettoes. The very picture of a femme fatale, Joseph thought.

She turned around and said, "You are a little late." Her face was model-perfect.

Joseph said, "I apologize. I had to use public parking." He walked through the foyer into a large room. The space had to be thirty feet wide and sixty feet long, with twelve-foot-high ceilings. Elegant, contemporary furniture was carefully positioned throughout the room. The living area, dining area, and kitchen were all part of the big room. Joseph walked directly to the woman with his hand out and a big smile on his face. "I'm Joseph Johnson."

She wore black leather gloves. She extended her hand, and with her Spanish accent said, "Hello, Joseph. I'm Natalia. Thank you for coming to my rescue. My closing for this place is scheduled in two days."

Joseph looked up and around the room and said, "This place is amazing! Congratulations. But I'm not sure why I'm here. I specialize in commercial insurance. I don't work with this type of property."

"That's what they told me at your office, but I told them that I only work with the best." She smiled and released his hand.

Joseph looked around the room for her purse or any other place where she may have a weapon. He walked to the windows. He felt comfortable turning his back to her that early in the meeting. "You have a fantastic view of the ocean and the bridge. I think you'll be happy here." He knew she was checking him out. He turned and said, "Will I need to prepare closing documents for your lender if you qualify for the insurance?"

She stepped closer to him, walking like a model, and said, "No, it's a cash deal." And then with a pouty face said, "If I qualify? You mean you may not want to take me on as a client?"

Joseph smiled and said, "It's not up to me. There is a multistep process we have to go through before we can bind coverage."

She turned away and said, "Well, I don't care about any of that. I'm sure we are compatible, and I want to celebrate right now." She crossed the room to the white marble kitchen counter and picked up two champagne glasses and a bottle of champagne.

Do not drink a drop of that, Joseph said to himself as he took a moment to look around the space again. *Jackson said she'd probably have weapons hidden in different places.*

As she peeled the foil from the neck of the bottle, she said, "What is the process to see if I am eligible for your insurance?"

She unwound the wire cage, draped a small towel over the bottle, and placed her thumb over the cork.

Joseph could tell that she had done this many times. "First there is the property inspection, and then you'll have to go through underwriting to determine if the risk meets the proper guidelines.

With an enticing smile she said, "I love this part." She gripped the bottom of the bottle and twisted it slowly until the cork released with a satisfying *pop*. Only a little foam escaped from the bottle.

Joseph joined her as she poured the champagne. They lifted their glass and said, "Cheers." *She is a true knockout!* He had trouble taking his eyes off her face. He turned away, walked to the windows again, and pretended to take a drink. He turned around quickly and said, "Wow! This is really good. What is this?"

"I already told you, silly. I only get the best." She placed her glass of champaign on the marble-topped island, which separated the kitchen from the open dining area. She smiled as she approached Joseph. "Well, let's get the inspection process started." Then she turned and walked away down a hallway and said, "Follow me."

Joseph followed her, with his eyes on the short, tight-fitting skirt. He felt a little guilty about taking the gift she offered him. *At least I know she's not hiding a weapon there. I bet she thinks her friends will bust in here any minute.*

She opened a door at the end of the hall, and Joseph followed her in. She turned and said, "Here is the master bedroom. This would be a good place to begin your inspection."

She approached Joseph and said, "Do you like what you have seen so far?" She found his hand, led him to the bed, and started to unbutton his shirt. "What can I do to get a good underwriting score?"

Joseph clasped her hands and gently pushed her back until she sat on the edge of the bed. He put the knuckle of his index finger under her chin and lifted it so their eyes met. She smiled, and Joseph said, "I don't believe you brought me here to insure this condo. And you should know that your friends won't be joining you."

He waited for the tell. And then, there it was. Her eyes flickered to one side. Joseph followed her gaze to the bedside table. She lunged for the drawer. Joseph grabbed a fistful of her long hair and jerked her backward. He shoved her face onto the bed and planted a knee on the small of her back. She squirmed and grunted under his weight. *She's tougher than she looks.* He used zip-tie handcuffs to secure her hands behind her back. Joseph waited for her to stopped struggling. Then he turned her over, dragged her to the side of the bed, and sat her up.

She said, "Hey, I thought we were going to have some fun."

"Let's see what kind of fun you had planned," Joseph said. He pulled open the table drawer and found a stun gun and a long, thin knife. He pointed the stun gun at her face.

"A woman needs to be able to protect herself," she said.

"You and I are going to have an honest conversation. Every time I think you're not telling the truth I'll zap you with your definition of fun. Capisce?"

"What do you want?"

Joseph sat down next to her. "Look, this doesn't have to get ugly," he said in a calm voice. "I don't want to hurt you, but make no mistake, one way or another you're going to give me what I want. Who are you, and why are you here?"

"I was hired by a group out of Italy to seduce you and then mess you up."

"Who and why?"

"The Bruzzelli family in Naples. They said you beat up a couple of their crew, and they want you to pay."

"Mess me up? How?"

"They wanted us to make you walk with a limp and cut up your 'pretty' face. They don't want to kill you because they want your skills." She smirked at him and said, "You do have a nice face. In our brief time together, I knew I couldn't hurt you. They told me that you're an expert assassin. We could work together. We would make a good team."

Joseph lowered the stun gun. Were you the one who was going to use the knife to cut up my face?"

She looked at him, but didn't answer.

Joseph said, "The way I see it, I only have two choices. I could do to you what you were planning to do to me. That would send a message to the

Bruzzelli clan. Or I could just let you go and hope you wouldn't come at me again." He stood up and paced back and forth as he contemplated his options. "I'd rather not break your leg and cut up your face, but that would be pretty easy and go fast once I stuffed a gag in your mouth. Your friends would find you lying in a pool of blood. Option two is no good because how could I ever trust you?" Joseph walked into the bathroom and came out with a washcloth. He twisted it as he approached her. "This will work. I think I'll break your leg first. You'll probably pass out, so you won't feel me carving up your face."

She said, "No, wait, I'll—"

Joseph shoved the washcloth into her mouth. She bucked and kicked her feet. Joseph said, "You better hold still or I might break both legs. She shook her head violently and let out a muffled scream. He pulled out the gag and said, "Look, you know I don't have a choice. It's nothing personal. We're both professionals."

"I have another option for you," she wheezed.

"What's that?"

"My purse is in the other bedside table. You know they don't want to kill you. They want you to work for them, so why would they kill you? My passport is in my purse. It has my name and address. Once you have that information, you know I won't double-cross you, because I know you would come for me and my family. I have no connection to the Bruzzellis. They hired me because their men weren't capable of taking you on. I have no loyalty to them. I'll tell them I had to abort the operation."

Joseph said, "What kind of operation are they running over there?"

"I don't know much. I'm an independent contractor just like you. My contacts in that part of the world are with the Sicilian mob. They told me the head of the Bruzzelli group is a psychopath degenerate named Dante Bruzzelli. The Bruzzelli group has a small port south of Naples, where they smuggle drugs and weapons in and out of Europe."

Joseph said, "Your plan won't work for me. They'll just send someone else. Why don't you tell them you did the job? You'll get paid, and they'll get off my back. I never see anyone from that group, and they have no reason to ever see me. They'll believe their revenge is satisfied and continue to take their cut from the work I do for them. No one will know what went down here, and everyone will be happy. Tell them it will be a few months before I'll be able to work again. If they push you, tell them exactly what went on here today, except that *you* got *my* hands in the zip tie after you zapped me with that stun gun and then broke my leg and cut up my face while I was passed out."

"I can do that."

"If I agree to your plan and let you go, you will owe me a favor."

"I will owe you a favor of your choice, and I always deliver. We could stay in touch. We could meet in Paris or Vienna sometime, maybe often, and have some fun." She smiled her sexy smile. "We're both professionals who understand each other. Wouldn't it be nice to hang out like normal people and enjoy each other's company? I know you like what you see. Believe me, I like what I see.

"We could celebrate our partnership right here, right now." She said and smiled again.

Joseph pulled his phone out of his back pocket. He took a picture of Natalia and asked, "What's your cell number?"

She told him, and he called her number. A muffled ringing noise came from the nightstand on the other side of the bed. Joseph walked there and retrieved her passport from the purse. He took pictures of every page.

Joseph held up his phone and smiled. "Now we know how to get in touch with each other."

Joseph pulled her up off the bed. She stood with hands secured behind her back. Joseph moved in close to her. He didn't touch her when he whispered into her ear. "I want to hear you say again."

She leaned closer and said, "I owe you, Joseph, and I can't wait to deliver." She lightly kissed his ear.

Joseph used her knife to cut the zip tie and said. "Let's watch each other's back. If you hear something I should know, call me. I'll do the same for you. We'll get together in Paris sometime soon and spend some time together."

She grinned at him and said, "That's a deal, partner."

Chapter Thirty-Three

⮞◉◉⮜

A FEW DAYS LATER, JOSEPH AND RENEGADE SAT ON BAR STOOLS IN A small café in Naples. Renegade said, "We're here a little early. I'm sure Jackson and Apache won't mind if we drink a cold one."

The bartender brought them two bottles of Peroni beer. Joseph pulled out his wallet and said, "I'll get these." He handed the bartender ten euros and told him to keep the change. He noticed a note that he had put in his wallet a few weeks before and read it again. *Find Luca De Luca.* The note reminded him of his visit with his father.

Renegade asked, "What do you have there?"

Joseph handed him the note. He told him about his visit with his father in prison and how his father had said, *You need to start at a Cairo shoe store.*

Renegade said, "Why are we sitting here?" He hopped off his stool and headed for the door.

Joseph followed him as he used his phone to find the location of a Cairo shoe store. He caught up with Renegade outside the café and said, "There's one a couple of blocks from here."

⭒◦⭒

A bell on the door clanged as they walked through the front door. Joseph approached a young clerk stocking the shelves. Renegade stayed in the front of the store, close enough to observe but far enough away not to interfere. Joseph asked the clerk, "Is the owner or manager here?"

"Can I ask why?"

"It's personal business. Tell him my name is Anthony Cairo."

The clerk disappeared into the back room. A few minutes later a smartly dressed, sophisticated-looking older gentleman approached him slowly. "Can I help you?"

"Hello. My name is Anthony Cairo. My father is Mario Cairo, and my grandfather's name was Vincenzo. I'm looking for someone who knew them. Can you help me?"

The man looked Joseph up and down. He seemed to be uncertain about talking to a stranger. Finally, he said, "That makes you Ciccolini's great-grandson. You look like him. What can I do for you?"

Joseph said, "My father told me to find a man named Luca De Luca to get some answers about my family's history."

"Yes, he is the one you should talk to. He lives in the caves of Matera. We all lived in caves in Matera until Ciccolini led us out of there to lives we have now in Naples. It's a long story, but this is where you need to start. Matera is about a two-hour drive through the mountains from here."

"Pass me a slice of that sausage one, Joseph said." Renegade handed the tray of pizza pie to Joseph. All four of them were working hard on their supper. The café was crowded. Their table was right in the middle of the bustle. Jackson said, "It feels like we're invisible here. Everyone has to know we're foreigners, but they're all ignoring us."

"Yeah, and I kinda like it that way," Apache said.

Joseph asked, "How was it out there on the water today?"

Jackson said, "There were plenty of whitecaps today when the breeze picked up this afternoon. That's a small boat for the open sea. I'm not looking forward to the trip back to Capri tonight in the dark. There are big boats all over that route. The commercial shipping vessels and huge yachts move fast. They have no idea we're even there." He took a big swig of beer and said, "I'm still not a hundred-percent sure what they have for security on their docks at night. We wouldn't be able to just tie up our boat and walk through the marina. We'll have to find another way in."

Joseph put his phone down, looked at his friends with a smile, and said, "Let's rent a yacht. I just googled it, and we can actually rent yachts of any size, with a crew." He picked up the phone and looked at the screen again and said, "It'll cost us some serious money, but we have it. A big boat would be a good base for us. We could make jet skis and scuba equipment part of the package. Hans will set it up. He can probably get us a couple of Zodiac inflatable boats." He looked at Jackson and said, "Call Hans and tell him everything you want. Just tell him where and when you want it, and it will be waiting. He's available twenty-four hours a day. Don't feel like you're bothering him. He'll drag seven percent of everything we spend and love every minute of it. Plus, he'll do it in a way that will never come back to us."

The three other men looked at one another and laughed. Apache said, "I knew I was going to like working with this guy." They all laughed again.

Jackson said, "I'll call him after supper. What did you guys find out today?"

Renegade said, "We confirmed that all those Bru—" He caught himself before he said the name. "All the executives live in the same neighborhood called Vomero. It's on the highest hill in Naples and looks exactly the opposite of the way everything looks down here in the city. The streets are ancient but clean. The homes are big and fancy. The view of the city and the bay is pretty cool, but the neighborhood butts right up against the foothills of Mount Vesuvius. Did you guys know that that thing is still considered an active volcano? It's the one that buried Pompeii. Not sure how the intel on where they live will help us, unless we take some time to pinpoint their exact locations and schedules." Renegade nodded to Joseph and said, "Tell them what else we found out."

Joseph said, "Jackson and Apache don't want to hear about that. It's not part of why we're here."

Jackson looked at Joseph and said, "You're part of our family now. Everything is important."

Joseph pushed his plate forward and said, "When I went to the prison to visit my father, I asked him about the ongoing battle between the Cairo and Bruzzelli families. He couldn't say anything there, but he passed me a note that said find Luca De Luca. He said to start at one of the Cairo shoe stores to find him. We went to one of the Cairo shoe stores this afternoon and talked with an elderly gentleman who knew my family and told us Luca De Luca lived in the town of Matera, a couple of hours from here."

Jackson looked at Joseph and said, "Tomorrow, you and Renegade—"

"I can go up there by myself," Joseph said. "I don't have to involve you guys with any of this."

Jackson frowned at Joseph, lowered his voice, and said, "Tomorrow, you and Renegade will go to Matera and find this Luca De Luca. Apache and I will get the yacht preparations squared away and plan a way to infiltrate the compound. Kent was able to get the blueprints of the compound. There's a conference room right in the middle of the base of the V that would be a good place to install some video cameras." He stood up to leave. Apache stopped eating and stood with him. Jackson said, "We're going to head back to Capri now. Call me tomorrow when you guys get back." Jackson and Apache left.

Joseph looked at Renegade and said, "What just happened there?"

Renegade said, "Never question Jackson. He wants us to give him information and make suggestions, but don't interrupt him to question his decisions." Renegade stood and walked away, leaving Joseph alone at the table.

Chapter Thirty-Four

THE RIDE TO MATERA ON THE NARROW, WINDING ROADS THROUGH THE mountains was both beautiful and perilous. The humming of their motorcycle engines cleared Joseph's mind of everything except thoughts of what he might learn in Matera. He was looking for answers, but didn't have specific questions other than *Who am I?* and *How does the Bruzzelli family fit into the picture? Why does it matter? It must matter if Dad gave me the contact. It must matter.*

Renegade either has a lot more experience than I do on one of these bikes or he's just crazy. Joseph tried to keep up with him by leaning his motorcycle into a harrowing curve of the road.

Finally they got to Matera and parked their bikes in the town center. It looked like many other small towns in Italy. Joseph knew they looked out of place and assumed they wouldn't get much cooperation from the locals. He stopped asking for Luca De Luca and started asking people to point them to the caves. They chose one finger that lead them out of town to an area that looked prehistoric. Doors had been carved into the rocks of the steep slope of the terraced mountain. After getting directions from a man, they continued walking upward along the dirt path. Some of the doorways were covered with tarps and others with aged wooden planks.

Joseph found the door with a rooster painted on the wooden planks and knocked on it. They heard movement inside, but nobody came out. Joseph knocked again. They waited a couple of minutes before the leather-hinged door opened. A thin older man with pure white hair combed straight back squinted at them in the bright sunlight. He had a soft, brown face, and his clothes were almost formal.

Joseph said, "I'm looking for Luca De Luca. My name is Anthony Cairo. My father is Mario Cairo, and my grandfather was Vincenzo."

The man looked up at him and said, "And your great-grandfather was the revered Ciccolini Cairo."

Joseph said, "My father sent me to you. He said you would know the answers to my questions about our family."

The man motioned for Joseph and Renegade to come inside. Renegade stayed just outside the open doorway. Joseph had to bend down to enter the room. There was enough sunlight coming through the open door to illuminate the small room. Luca sat on a three-legged stool beside a small wooden table. Joseph sat on the other stool. Luca picked up a pitcher with one hand and a handmade clay cup with the other. He filled the cup with red wine and gave it to Joseph. He filled another cup for himself. He took a sip, then said, "I know who you are and know you're from Boston. You came a long way, son. I hope I can give you what you seek. I will try." Luca smiled a welcoming smile and gazed at Joseph with a look of genuine concern. Joseph felt comfortable in the presence of this pleasant man.

Joseph said, "There's an ongoing vendetta between the Cairo family and the Bruzzelli family. I was hoping to find out why and how I can end it."

Luca smiled and took a sip of wine. He looked at Joseph with his kind, dark eyes and chuckled. "That, Anthony, is quite a story and an impossible task. The story starts hundreds of years ago right here in these caves. Your family—our family—lived here along with dozens of other families. The Cairo families raised sheep and goats. The men were shepherds who watched over their flocks in the pastures on top of this mountain. Back then, each family had their own way of contributing to the cave community. I don't know when it started, but the Bruzzelli family became the family that would take but never contribute anything. At times there was violence involved. Your great-grandfather, my uncle Ciccolini, created a cave watch group to protect themselves from the Bruzzellis. There were no police in those days. The community had to take care of itself. The Bruzzellis eventually outbred the rest of the families. Their power and intimidation took over the community. The Bruzzelli group took a piece of something from everyone. As time went on, their population grew, and so did the violence.

"Ciccolini left the caves as a young man to look for opportunity. He was our leader even at his young age. He told the elders that he would find a new place for the Cairo families to live. When he left, he told them that he would return with some good news. The three years he was gone were the worst years in the caves. The Bruzzellis' violence and oppression grew more ruthless every day.

"Ciccolini came back to the caves with a story of hope and opportunity. He had traveled to Naples and gone to work as a cobbler. In a short time, he created a specific type of work boot that all the men of Naples wanted. He hired people to make the boots and changed the way boots were made by designing and making different sizes of boots instead of making custom boots for each customer. He actually invented the first assembly line in Italy. The Neapolitans bought his boots. He expanded by hiring more and more workers.

"When he came back to us with his story of wealth and opportunity, most of the Cairo families left the caves and followed him to Naples, where he had jobs and homes waiting for them. His leadership created opportunities and freedoms for us that we had only dreamed about. Ciccolini's vision went a step further. He opened shops that sold his boots. He took his Cairo family members out of the factories and made them owners of these shops. There are still Cairo shoe stores all over Naples. He kept evolving his business by making a shoe to complement his boot design, and then he created different types of boots and shoes. A few of his nieces became fashion designers of women's shoes, and a whole new market opened up. Cairo shoes were shipped all over Italy."

Luca took a drink of wine, then stood up, walked across the small room and opened a cupboard door. He pulled out a loaf of bread, placed it on a plate and brought it to the table. He sat down and tore off a piece of bread and pushed the plate to Joseph. Luca dipped his bread into his cup of wine and ate it. Joseph did the same. Luca ate more bread without saying a word. Then he poured himself some wine and filled Joseph's cup.

Joseph was mesmerized by his movements, his voice, and his story.

Luca said, "That's when the Bruzzellis left the caves. They brought their violence and intimidation with them to Naples. Those were the early days of what we now call the mafia. Just as Ciccolini created a modern business, the Bruzzellis created the modern mafia. Their numbers continued to grow, and so did their control of Naples. The Bruzzelli family was especially brutal with the Cairo families because of jealousy. The Cairo's are honorable, beautiful people. The Bruzzellis are the opposite—ugly, mongrel bastards. Anytime they had a chance to control a Cairo, they took it. Ciccolini saw the writing on the wall and sent his son, Vincenzo, my best friend at the time and your grandfather, to America. Vincenzo ended up in Boston. He found work on the docks. Eventually, he opened an import/export business. His biggest import was Cairo shoes, but he also imported Italian wine and olive oil. Americans couldn't get enough of Italian fashion. His business and his control of the Boston docks grew and grew. The shoe business slowed considerably over the years because of the influence of cheap labor in Asia, but the high-end fashion business is still strong and controlled by Cairo descendants. Because most of the designers are women, the Cairo name has been lost from the finished product.

"Vincenzo saw the need to protect his business in America, so he started what Ciccolini had started in the caves—neighborhood watch groups. He and your father ran the import/export business and kept their neighborhood safe from other Italian and Irish mobs in the area. Even though their cartel was similar to a mafia organization, your father's motives were aimed at protection of his neighborhood. He controlled the docks and the construction sites to make sure his neighbors got a fair shake with the unions for the jobs there.

"For unknown reasons your Uncle Geno befriended a few Bruzzelli men when he came back for a visit and brought them to America. Now the Bruzzellis will do everything they can to destroy the Cairo legacy in America."

"What do they have going on in Naples?"

"Their main business is shipping. They have a small, private harbor south of Naples. They're expanding their business. They use their harbor to unload, store, and ship drugs and illegal weapons all over the world. They're in bed with arms dealers in Russia, opium dealers in Afghanistan, and drug cartels in Central America. Most of the drugs from Central and South America go through their port before they're distributed to the rest of Europe. They can ship anything to anywhere and are paid very well for their expertise. They also have their thumb on everything going on in the Naples area."

Joseph asked, "Why are they so successful? Why would the Afghans pay them to ship their goods?"

"Because the world wants Italian fashion, cars, wine, olive oil, and other goods. It is easy for them to hide the Afghan heroin in a shipment of Chianti to America, for example. Afghanistan doesn't have anything else to export. A shipment coming from there would have red flags all over it."

"Don't the Italian authorities know what's going on?"

"The Bruzzellis control all the politicians and police in and around Naples. Plus, they're smart, because they unload the contraband from freighters in international waters, then bring it into their port for storage. They supply Europe and the Mideast using their boats. For exports to the U.S. and other parts of the world, they meet freighters in international waters, where they load the illegal goods that are hidden among normal exports from Italy.

"The heads of the Bruzzelli family live like kings in Naples, taking whatever and whomever they want. They're breeding bastard children like rabbits to increase their control. Their leader is a man named Dante. He runs the show, and I can tell you from personal experience he is an evil, evil man.

"That's the story, young Anthony. Please know that your past is a proud history filled with brilliant, good people who have never been able to escape the evil shadow of Bruzzelli violence. To answer your question about how you could end the vendetta … You can't. If the great Ciccolini couldn't do it, no one can."

Joseph could tell that Luca was done talking. He said, "Thank you, Mr. De Luca. This is what I needed to find out. How are you? Is there anything I can do for you?"

Luca laughed. "Give me back my youth and my best friend, Vincenzo. We were quite the team. Outside of that, no. I am safe here. I have friends that keep me informed."

"Where is your family?"

"My family is gone. My beautiful wife has passed, and the Bruzzellis took my daughter, Sophia, a long time ago. There's nothing I can do about that. I can't fight them. I tried to find her in Naples years ago, but was warned to stop or else Sophia would be killed. I've given up wondering what happened to her." Luca lowered his head for a while, then looked up at Joseph and said, "You could come back and visit me sometime and bring me some news."

Joseph stood and said, "I will do that, Mr. De Luca, and the news I bring will be good news." Joseph noticed Renegade standing in the doorway and felt good he was there with him, even though he knew that Renegade couldn't understand a word they said.

Luca De Luca stood, extended his hand, and said, "It's been a pleasure."

"Mine, too," Joseph said, then headed to the door. Before he walked out, Luca said, "One more thing, Anthony." Joseph stopped and turned around.

Luca said, "Your father did not kill Vincenzo. That is a typical Bruzzelli lie. They killed your grandfather and made your father take the fall for it so they could put Geno in his place. I'm sure they made threats about what they would do to your mother, your sister, and you. He took the fall to save all of you. He had to give in and watch them put Geno in his place."

Joseph was dumbfounded. *Dad didn't kill grandpa!* He screamed to himself. *Why didn't I see that? It was right there in front of me.* His mind raced as he stood in the doorway of the cave. He had one foot in the cave and the other foot in the outside world, the two worlds pulled together by this humble man. *That's why I made this trip. That's the answer to the question that I never even thought to ask.*

Joseph looked at Renegade, then at Luca De Luca. Tears stung his eyes. He walked back into the cave and gave his great-uncle a tight family hug filled with love and appreciation. Then he stepped back and said, "I will fix this, and then I'll come back for you."

Luca De Luca said, "I know you will, Ciccolini. I know you will."

Chapter Thirty-Five

HE HOT CUP OF COFFEE COMPLEMENTED THE MORNING'S CALM, COOL
start. Claire warmed her hands with the big mug. The sun peeked over
the horizon, waking up nature all around her. The breath of a cool breeze
rustled the live oak leaves. She had a wool shawl on her shoulders, and her
feet were in warm slippers.

Anna Tobin walked out of the big kitchen on to the outdoor stone patio
of the Tobin family's house, which was part of the estate on their vineyard
outside Paso Robles, California. She approached Claire and asked, "Is there
room for me out here?"

Claire smiled. "Please join me. What's down the back slope of that
mountain?"

"There's nothing there but scrub brush and some of Jackson's surveillance equipment. He keeps his men on watch here twenty-four-seven so we
always feel safe. You know that he's why we're all here, together and safe?"

Claire said, "Mandy told me a little. She said you and Max were separated
after your parents died and you were too young to remember them or each
other. And poor Sophie had to live on the streets to escape her foster farther.
It's no wonder you love this place and love being together."

"Sometime I'll tell you the whole story, which includes a bank hiring
people to kill Armando and Chechen mobsters trying to kidnap Sophie.
The mobsters have even been here in Paso Robles looking to take revenge
by killing Sophie. It's a long, horrible story that ends up with Reed Jackson

and his men protecting us. Speaking of Jackson, have you heard from Joseph this morning?"

"Yes, I just got off the phone with him. He and Renegade went to a small town near Naples to look for a man who could tell Joseph about his family's past. He found the man, and he has a long story to tell me when we can talk longer. He said they'd come back in a few of days."

Anna said, "That's good. It will be good to get those bad men out of the picture and off your back."

"Yes, it will. I'm not sure what I'm getting myself into here, but I know I want to be with Joseph, or Tony, as Max knows him. That's one of the many things we need to sort out."

Anna said, "He's been through a lot in his life. I guess we all have in different ways. Have you talked with Mandy's mother, Deshi, yet?"

"Last night and in the tasting room, but just for a few minutes. She seems like a sweet lady. So she and Reed Jackson met when you and Armando were married last year, and they fell madly in love? And the same night your brother, Max, fell in love with Mandy, her daughter? That must have been some party."

"Yes, that's what happened right over there, beyond that fence in the pasture. Except that Max and Mandy had been flirting with each other for a couple months before that night. We had a dance floor with a small stage and a band. Jackson and Deshi met for the first time on the dance floor, and they haven't been apart since then."

"Did Max ever talk to you about what Joseph was like growing up?"

"Max told us that Joseph was the only person in his whole life that was nice to him. He had Max over to his house a couple times and tried to include him in things at school. But, Max admitted, he just didn't fit in. Joseph had his big family and mostly hung around with older boys. He said Joseph was a good golfer. One summer they hung out and played golf nearly every day."

"You know, I was just thinking … You should talk with Deshi about how she handles things when Jackson is away. It sounds like Joseph will be working with them on some exciting, but dangerous, missions."

Claire asked, "You all know about that?"

"Yes. We've fought assassins a bank hired and a group of Chechen mobsters together. We're all like a big family. Jackson doesn't keep anything from us. He has created a fortress here for our protection, and he always has a couple of his men staying here keeping their eyes on what's going on. I'm glad you're here. You're safe with us. We all want you to stay as long as you can, even after this mess gets sorted out."

Claire said, "Thank you, Anna. All of you have been great. I love it here and really enjoyed helping Sophie and Deshi in the tasting room the last few days."

"They said you were a big help. I understand you're planning to go out in the fields bright and early tomorrow morning with Mandy and Armando."

Claire laughed. "Yes, I am. Mandy has me all suited up with some of her overalls and boots. It will be a whole new experience for me."

Anna looked down at the baby monitor in her hand. "It looks like Bella is ready to get up for the day. I'll grab her and see you inside for breakfast."

Chapter Thirty-Six

⟾⟾◈◈◈⟽⟽

EARLIER THAT DAY, HANS BRECKMAN, THE SWISS BANKER, CHARTERED a yacht for Jackson out of Rome and had it delivered to the port of Naples. Jackson instructed the yacht's captain to cruise up to the Gaeta Naval Base, between Naples and Rome, to get some supplies. Jackson's CIA contact arranged for a supply pickup at the U.S. naval base in Geata, Italy.

The aft section of the upper deck was the largest open space on the one-hundred-twenty-foot-long super yacht. It was early evening. The yacht cruised south, a mile from shore with Jackson, Apache, Renegade, and Joseph sitting at a dinner table on the afterdeck.

A waiter and a waitress arrived at their table with a plate of food in each hand and placed the dinner plates in front of the four men. At the exact same time, the servers lifted the silver-plated covers off the plates. Steam from the hot meal and a savory aroma gave the four men permission to dig in.

Apache didn't wait long. With his mouth full of tenderloin, he said, "I gotta say it again. It was a good idea bringing Joseph along for this op, boss. This is some high-class shit we got going on here."

No one added to the conversation. They were too interested in their food and the sights around them. A few minutes went by before Jackson asked Joseph, "What did you learn from your trip to Matera today?"

"Renegade drives fast." Joseph chuckled. "That place was pretty weird. There are people who actually live in caves there. Luca De Luca was one of them. He told us the history of the Bruzzelli and Cairo feud. The Bruzzellis deserve everything they're going to get. But the best information was that De Luca is sure my father is an innocent man who was forced to take the

179

fall for killing his father to save my sister, my mom, and me. The Bruzzelli crew needed Dad out of the way so they could put Geno in his place."

Jackson said, "Why don't you call your lawyer contact in Boston and ask her to put an investigator on a path to find an alibi for your father on the day your grandfather was killed. If your father wasn't at the crime scene, he had to be somewhere else. Chances are there are witnesses who could vouch for that. We need him out of Souza for this plan to work. I'll ask Kent to do what he can on his end.

"After dinner we're going to take out the Zodiacs and scuba gear. It will be a good chance for us to test our gear. When we get back, we'll tell the yacht crew that we want to go back out at three o'clock in the morning to try to find a specific sea creature that only comes out at night. On that outing we'll pay a visit to the Bruzzelli compound.

"We know from the blueprints that there's a large conference room right in the middle of the base of the V, at the top of the hill. Renegade and Apache will find the room and install some video and audio bugs. While they're doing that, you and I will find out what's in the other buildings in the compound. Kent told me that Interpol has been tracking a large quantity of C-4 plastic explosives that came from Russia. They asked us to find it and destroy it."

Jackson stood up. "I'll tell the captain our scuba diving plans. Come to my quarters in fifteen minutes to have a look at the other gear we have."

Several hours later the two Zodiac boats' motors were silent as the four men paddled the rest of the way to shore. They were a quarter mile from the south edge of the Bruzzelli compound. The two boats caught the same wave, which pushed them onto the beach. In a few seconds they pulled the boats across the beach and into the brush that bordered the beach.

Jackson handed a pair of night vision goggles to Apache and placed the second pair on his head. He whispered to Joseph, "When we work in two-man teams, only one of us wears these. The other man is responsible for seeing what the goggles don't show in their narrow view. You will stay one step behind me at all times. That will never change unless one of us says the word *split*. If you hear that word, change direction and move as fast as you can for at least five seconds before you take cover. Then stay down and use your communications gear to find out what happened."

"Copy that," said Joseph.

Jackson turned to Apache and Renegade. "Stay behind us until I give you a signal. We'll go in first to make sure the first part of your mission is clear. You're on your own after we separate. We'll meet back here in seventy minutes. Work fast, men, work smart." Jackson lowered his head and hunched forward as he moved into the brush. Joseph was on his heels.

Hidden in the brush on the edge of the compound, Jackson scanned the docks, buildings, roads, and walkways ahead of them. He said, "Anything?"

Joseph replied, "Nothing."

Jackson lifted his shirt cuff to his mouth and said to Apache and Renegade, "Advance to our position."

When they arrived, Jackson said, "It all looks clear. We're going to check the buildings across the compound on the other side first, then come back to check the buildings on this side. It looks like your best path up to the base of the V is on this side. Stay off the path and keep close to the buildings on your way up the hill.

"Watch the scene and wait for us to get behind that truck." Jackson pointed to a flat-bed truck halfway across the compound. "After we're settled there, we'll watch your movements all the way up the slope, and then we'll go to work." Apache and Renegade nodded.

The door to the first building they came to was unlocked. Joseph followed Jackson inside. It was a big warehouse with forklift trucks off to one side and rows of crated supplies on pallets stacked on top of one another several feet high on both sides of the aisles. Jackson whispered, "We're looking for guards and black metal drums with orange writing on the side. The writing will be in Russian." Joseph followed Jackson up and down each aisle, looking for the Russian containers.

Quickly, they entered a second building. That building was completely dark inside, so Joseph's eyes were no help with searching for the Russian containers. He stayed right behind Jackson as they crept up and down the aisles. They exited the second building and entered the third and last stand-alone building on the far side of the compound. There was enough light for Joseph to help look for the containers as they crept up one aisle and down another. No Russian containers.

Jackson looked at his watch before they exited the third building. He whispered, "I'd like to see what's inside that big room, up the hill, at this end of the V structure. Joseph stayed behind Jackson as they scrambled up the steep, grassy slope. The door was locked. Jackson whispered, "Shit!" Joseph said, "I can pick that lock in fifteen seconds."

A few seconds later, Jackson inched the door open. Hunched over, he took one step through the door. He stopped. Joseph stayed outside, scanning the paths and other buildings. Jackson backed out of the building and closed the door. He looked at his watch and said, "We'll go down the way we came and then go over to the other side of the compound to check out the buildings there.

Inside the first building they found the black Russian drums with orange writing. Jackson said, "Go open the door just enough to monitor the compound. I need to open one of these containers. I'll come to you when I'm done." Joseph hurried to the entrance door.

Jackson soon returned to Joseph and said, "We don't have enough time to look in the other two buildings here, but I want to see what's in that big room on this side of the V structure. When we get there, you'll pick the lock, then I'll look inside while you watch for activity. Just like we did before."

A few minutes later, Jackson and Joseph returned to their boats. Jackson said, "We're a little early." He pulled a note pad out of his backpack in the boat. He drew sketches of the compound and scribbled notes all over the page. Apache and Renegade returned, and a few seconds later they were paddling their Zodiacs away from the shore.

The next morning Apache was the last one to enter the large master bedroom suite that was Jackson's room, that doubled as The Agency men's operation headquarters. Jackson had a laptop computer wired up with headphones on the coffee table.

A waiter knocked on the door and pushed a cart into the room. He walked straight to the breakfast nook and set the table. Then he opened the curtains, revealing large sliding glass doors leading to a private deck. The waiter asked, "Should I opened the doors, sir?"

Jackson said, "No thank you. We'll take it from here."

"Very well," the waiter said and left.

The four men looked at one another and smiled. Apache said, "I can't wait to tell the other guys how we're roughing it." Even Jackson smiled.

Jackson sat down on the couch and looked at the laptop monitor. He said, "Still no activity in the Bruzzelli conference room. It would be good to have someone walk into the conference room so we could test the equipment you installed last night." Jackson stood up and placed the laptop on the breakfast table. He pulled both sliding doors open. The fresh ocean air filled the room. Jackson sat down at the table. The rest of his men joined him.

After a good start on the lavish breakfast, Jackson looked at Apache and Renegade and said, "Guess what? Joseph can pick a lock in ten seconds." The men looked at Joseph.

Joseph said, "Can't everyone? That's one skill I learned from the Bruzzellis that has paid off over the years. It's mob course one oh one."

Jackson showed them the sketch he had made on his notepad. He pointed at it and said, "This is the door where Joseph picked the lock. It opened into a dormitory filled with young girls.

"We'll need to go back to the compound tonight to set the rest of our cameras." Jackson pointed to his drawing again and said, "We need to see who's in these five rooms on both sides of the structure that lead up to the base of the V, where the conference room is located.

The four men sat around the cleared breakfast table. Joseph sat in front of the laptop with headphones on. He had a pen and legal pad ready to go to work.

Apache and Renegade had placed two cameras in the Bruzzelli conference room—one in the front and one in the back of the room. Jackson and his men stood behind Joseph as he switched the pictures from the cameras. They had a hi-res view of the men in the conference room.

Groups of men started filling the conference room. There were nine men sitting at the table in the middle of the conference room. Several other men stood behind them with their back to the wall of the oval-shaped room. The man seated at the head of the table had a piece of paper and a pen in front of him. He said, "Let's get this started. First up today is an update on the new harbor construction project."

The audio was loud and clear. Joseph pointed to the man who was talking and said, "That must be Dante Bruzzelli, he's the godfather of the Naples mafia." Joseph wrote down in English what Dante was saying for the men behind him to read.

A lengthy conversation followed. Joseph couldn't keep up with the discussion, so he just wrote down key words. As the dialogue continued, Dante Bruzzelli crossed items off his list. Words on Joseph's pad included payoffs, eighty percent complete, need more warehouse space, Afghan heroin, cocaine shipped from Mexico, Russians, Chechen girls, Boston girls, race in Sicily, dinner plans, and entertainment.

Joseph stopped writing when Dante said, "Tell me we've taken care of that Cairo punk with the pretty face."

Joseph wrote down the word *Cairo*.

One of the men seated at the table said, "I heard back from Natalia. It's done. She used a taser gun to knock him out while they were in bed. She zip-tied his hands behind his back and propped one of his legs on chair while he was recovering from the electric shock. With his leg at full extension, she jumped onto his knee. His knee broke, and he passed out. While he was out, she used a fillet knife to carve up his face. She said there was blood all over the place."

"Let's see the pictures."

"She didn't take any photos. But she said he'd be laid up for a few months."

"Have you paid her?"

"Yes. She required payment in full before she accepted the contract."

Dante said, "I don't like this Ciro. Remember, this is on you if she failed." He turned his attention to another man standing at one side of the room and said, "Where are we with those gypsy kids up in our neighborhood?"

The man responded, "I'm going to let Brando tell you how he fucked that up."

All eyes turned to one of the men standing off to the side. He was a head taller than the rest, and the features of his face were much softer than those of the hard-looking men around him.

Dante Bruzzelli said, "Aren't you the one I specifically told to root those mutts out of Vomero and make it clear to them never to come back?"

The younger man stepped forward into the light. With a confident tone he said, "We could have run those kids out of there, but I saw a much bigger problem that I thought needed to be addressed."

Dante laughed. The men at the table followed his lead and laughed at Brando standing in the spotlight. With the laughter gone and with a menacing look Dante said, "You saw something bigger than what I told you to do?"

Brando took another half step closer and looked at Dante. He said, "Those kids couldn't have been more than twelve years old, and they were all carrying weapons. That deserves our attention. I followed them down to Scampia, where they reported to their bosses. I spent the night there and got reacquainted with some of my old contacts.

"Things have changed there, and those changes are a threat to us. There are Columbian and black gangs using those kids, and many more just like them to run their smack and who knows what else. Those kids have no concern for life or for the consequences of getting caught. I was told they'll walk right up to a man, woman, or even a policeman and shoot them in the back of the head in broad daylight, right in the middle of the street. We're close to losing complete control of what's going on there. If we lose control there, it could start a domino effect all around us."

Dante sat up a little straighter and leaned forward. "How do you know so much about what goes on in Scampia?'

"I grew up in the Vele di Scampia before they tore it down."

"Pull a seat up to the table." Dante's words sent the men against the wall scrambling to get a chair for the young man. Brando sat between two of the older men. Dante said, "What do you suggest we do?"

"You could take them by surprise very easily. My friends showed me three locations where they run their operations. They have a little protection set up, but not much."

Dante didn't take his eyes off Brando. "Who are you?" He waved his hands to the men sitting at the table and said, "Which one of us is your father?"

Brando said, "You are."

Dante gave Brando a closer look. "Who's your mother?"

"Sophia De Luca."

Dante leaned back in his chair and said nothing. He seemed to be scanning his memory. Finally, he nodded, as though he'd remembered something. Then he looked at another man at the table and said, "This shit in Scampia. That's your territory. What do you think?"

"I have to agree with Brando. Things are a mess down there with those young kids playing gangster. The gangs I know selling in that neighborhood buy their product from us. I wouldn't be surprised if there are other gangs, like the Columbians or blacks. We've had to go in there in the past and clean things up. He's right. We should probably do it again."

Dante said, "Two nights from tonight we'll go in there and kill them all." He looked at the man sitting next to him on his right and said, "I want you to take responsibility for this." Then he looked back at Brando. "You go down to Scampia today. I want you to figure out the where and when and then get back to us with the details. Two days from today, in this room, we'll go over your plan. Then that night we'll hit them. Do you want anyone to go with you?"

"No. It's better if I go alone. I'll stay with my mom. That'll be a good cover."

Dante looked around the room. "That's it for today, gentlemen." He turned to another man. "Vito, I want to talk with you before you leave." The rest of the men filed out of the room.

Joseph took off his headphones, picked up the legal pad, and reviewed his notes. The men behind him were engaged in conversation when Joseph noticed Dante and the man he called Vito talking. Joseph put the headphones back on and put his pen back to work on the pad.

Joseph began summarizing the Bruzzelli meeting, using his notes to remind himself about what to report. Jackson took notes of his own as Joseph delivered the details of what he had heard. When Joseph finished his report, all eyes turned to Jackson, who was still writing in his small notebook. Eventually, he stopped writing and looked at his men. He said, "This is turning into something bigger than any of us anticipated. I have some ideas. I need to talk with Kent. It's a little early, but I bet he's at Langley by now. Jackson picked up his phone and walked out on to the veranda. He turned back to his men and said, "You guys take the afternoon to get some shut-eye. We'll meet at seven o'clock for dinner again like last night. We're going back to the compound later to set up the other cameras. We need more intel."

Joseph went to his cabin. He had a veranda off his bedroom with a table and chairs. It was a beautiful afternoon. The sights of Italy made him think of Claire. He looked at his watch. *Two o'clock. That would be five o'clock in the morning West Coast time. A little too early to call.* That was when his phone buzzed. He looked at the caller ID. *Claire!* "Hey, baby, what are you doing up so early? I was just getting ready to call you."

Claire laughed. "I know. I felt the tug of our invisible string. What were you going to say?"

"I was going to tell you how much I miss you and how I wish you were here. We have a huge, beautiful yacht for our home base. Someday we'll rent one of these just for ourselves."

"Jackson's girlfriend, Deshi, already told everyone about the yacht. We want to join you guys. How's it going? When are you coming home?"

"The more we learn about this place and these bad guys, the more complicated our mission gets. I don't think we'll be coming home for a while. We're meeting again in a few hours for dinner to hear what Jackson has planned. But before then I need to talk with Jackson about something that will make our mission even more complicated. I'm not looking forward to that. Why are you up so early?"

"I'm working in the vineyards this morning with Armando and Mandy. I'm going to help the crew with canopy management. You should see me in the overalls Mandy gave me."

"I would like to see that. Send me a picture. I could use a little shot of your cuteness right now. It sounds like you're having fun there."

"I am. It's really great here. Everyone is so cool. But I have to get going. I don't want to be late. I love you. Stay safe, Joseph."

"Okay. I love you, too."

Chapter Thirty-Seven

JACKSON CALLED, "IT'S OPEN."

Joseph walked into Jackson's room and said, "Gotta minute? I wanted to run something by you."

"Sure, of course. What's up?"

Hesitantly, Joseph said, "I know this op keeps getting bigger and more complicated, but I have some additional information that may be important. The younger man, they called Brando, we saw in the Bruzzelli meeting may be my cousin. Luca De Luca told us that the Bruzzellis took his daughter a long time ago. Her name was Sophia De Luca, the same name Brando used when Dante asked about his mother."

Jackson said, "That is good info. I just got off the phone with Kent, and I want to go over what we talked about with you."

Joseph felt relieved that Jackson was interested in his news. He followed Jackson to the veranda.

"Kent is going to get back to me shortly. He likes the idea of letting the Bruzzellis clean up Scampia and then having the Italian authorities round up the Bruzzellis and charge them all with first-degree murder. That would put them all behind bars for life. At the same time the police are securing Scampia, we would take care of the bosses at the compound. He wants to get Interpol on-board and then get back to me. We've decided not to include the Naples police until the last minute because the Bruzzellis have contacts there. With Scampia cleaned up and the Bruzzelli thugs behind bars, the police would be able to take back control of that area and restore the rule of law.

"I'm going to have the rest of my crew fly here ASAP, today if possible. We're going to need everyone on-board to make this work. Deshi has been bugging me about coming here with them. Has Claire asked you about that? I think they're working together."

"Claire did bring it up."

Jackson said, "If you could turn Brando, we could use his knowledge to help us.

I have a few more calls to make. You try to get some shut-eye. It's going to be another long night. We have to get all the cameras set tonight to see what's going on in there. Try to figure a way to engage and turn Brando. He could be a great asset. We'll both have something to report at our dinner tonight."

Joseph said, "Sounds good. Before I take off, I'd like to go over some additional notes I took after the Bruzzelli meeting ended. Dante had a private conversation with one of the men. I rewrote the conversation." Joseph handed Jackson a piece of paper.

Jackson read what was written on the paper. He looked at Joseph and said, "This is good. We can use this."

Joseph headed for the door. "I'll see you at dinner."

Chapter Thirty-Eight

⇒◈◈◈⇐

THE STREETS IN THE NEIGHBORHOOD OF SCAMPIA WERE MOSTLY deserted the next morning. Joseph found a parking spot for his motorcycle. Based on what he had heard during the Bruzzelli meeting the day before, he assumed that Brando would be staying with his mother. Joseph had learned a long time ago that gangsters don't get started very early in the day; he felt confident that Brando would be there.

Some neighborhoods in Boston looked just as distressed as these streets. Joseph thought as he walked on to find Sophia De Luca's apartment. The few people he passed on the street eyed him as if they knew he didn't belong there. Those looks confirmed his decision to get this done early in the morning.

When Joseph found Sophia's apartment building, he climbed three flights of stairs to a long hallway that had metal doors on both sides. The dirty corridor had a nasty smell lingering in the air. He wondered what life was like on the other side of the doors he passed.

He found apartment number three hundred twelve and knocked on the door. A quiet voice said, "Who is it?"

Joseph said, "Tony Cairo."

"What do you want?"

"I'm visiting from America. I think we're related, and I wanted to say hello." Silence. Joseph said, "Luca De Luca sent me."

Locks clicked and a chain rattled. The door opened slowly, and a woman peeked out. She wore a shabby red terry cloth robe. Her uncombed dark brown hair fell to her shoulders. The timid expression on her face made

Joseph sensitive to his early morning disruption. He wanted to make her feel comfortable right away. He said, "I'm sorry to bother you so early this morning, but I'm on a tight schedule, and I couldn't get your phone number. I went up to Matera a couple of days ago and talked with your father."

She looked puzzled. "I haven't seen or talked with him for twenty years. I didn't know he was alive."

"He lives in a cave at Matera. He told me your mother passed a few years ago."

A young man stepped up beside the woman. Joseph recognized Brando right away. "Everything OK here, Mama?" he said in a deep voice.

Joseph smiled at him and offered his hand. "Hi. I'm Tony Cairo. Your grandmother and my grandfather were brother and sister. I'm visiting from America, and I wanted to stop by and say hello." Joseph gave them a big smile and stuck out his hand to Brando. He took Joseph's hand tentatively.

"I'm Brando Bruzzelli." He looked at his mother. "I didn't know we had relatives in America."

His mother said, "I didn't either. Please come in, Mr. Cairo."

The apartment was cramped. A rumpled blanket on the couch and Brando's sleepy look indicated that he had slept there the night before.

Sophia led Joseph to a Formica-topped kitchen table that was half in the kitchen area and half in the living area. She moved some papers and clean dishes off to the side and said, "Please sit down. I have some coffee made."

Joseph could tell she was uncomfortable because of the surprise visit, the state of the apartment, and her disheveled appearance. He wanted to keep everything upbeat and positive. He said, "Thank you. That sounds good." Brando sat down across from him. Joseph said, "I told your mom that I visited your grandfather a couple of days ago."

Brando still looked uncertain, but finally he said, "Tell me about him and how you found him."

"My father, who lives in Boston, told me to look him up. He said someone from one of the Cairo shoe stores would know how to get in touch with him."

Brando seemed skeptical. "What brings you to Naples?"

"I'm here on business and had a little time to do some touristy stuff." "What's my grandfather's name?"

"Luca De Luca. He's a cool dude. Everyone in Matera knows him. I had a couple glasses of wine with him. He told me some really interesting stories about the Cairo families. He mentioned that he hasn't been able to go to Naples and hoped I would be able to find your mom. I'm not sure he knows about you, but I'm certain he would want to meet and get to know you." That seemed to soften Brando.

Brando's mom placed a cup of coffee on the table for him. Brando said, "Do I have any other relatives I should know about?"

Joseph didn't know if the question was his to answer.

Sophia said, "That's something we can talk about later."

Joseph wanted to change the subject. He took a sip of the strong black coffee and said, "I've rented a yacht as a home base while I'm here. I'd like both of you to take a short cruise and have lunch with me today. I have some boxes of what may be considered family treasures that are yours. I rented a motorcycle to get around here, so I couldn't bring them with me. Please say you will have lunch with me." He could tell the words *yacht* and *treasures* had hit the mark, just as he had hoped.

Brando looked at his mother. Keeping her gaze on Brando, she said, "I guess I could ask Cristina to cover my shift today."

After a short pause Brando said, "Could we make it an early lunch? I have a lot on my plate today."

Joseph replied, "Of course. How about ten o'clock on dock A. I'll be waiting for you there. I'll tell the staff to prepare lunch for us at eleven, and I'll have you back in port by noon."

Brando looked at his mother. She nodded. He said, "I guess that will work. It would be a nice break for Mama. Give her some time with you." Then he smiled for the first time and chuckled. "I'd kinda like to see this yacht, too."

Joseph flashed a smile. "Great! It's settled then. I'll meet you at ten." They all stood up. Joseph surprised Sophia with a big hug, then shook Brando's hand. Joseph said, "It's a real honor to have met you both. I'm looking forward to our visit later today. He smiled at both of them and left. *Mission accomplished*, he said to himself, grinning, as he descended the stairs.

Chapter Thirty-Nine

Later that morning Joseph stood next to Sophia and Brando on the upper deck of the yacht. With both hands on the railing, Sofia leaned back and let the wind sweep across her face. She had dressed up for the occasion in a blue dress with a wide, white belt. She wore white, low-heel shoes and carried a matching white purse. There were scuff marks on her shoes and purse. Brando stood on the other side of Joseph. He watched smaller boats in the distance and eyed the coastline as their yacht cruised parallel to the shore.

Brando said, "That was a sweet tour of your boat. What kind of business are you in that you can afford such luxury?"

Joseph said, "I'm involved in several businesses. My main business is commercial insurance, and I have ties with our family business, but that's about to come to an end." Joseph watched Brando take in that information and waited for him to put the pieces together. Joseph had planned the timing of their cruise so they would pass the Bruzzelli compound at about this time. He pointed out the compound and said, "Do you recognize those buildings from out here?" Joseph watched Brando's expression change. He looked at Joseph and said, "Yes, I know that place. Why?"

"I'm the one that the men who meet there talk about." Joseph smiled. "I'm the Cairo kid with the pretty face. As you can probably see by now, I turned their hired assassin, Natalia." Brando's and Joseph's gaze met and lingered there for a while. Then Joseph took Sophia's arm. "Come on, lunch is ready." He ushered them to their table on the afterdeck, which was set for six. Two servers arrived with pitchers of water and took their drink orders.

After the servers left, Joseph said, "I have a story for you. It's your story, and it's about how we can change it. Please stop me if I get anything wrong." Sophia and Brando exchanged glances, then looked at Joseph.

Joseph turned to Brando and said, "Your beautiful mother was taken from her family when she was fifteen-years-old by men who worked for your father. I'll bet she was the prettiest girl in town, and the fact that she had Cairo blood in her family lineage meant she never had a chance at a normal life. Dante Bruzzelli made sure of that." Joseph turned to Sophia, who had a startled look on her face. Joseph said, "Brando has come up through the Naples' mafia ranks very quickly because he is smart, but that's about to change. Just yesterday Dante found out that Brando is his son and yours. Even knowing that Brando has Cairo blood, Dante still gave him some additional responsibilities. But that will soon come to an end." Joseph waited for Brando to tell his mother that Joseph was wrong, but he remained silent.

The servers arrived with three glasses of iced tea. One server said, "Your lunch will be out soon."

"Thank you," said Joseph. He took a sip of tea, then looked at Brando and said, "You are probably wondering where I'm going with this." Joseph didn't wait for a response. "I want to give you the words your grandfather Luca De Luca gave me a few days ago. He said, 'Know that your past is a proud history filled with brilliant, good people who have never been able to escape the evil shadow of the Bruzzellis.' You and your mother are part of that history. I'm offering you a way out of the Bruzzelli outfit and a way out of the slums of Scampia for your mother."

At that moment Claire and Deshi stepped on to the deck. Joseph stood and said, "This is my girlfriend, Claire, and this is our friend Deshi." Brando stood and offered his hand. Joseph said to Claire, "Please sit here. Brando and I have some more things to talk about." Claire and Deshi sat down and engaged Sophia in conversation.

Joseph led Brando along the walkway on the side of the yacht to where Reed Jackson was waiting for them outside his suite. Joseph said, "Brando, let me introduce you to my associate, Reed Jackson."

The two men shook hands. "Hello, Brando. Glad to meet you." Joseph could tell by Brando's silence that all this was coming at him fast. The surprise knowledge Joseph had of the Bruzzelli compound, the brief family history lesson, and now the intimidation of Jackson's formidable presence was a lot for the young man to take in.

Brando turned to Joseph and said, "What's this about?"

Jackson said, "Interpol, the top Italian anti-mafia prosecutor, and the Naples police are going to let the Bruzzelli outfit execute your plan to clean up Scampia. Then they're going to round up the Bruzzelli thugs after they have killed the rival gang members and then put the Bruzzellis away in prison. With Scampia cleaned up and the Bruzzellis gone, the Naples police will be able to restore law and order in that neighborhood. We're offering you a chance to work with us to make that happen and to free yourself from the mafia life completely."

Brando said, "I don't think you guys have a clue about what's going on here. The guys who are going to Scampia are just some of the soldiers. The bosses won't get any dirt on their hands, and they'll start it all over again. Besides, I have a good life, and I have plans for getting my mother out of Scampia very soon. I appreciate your offer, but count me out."

Jackson said, "Just so you know, we're taking all the bosses out at the same time as the Scampia cleanup."

Brando laughed and pointed to the shore. "You're going into their complex and taking them all out?"

Jackson said, "That's right. We've been inside the compound a couple times the last few days to set things up. We're going to take them all out without hurting any of the girls. This is all going to happen with or without you. You can be one of the good guys, live an honest life, and get your mother out of the slums. Or you can dig the hole you're standing in right now a little deeper every day that you're alive, continue to be part of a business that destroys everything it touches, and allow that piece of shit Dante Bruzzelli to hold control over you and your mother.

"If your cousin—"Jackson nodded at Joseph—"hadn't spoken for you, you'd either be a dead man walking or on your way to being behind bars for the rest of your life. We want to show you something." Jackson motioned Brando into his suite, where he had a computer set up. "Sit down and listen to this."

Brando sat down, and Joseph pressed Play on the computer. The screen came to life, showing the time in the Bruzzelli boardroom when the meeting from the day before was adjourned, when Dante said, "Vito, I want to talk with you before you leave." Brando leaned closer to the screen. He saw and heard Dante say to Vito, "That Brando kid is one of your crew, right?"

"Yes, he's the banker I've told you about."

"Did you know that he's got Cairo blood?"

"No. He's got our name. And I'm sure he doesn't know he has Cairo blood. That generation doesn't know or care about the bad blood between our families."

"I care. Do you have anything on him?"

"He's a loner… He does have an interest in a small winery up in Tuscany. His partner runs a small operation. Brando has worked it for several years."

Dante said, "Send some guys up there to make his partner an offer. We're gonna take pretty boy down a couple notches. After we get Scampi cleaned up, if he lives through the cleanup, put him down there on the streets. His banking days are over."

"No problem. I have a couple of guys who will want to settle a score with that partner of Brando's."

Brando closed the laptop and shook his head. He looked at Joseph, then at Jackson. "That spells it out pretty clearly. Count me in. I don't owe them anything. What do you want me to do?"

Joseph slapped Brando's shoulder. "Good to hear. Let's join the girls. We'll go over the details after lunch."

Jackson led the way back to the luncheon. Joseph gave a thumb's up to the ten men from The Agency who were seated at a separate table having their lunch.

Chapter Forty

A FTER LUNCH ALL THE MEN AND THE THREE LADIES ADJOURNED TO Jackson's suite, where they had more privacy. The large cabin was full. A few of the Agency men stood out on the veranda, but were still close enough to the rest of the group to be involved. Joseph introduced Brando and Sophia to the men from The Agency.

Jackson said, "What started a few months ago as a small job to find out who Joseph Johnson is turned into an important mission to support Interpol, the Italian Anti-Mafia Commission, and the Naples police. We welcome Brando and Sophia into our group and appreciate their help in ridding Naples and the rest of the world of the Bruzzelli scourge. The Bruzzelli bosses are expecting a call from Brando tomorrow morning with a plan for sending their soldiers into the neighborhood of Scampia tomorrow night. Their plan includes killing drug dealers and their associates who compete with them. The Naples police department and the Italian Anti-Mafia organization will wait for the Bruzzellis to finish killing their competition. Then they will move in and arrest or kill the Bruzzelli soldiers if they resist arrest. The Anti-Mafia squad predicts a warlike gunfight.

"While that is going on, we will execute our plan to eliminate the Bruzzelli bosses, who will be sleeping in their rooms at the compound. Tonight, we'll monitor the cameras we set last night to fine-tune our plan. Our mission will be to execute the bosses in a way that doesn't harm the young girls they've enslaved. According to the Anti-Mafia prosecutor, these men are responsible for hundreds, maybe thousands of murders and many other crimes. There will be no trials, no attorneys, no judges, no jurors intimidated by the mob, no plea deals, and no press. The charge is murder, the verdict is guilty. Their punishment is death.

"In addition, there's a large warehouse filled with girls who they rape on a daily basis. We'll set them free, then destroy their port, all the buildings in the compound, and the boats used to transport their illegal goods."

Jackson looked at Brando. "Brando, we'll ask you to help us monitor the activity in the Bruzzelli compound to help us prepare our plan. You and Sophia can stay on the boat tonight. That way we know you'll both be safe. You can make tomorrow's call to your boss from the yacht."

Brando looked at Sophia and said, "No problem."

Chapter Forty-One

⟤⟡⟢

THE NEXT MORNING JOSEPH, JACKSON, AND BRANDO HUDDLED IN A corner of Jackson's suite on the yacht. The doors were closed.

"Hi, Vito. It's Brando. I want to give you the details of the plan for tonight. I'm going to text you three addresses, where—"

"Hold on, Brando! Dante insists you to come to the briefing today to tell everyone your plan."

Brando looked at Jackson. Jackson nodded. "No problem. I'll see you there. Is there anything else I should know?"

Vito said, "You should be prepared to be with the men who are going into Scampia tonight."

Brando looked at Jackson again to get a confirmation and said, "No problem." Brando ended the call.

Jackson looked at Joseph and then asked Brando , "How do you feel about that?"

"I don't have a choice. Listen, you guys can trust me."

Joseph said, "We aren't worried about that. We're worried about what could happen to you. There are too many variables we can't control."

Brando said, "I can handle the afternoon meeting, no problem. But I don't know what to expect after that."

"That's the problem," Jackson said.

"Look, those guys are all idiots. I'll be able to take care of myself."

Jackson said, "Like you said, we don't have a choice. I'll tell the captain to take us to the port in Naples to drop you off. Then we'll go to the Gaeta naval base to pick up the detonators and a couple more Zodiacs. We have eyes in the Bruzzelli boardroom, so we'll be able to monitor how it goes for you and find out if there's any conversation about you."

Jackson pulled out his phone and said to Brando, "What's your number? I'll call it so we have each other's contact information. Joseph, you call him, too."

Jackson and Joseph dialed Brando's number. Brando's phone rang. Jackson said, "Add us to your contacts list so you can give us an update if you get a chance. Also, link us to your location services. We'll do the same with you. That way we can keep tabs on each other."

⸺◦⸺

When the yacht pulled into the port, Brando and his mother stood on the bow, watching the crew tie up the vessel.

Brando held his mother's hand and said, "I have to do one last thing with these guys. If everything goes as planned, we'll be free of the Bruzzelli curse forever. If something happens to me, I want you to go to Montalcino. Pascal will need your help. You will be his new partner. One more thing. If I don't come back, you'll meet my friends Lia and Gina. Tell them I love them."

Sophia hugged Brando. "Nothing better happen to you. Please come back to me."

"I will, Mama."

Chapter J

LATER THAT NIGHT, OVER A HUNDRED MEN, ALL WITH THE LAST NAME *Bruzzelli*, were gathered in an abandoned garment factory in the heart of Scampia. For the first time, I realized that this attack would be a complete bloodbath. Our men had been divided into three groups. One group was assigned to each location that I had identified as headquarters for the gangs that competed with the Bruzzelli mafia. I was in one of those groups. I recognized a few of the men, including Enzo, who was the one that botched the truck heist the first time I met Pascal. He was in a different group. Enzo spotted me and grimaced. He lifted one hand, crooked his fingers into the shape of a gun, pointed it at me, and pulled the invisible trigger. I turned away.

The man who was in charge of my group stepped up to me and said, "You're the only person in Scampia tonight without a gun. Here." He handed me a pistol. "Do you know how to use this?"

I looked at the pistol and thought, *It can't be that complicated, and I'm not planning to use it.*

The man must have sensed my uncertainty. He said, "Here's the safety. Just point and shoot. You have six rounds; use them wisely."

"Of course."

"I better see you usin'n it. Dante told me to keep my eye on you, Cairo."

I looked into his eyes and thought. *Was that a threat?*

The man turned away and yelled at everyone in our group, "Gather up over here."

We huddled in one corner of the warehouse while the other two groups did the same. Our captain said, "Our target location is just a few blocks from here. It's a deserted warehouse. Outside, there will be addicts hanging around the front of the building looking to score. Half of us will walk right past them through the front entrance. No shooting until I take the first shot. Based on what we saw earlier today, inside there will be dozens of men and boys standing around counting money and packaging drugs. They won't be prepared for us. After I take the first shot, shoot everyone you see. Kill them all.

"The other half of our group will be in back of the building. When the roaches try to escape out the back, shoot them dead. Everyone. We don't want any witnesses. Take all the cash and drugs you can carry and get out of there fast. We'll meet back here."

I looked at my watch. It was midnight. The two other groups were waiting for us to move out. Our captain thrust his fist into the air and yelled, "Kill them all!"

The swarm of Bruzzelli gunmen poured out of the warehouse to unleash hell on the streets of Scampia.

Chapter Forty-Two

We hid in the brush on the perimeter of the compound. I checked my watch. Midnight. Renegade and Apache ran out of the compound and back to us. Renegade said, "We took down one man on the docks and the two men stationed at the front gate. We didn't see anyone else."

Jackson said, "Good." He gathered all the men around him. "OK, a quick review. The Russian C-4 is in the closest building to us. We'll start there. Those of you who are assigned an executive's room, take one charge of C-4 and one detonator. I'll go with you up to the base of the V, where we have identified the bedrooms of the nine Bruzzelli executives. There'll probably be a girl in each one of the executive's room. Get the girl out of the room first. I'll be outside pointing them in the right direction. Wait until the girl is out of the room, and then eliminate the Bruzzellis. Place your C-4 packet in the room and set the detonator for one-thirty A.M. and meet back here. Cochise and Geronimo will stay here to set the detonators for the rest of the C-4 packets that we'll distribute around the compound and port. Joseph, you're assigned to Dante Bruzzelli's room. After you kill him, go to the girls' dormitory and make sure they're all out of there. Tell them about the buses waiting for them at the end of the compound's lane. At one-thirty, when the C-4 explodes, we should be back on the yacht watching the fireworks."

We moved like darting shadows up the hill of the compound and spread out outside the executive's rooms, with one man in front of each door. Jackson raised his hand as a signal for us to enter the rooms at the same time.

I opened Dante's door. It was dark and quiet in the room. I used my night vision goggles to find Dante. He was asleep on one side of the bed. A girl was asleep on the other side. I crept close to the bed, lifted the goggles, and turned on the light. Dante jerked awake to find the tip of my silencer in his mouth. The girl awoke slowly and shielded her eyes from the bright light. I told her, "Go down to the dormitory with the other girls and wait for me. I'll be there in a few minutes to lead you out of this place."

Dante gaped at me. I turned my head away as if I was going to shoot him, but didn't pull the trigger. Instead, I taped his mouth shut and wrapped tape around hands and feet. He watched as I set the explosive device on the headboard of his bed. His eyes were filled with terror. I laughed at him and said, "I'm Anthony Cairo. My father is Mario Cairo, and my grandfather was Vincenzo. I'm the one with the pretty face. Yes, I turned Natalia, using my Cairo charm, and told her how to lie to you. She knew you Bruzzellis are all weak, stupid men." His eyes darted around the room.

"Tonight's the night when all the Bruzzelli cowards die. That includes your men here and all the Bruzzelli bastards running around Scampia tonight. Then I'm going to sell your wife and daughters to the Chechens. They'll be servicing men just like you, and it's your fault." I slapped his face hard. "Die with that, you piece of shit. Think of me as Ciccolini Cairo coming out of the grave to take our revenge."

I pivoted when the door opened behind me. It was Jackson. He looked at me and said, "Finish it."

A round red-and-white target appeared on Dante's face just before two bullets hit their mark. I hurried out the door and down the compound's slope to the girl's dormitory.

The girls fled up the lane to the place where two buses and several social services workers waited for them.

We returned to the yacht, pulled up the Zodiacs, and gathered on the top deck to watch the fireworks. The C-4 explosives lit up the night sky with thundering blasts of sound and brilliant flashes of light. We all cheered and hooted. The show was over in seconds. Watching the Bruzzelli empire go up in flames was something I would never forget.

Jackson walked away from the railing and worked his phone. I followed him. "Any word from Brando?" I asked.

"No. I was just checking his location. He isn't moving. He's still in the Scampia neighborhood." Jackson looked at me and said, "Let's take one of

the Zodiacs to Naples Bay and hoof it into Scampia. We're close right now."
He looked at his watch. "We could be there in ten minutes."

I said, "I'll load the Zodiac. What weapons and equipment do you want?"

That's when Jackson's expression changed. He said, "A true warrior
doesn't need a weapon." His eyes focused their strength on mine. I felt this
was a teaching moment and accepted the opportunity. He said, "Weapons
are only a burden. If you ever need one, take it from the weak. When we get
back, I'll spend some time with you to improve your skills. You have a good
base, but your natural abilities are in the way. You need to understand the
importance of speed as a weapon. I can teach you how to achieve a warrior
level of speed. When we were in the ring at your boxing club, you saw the
potential. I'll show you a technique and a way to train to harness this power.
Speed is the true warrior's weapon."

A few minutes later we were on the water and Jackson had the Zodiac's outboard engine on full throttle as we skipped over the swells in the
darkness. I looked back at the yacht. Brando's mother stood on the bow,
watching us speed away.

Jackson and I tied up the Zodiac at one of the small-craft docks in Naples
Bay. We both had our phone tracking Brando's location. We hustled toward
the ping of his phone and toward the sound of gunfire. It sounded like a
war zone.

Jackson said, "We split up here. You lead. We're heading into a hornet's
nest, and it's better if we separate. I'll stay one block behind you. If either
one of us runs into trouble, the other one will have a chance to react. This is
a time when patience is key. Assume that both the police and the gangsters
are our enemy. We want to avoid them at all costs. Our mission is to stay
invisible, find Brando, and get the hell out of there."

I headed out, as he had instructed me, stayed in the shadows, and slowly
worked my way to Brando's phone. Whenever I turned around, Jackson
briefly showed himself to confirm our connection. We moved closer, one
city block at a time. The popping sounds of gunfire slowed. *Play it cool.
Keep it slow,* I said to myself.

The closer we got to the ping of Brando's location, the more activity there
was around us. The police seemed to have the upper hand. Gangsters ran in

different directions as a whole regiment of police swept them up. I turned back to find Jackson. He appeared from behind the edge of a building a block behind me. I motioned with both hands down to tell him to hold his position. We slipped back into the shadows.

After the gunfire stopped, we slowly advanced. I checked my phone. I was within two blocks of Brando's phone. Flashing lights from ambulances and squad cars lit up the area ahead of me. I moved a little closer. The ping from Brando's phone showed his location in an area directly in front of me, in the middle of an intersection. The intersection was littered with black body bags lying side by side. There had to be fifty to sixty dead bodies there. Brando's phone location was right in the middle of the carnage.

Somebody shouted behind me, "Show me your hands!"

I turned with my hands in the air. Two police officers had their eyes and their pistols aimed at my head. I said, "Hold on, I'm not part of this."

Jackson appeared out of nowhere, behind the two officers. He was a head taller. He applied a specific grasp to the back of their neck. The officers' eyes rolled up. They were paralyzed. In a few seconds they collapsed onto the pavement. We dragged them into a dark alley.

"What the hell was that?" I asked.

Jackson worked quickly. He used the two police officer's handcuffs to secure them, and then he said, "There's a nerve close to the spine that will temporarily paralyze the body when enough force is applied to the right spot. At the same time, you can clamp the two large arteries that carry blood to the brain. When you do that, the person will pass out in a few seconds. We call that the sensei chokehold. Usually, it's done with a headlock. It's quick and very effective when done right. I'll teach you the technique when we start your training."

Chapter Forty-Three

THE NEXT DAY, TRACI LORENZ WAS ON HER WAY TO SOUZA CORREC-
tional Center outside of Boston.

It was a brisk fall morning with a bright blue sky. The early morning Saturday traffic was noticeably less than the midweek mess.

This time Traci was better prepared for her visit. She had researched the protocol for getting around and parking at the entrance. Her passenger was quiet, timid. Traci wanted to engage, but didn't have a clue about how to start a conversation.

At the same time of day, a group of six men with their hands cuffed behind their back were led to the holding cells on the third floor of the Annex Building, located behind the Boston City Police Department. Only the most notorious and dangerous criminals saw the inside of those walls. The ten cells were built of old-school, vertical iron bars that separated the cells. The rear walls of each cell were made of red brick, with barred windows fifteen feet off the floor.

Two police officers accompanied each prisoner. There was no resistance by the detainees. The officers led each of the six prisoners into one of the cells. Once inside, they backed up against the front of the cell. A police officer removed their cuffs one by one through the bars.

Traci Lorenz slowed her vehicle to a stop in front of a sign that read "Visitor's Parking." The lot was small, and hers was the only vehicle there. They had arrived early, too early to start the process.

Her passenger was silent as she looked straight ahead through a chain-link fence at the brown brick side wall of Souza Correctional Center. This side of the prison had no windows. A dark brown metal door was the only feature that disturbed the monotonous lines of dirty, worn bricks that formed the wide, tall wall. A flat roof added to the bland architecture one would expect from a federal maximum security correctional facility.

"When was the last time you saw your husband, Mrs. Cairo?" Traci asked.

"It's been two years and three months since he told me to stay away. I know he said that for my benefit, but it hurt me then and every day since." She looked at Traci. "How did this happen? Why are you involved?"

"It all started with your son. I met him —"

"You met Tony?"

"Yes. We came here a few months ago to visit Mr. Cairo. Tony wanted to talk with him about the Cairo family history and about getting him out of here. Your son must have some high-ranking contacts to make this release happen so fast. And the truth is, your husband was innocent of the crime. He was set up by his brother and took the fall to keep you and your children safe."

"How is Tony? I haven't seen or talked with him in almost eight years."

"He is a strong, confident man. You raised him well." Traci checked her watch and said, "It's time for me to go in there. I have to sign for him because he is being released in my custody. You stay here. Hopefully, I'll only be a few minutes."

Traci pressed the intercom button on the fence gate and said, "Traci Lorenz here to sign for Mario Cairo." She looked up at the camera. The gate buzzed open. It was a short walk to the brown door.

A few minutes later the brown metal door opened again, with Traci leading Mario Cairo into the bright, free world outside. After a few steps Mario stopped. He looked up at the blue sky and took in a long, deep breath of the cool, fresh air. A flock of geese flew in a V formation above them. He lifted his hands above his head and yelled a loud, strange noise. Traci waited. Mario closed his eyes and took in another deep breath of freedom and dropped his hands. He gave her a broad smile. Traci saw Joseph's eyes in that smile. He said, "That felt good."

"I'm sure it did. I have a surprise for you. This way."

As the chain-link fence gate closed behind them, Mrs. Cairo got out of the car. Mario ran to her and swept her off her feet with his embrace. They twirled around and around. Mario was a big man. He easily lifted her and cradled her in his arms. Traci stayed back to let them have their time.

Eventually, they climbed into her car, Mario and Charlotte in the back-seat and she behind the wheel. Traci pulled out an envelope from the side of her seat and gave it to them. "This is from Tony."

Mario opened the envelope, unfolded the single page, and read out loud:

Papa,

> *I knew you could never hurt Grandpa. I wish you had told me the truth a long time ago. I found Luca De Luca as you suggested, and he told me the whole story.*

> *You'll be happy to know that just as you are getting out of that place, Geno and all ten Bruzzelli men are in jail. They'll be taking your place in Souza very soon and will be there for the rest of their lives. And, all the Bruzzellis in Naples are either dead or will be put away for the rest of their miserable lives.*

> *My friend Traci is going to take you back to the old neighborhood where a home is set up for you. She will also give you access to a bank account with enough money to get you started.*

> *Sean told me Mama's smile is still the prettiest thing ever seen on the Hill in Providence. Give her a kiss for me.*

> *I have a few things to straighten out in Italy. I'll be in touch,*
> *Tony*

—◦◦◦—

Geno Cairo and Mateo Bruzzelli watched their six soldiers back against the bars of their cell to have their handcuffs taken off. Mateo looked at Geno and said, "That's all of us."

Geno asked the men in the other cell, "Did they tell you guys why we're here, what they have on us?"

One of the men said, "They pulled me out of bed after they broke down my front door. I didn't have time to move. They cuffed me and dragged me out without saying one word."

Another man said, "I was awake and saw them coming. There were four men wearing business suits waiting outside my back door. They used some of that kung fu shit on me, then cuffed me. They didn't say anything."

Geno said, "It sounds like we all got the same treatment at the same time. There were guys dressed in suits at my house, too."

Mateo paced back and forth in his cell, half talking to the others and half talking to himself. "They have to give us a phone call. I'll call Naples. They'll have us out of here before dinner." He snickered and looked at Geno. "We'll go back to that place that knows how to make a proper sausage meatball, and we'll laugh at these meatballs who think they can get away with putting us behind bars."

Eleven heads turned when a door opened at the entrance by the stairwell. Two men wearing crisp, tailored suits entered the room and walked right past the men in the cells. Mateo, Geno, and a couple more yelled, "Hey, what's goin' on? Why are we here? We want our phone call!"

The men in suits didn't acknowledge them. They walked to the other side of the room, pulled a large television set out of a closet, and rolled it in front of the men, who were still yelling at them. The men in suits didn't look at the prisoners or say a word. They plugged in the TV, pressed a button on the remote, and walked out the same door they had come in a few minutes before.

All eleven men moved to the front of their cell, gripped the bars, and waited for the TV to come alive.

A date popped up on the screen. Geno and Mateo looked at each other, trying to remember that date. Then the following words appeared next on the screen:

COPP'S HILL BURYING GROUNDS,
funeral service and cemetery,
Boston, Massachusetts

Mateo looked at Geno. Geno nodded to confirm the connection.

The video started with vehicles pulling up to the side of the Lochlann Lynch headstone. The quality of the images looked like a made-for-TV movie. The picture and sound were exceptional. Geno saw himself and heard his own voice in the conversation regarding making an offer to the other two bosses. He saw when he and Mateo pulled guns from their coat and shot his two friends in the head. The video showed the entire scene when the Bruzzelli men came from behind the gravestones and ambushed the men waiting by the vehicles.

He and his men watched the massacre at the Lochlann Lynch site continue as six more men were gunned down in cold blood at the gravesite. They saw themselves emptying their magazines into the bodies of the dead men lying on the ground as they walked back to their vehicles. There was no mistaking the identity of anyone at the scene.

Chapter Forty-Four

MALVOLIO BRUZZELLI OPENED THE DOOR AND SAID, "YOU WANNA SEE me?"

A big man with thick, dark hair and deep, black eyes stood behind a desk. He said, "Sit down."

Malvolio had never been summoned like this to the godfather of the Sicilian mafia's office. He wondered what was going on.

Malvolio sat on a chair that was in front of the desk. The man swaggered around the corner of the desk and stood next to him. He was uncomfortably close to Malvolio. He peered down at him and said, "We just got word that your father, Dante, is dead along with dozens more from his crew. Nearly every other man associated with the Bruzzelli organization in Naples is either in jail or in a body bag. Their marina, the boats, and all the buildings in the compound have been completely destroyed."

Malvolio said, "What happened?"

"We know the Naples police killed or arrested the Bruzzelli soldiers who were down in the neighborhood of Scampia, but there had to be somethin' else goin on. Your father and his eight captains were killed in their rooms at the Naples compound. You need to get back there to take control of whatever's left. I'll send ten of my men with you.

"You have to find out who did this to your family and take revenge. Make who was part of this and everyone around them pay. It's bad business for us if you don't get your family shit sorted out. If you're not up to it, we'll move in.

"Someone had to be working with the police. Find out who." The godfather of the Sicilian mafia paused to think. He moved even closer to Malvolio and pointed down at him. "You're going to have to get your hands bloody for this one. Turn over every rock you can find and watch what slithers out. Look at those assholes from Rome. They've always looked down on us. Look for any ongoing vendettas your family has had with other families. This is your chance to take over as head of the Naples organization."

Malvolio sat in silence for a while to let that all sink in. He thought about taking his father's place as godfather of the Naples mafia. If he played his cards right, he would live the life of a king like Dante did. He thought about his Uncle Vito's young wife and his pretty daughter, Lia. *They're mine now*, he thought. Then Malvolio looked up and said, "When can we leave?"

"You know you can't go to Dante's house. The anti-mafia squad will be looking for you."

"Yeah, I know. I'll use Vito Bruzzelli's place as my headquarters. That's where I've been staying when I've gone back the last few years. There's a couple things there that need my attention."

Chapter Forty-Five

———❦———

A WEEK LATER IN MATERA, ITALY, IT WAS MIDAFTERNOON. LUCA DE Luca heard a knock on his door. That was unusual. He rarely had visitors. The last time was when that nice young man from Boston visited him. Luca didn't think he would see him again for a long time. There was an unwritten rule in the caves. Social engagements should occur either early in the morning or in the evening and not in one's home. The caves weren't meant for entertaining. Social interactions took place at one of the many open-air piazzas or in a café. A visitor now was most likely bringing bad news. Luca hustled around his small home, changing clothes and tidying up the place.

———❦———

Just outside Montalcino, Italy, Lia and Gina walked out of Pascal's barn. They had to squint their eyes in the bright midday sun. Pascal yelled at them, "Over here." He had set up a late lunch under the big shade tree. The girls joined him at the picnic table and smiled at the spread Pascal had prepared.

"This looks really great, Pascal," Gina said. "Thank you for taking such good care of us.".

"Have a seat. You girls slept late today."

"It was pretty late," Lia said, "or I should say early this morning, when we turned in."

Gina said, "It would have gone faster if Brando had been with us."

"I know. He is missed, but you two did great. Thank you for helping me out. Eat now. I made this especially for you."

Lia and Gina sat on one side of the picnic table, and Pascal sat on the other. Pascal pushed a plate of fresh olives and cheese to them.

"I forgot to tell you that Brando's mother called," Pascal said. "She's planning to come here with her father and another couple. I told her you were here, and she said, 'Good. I have a message for them.' You girls enjoy your lunch and take it easy the rest of the day. We'll go back in the vineyard tonight and finish the last of the Trebbiano from lot number four. I need to get some things ready for tonight's harvest."

The leather-hinged door on Luca De Luca's cave swung open. The sight of Joseph surprised Luca. He smiled and said, "I didn't think I would see you again this soon."

Joseph said, "I have a couple of surprises for you." He stepped to the side and pulled Sophia by the hand to the doorway. Joseph expected them both to smile and jump into each other's arms. But Sophia's face looked the same as it had earlier that day when they drove through the mountains on the way to Matera when Claire asked Sophia, "Aren't you excited to see your father again?"

Joseph saw Sophia's face in the rearview mirror. With Claire's innocent question, the expression on Sophia's face had changed from her usual sweet expression to a look of sadness. After a short period of silence, Sophia said, "I feel ashamed."

Claire looked back. "What? Why?"

"I'm ashamed of what I let Dante Bruzzelli do to me, how he defined my life. I remember the day it all started like it was yesterday. It was a school night. Mama, Papa, and I were eating our supper in our home in Naples when the front door crashed open. There were three of them. They beat Papa unconscious and hurt Mama. They told Mama that Dante had his eyes on me for a long time, and today was the day. They took me away." She looked at Joseph. "To the place you pointed out to Brando when we were on the yacht."

Sophia turned to Claire. "Dante slapped me around for weeks. He told me that he would kill my parents if I didn't give him what he wanted. I believed him and gave up fighting. I lost track of time and lost hope of ever going back to my old life. He kept me in that compound until Brando was ready to be born. Dante came to the hospital to name his son. That was the last time I saw him.

"They took me to an apartment in Scampia and threatened violence against me and Brando if I ever left the neighborhood. For twenty years I tried to stay invisible and hoped he would forget about us. It's ironic to think that Brando avoided the mafia life in Scampia, but it found him at that nice school in Vomero."

She looked out the window. "I should have fought more. I should have tried to escape harder than I did. All this time I have felt what happened to Mama and Papa was my fault."

Joseph took his eyes off the road to glance at Claire. He expected her to say something more, but she was crying. Joseph said, "There was nothing you could have done, Sophia. Nothing. You couldn't fight them. Your parents couldn't fight them. They were evil men, but they're all gone now."

"I know. I know everything you say is true, but those thoughts have been with me for more than twenty years, so I doubt they'll ever leave me alone."

Luca's sad expression looked exactly the same as Sophia's as he studied his daughter's face. He may have had the exact same shameful thoughts about himself running through his mind.

Eventually, the corners of his mouth lifted into a smile, and Sophia's smile followed. Luca walked out the door and embraced his daughter. They held each other for a long time as Claire and Joseph waited in silence.

There on the side of the steep, terraced mountain, the bright afternoon sun warmed their reunion. People on the narrow dirt path gathered around them, smiling as they waited for the scene to play out. Eventually, father and daughter stepped back, beamed at each other, then moved in for another hug. Their growing audience broke out in applause. Joseph and Claire joined them.

Luca stepped back. He acknowledged the people watching them and proclaimed, "This is my daughter!" The group applauded again.

Sophia and Luca went into his small home. Joseph and Claire stood in the doorway.

"There is so much I want to know, so much I have to say," Luca said while holding both of Sophia's hands. Then he looked at Joseph. "You did it. Are we safe?"

"Yes. They're all gone."

Luca noticed Claire in the doorway. He looked at Joseph again. "You said you had two surprises for me. Is this the other one?"

"No, this is my girlfriend, Claire." Claire smiled and waved. "The other surprise is you can come with us right now. Sophia is going to start a new life in the hills of Tuscany. We'd like to take you with us."

Luca closed his eyes and lowered his head. He still held both of Sophia's hands. He looked up at Joseph and said, "I will follow you."

Chapter Forty-Six

A FEW DAYS LATER, IN THE COURTYARD OF AN ABANDONED MONASTERY outside of Montalcino, Italy, Joseph followed a real estate agent out of the wide, arched entrance to a stone-paved patio that was used as a parking area. The buildings of the monastery sat on top of the tallest hill of the countryside, which bordered Pascal Barone's winery. The view from the top of the hill was a three-hundred-and-sixty-degree mural of patchwork shades of green formed by vineyards, meadows, and forests. The top half of the canvas offered subtle shades of blue created by the wide Tuscan sky.

The agent said, "Well, what do you think?"

"The place looks like it needs a lot of work, but it has potential. Are you sure the listed price includes all the buildings and all the land?"

"Yes, it's a package deal. The Italian government is strongly encouraging foreign investment in these abandoned treasures."

Joseph and the agent walked to his car. He said, "I'd like to check the place out with my friends the rest of the day. Could we have access?"

"No problem. I'll come back tonight to lock up. I look forward to your phone call tomorrow."

As the agent drove away, Joseph looked back at the monastery. He was just as amazed at the sight of structure as he was with his consideration to buy the monstrosity. He walked back through the arched entrance into the open courtyard. Tall stone walls built to defend the convent formed the outside wall of the large piazza.

Claire, Sophia, Luca, Pascal, Lia, and Gina were waiting for him. Claire asked, "What did you say?"

"Not much. He said we could have the place to ourselves for the rest of the day. He'll come back tonight to lock up."

Claire held the three-page property listing in her hand. She read, *"Nestled in the picturesque and tranquil Tuscany hills, the castle Montassero was initially built as a monastery in the 11th century. Coveted for its wonderful location and beauty, it was purchased by the noble Bevilacqua family and converted into a castle to be used as the family's country residence.*

Castel Montassero allows its owners to experience authentic Tuscan life. Walk into the past and see the high stone walls that once protected this ancient hamlet from invaders. Marvel at medieval frescoes, splendid buildings, and the courtyard, which could incorporate shops, a tasting room, café, and a restaurant.

The property includes the original structure of wooden beams, brick walls, stone arches, a chapel, stone barns, and even the ancient well, all of which offer a unique experience. Look out any window and enjoy seeing the rolling Tuscan hills, vineyards, and woods. This is truly the most beautiful part of Italy."

Pascal said, "That all sounds correct. My house is just down the slope from here and was part of the estate centuries ago. The Bevilacqua family deeded the house and vineyard to my family before they abandoned the property."

The group followed Joseph from room to room on all three floors of the structure. They stopped in a large room on the third floor with floor-to-ceiling windows on five sides of the octagonal room. The view through the windows was too beautiful for words. They marveled at the sights without a sound until Claire said, "I claim this room for our bedroom!" She laughed with their new friends.

Joseph grabbed Claire's hand and said, "If we're going to do this, we have to do it together and go all in. Joseph looked into the eyes of each person in the room. "We could fix this place up, expand Pascal's vineyard, and help Pascal make fantastic wine while we make a life here. Claire and I have the money to make it happen, but we won't go forward unless we are all together. We can talk more about the details later, but before we go forward …" Joseph looked at Pascal. "Would you want to expand what you already have? And would you want us here helping you?"

Pascal waved his arms and said, "Of course I would. Lia and Gina know I need help, and I know we can work together well. It's a pleasure for me to be part of this group."

Joseph asked Sophia and Luca, "Can you see yourselves living here and being part of this?"

Luca and Sophia looked at each other with big smiles. Luca said, "We are all in!"

Joseph turned to Gina and Lia. "We need you both with us to make this work. Are you in?"

They laughed. Lia said, "I love everything about this place and I don't have anywhere else to go."

Gina said, "The first time Brando brought us here, we swore that we would never leave."

Chapter Forty-Seven

REED JACKSON AND DESHI WERE BACK IN PASO ROBLES, SITTING AT THE large table in the dining room of the Tobin Family Estate. The soft evening sunshine beamed through the windows of the big room and touched everything there. Anna, Armando, and Bella sat across the table. Mandy, Max, and Sophie were seated as well.

Servers brought steaming plates of grilled salmon into the room. Plates of pasta, broccoli, and brussels sprouts were scattered around the table. The servers poured wine and water. Maria asked, "Does everything look okay, Miss Anna?"

"Yes, Maria, everything looks fabulous. You all have your dinner now. We can manage from here."

Sophie said to Jackson and Deshi, "You have to tell us all about what happened in Italy."

Jackson said, "Almost everything went the way we planned. We freed fifty-four young ladies from those mobsters. That Italian cartel was working directly with the same Chechen group involved in human trafficking that we fought in Munich. Now those girls are free, and that cartel is gone.

"The cartel had been transporting illegal drugs, weapons, and explosives all over the world. We used Russian explosives that they had stored in one of their warehouse buildings to blow up several buildings, a small port, and the boats they used to transport the contraband. The Naples police and the Italian Anti-Mafia squad arrested seventy-seven mobsters, and close to thirty more of them were killed in the Scampia operation.

"The mafia cancer that has infected Neapolitans for decades is gone. The city of Naples can begin the rebuilding process."

Jackson's phone vibrated. He looked at the screen and said, "It's Kent. I better take this." He excused himself and went through the kitchen, outside, to the patio.

Deshi said, "The yacht was amazing. Our chef prepared the best Italian meals I've ever had while we cruised the Mediterranean between Rome and the Amalfi coast. The whole experience was simply breathtaking every second of the day. We all have to go back there someday. You would love it."

"Were you able to visit some of the ports along the coast?" Mandy asked her mother. "I always wanted to see the ruins of Pompeii."

"No, we stayed on the yacht." Deshi smiled, winked, and then added, "This time."

Max asked, "Any chance we'll see Joseph and Claire in the near future?"

"It looked like Joseph was on a mission to get his aunt, Sophia, and her father back together, and settled somewhere in Tuscany. They had been separated for over twenty years. They have an interest in a small winery not far from the town of Montalcino. Not sure what they're going to do there. But with Joseph and Claire in the mix, I'm sure things will work out."

"What was Sophia's son like?"

"Brando was—" Jackson came back into the room. Deshi asked, "What did he say?"

Jackson sat down. "Kent gave us two new assignments. The first target is the Mexican drug lord El Escorpión. The Mexican government has given up trying to capture or kill him. His organization is responsible for thousands of murders and ninety percent of the illegal narcotics brought into the U.S. Kent didn't have much intel other than we know that Escorpión is building a complex on the east side of the Baja Peninsula that borders the Sea of Cortez. Most of the area is desolate mountains and desert. There are a couple of small towns and a couple of hotels in the area. He suggested we make a resort there our home base because it's a place where Americans go to deep-sea fish and soak up the sun. We would fit in there while we do our recon. The other op is in Africa. The target is a strong-arm dictator who commits unthinkable atrocities, including genocide against rival ethnic groups. He is scheduled to meet with the leaders of the other African nations later this year in Cape Town."

Mandy grabbed Max's hand and asked, "Can we go with you to Mexico and hang out while you guys do your spy stuff?"

Anna looked at Sophie and Armando and said, "We're going, too. Bella needs some beach time."

Jackson said, "We'll have to play that one by ear. If there are no safety issues, I think we could figure out a way to make that work. Remember, our job is to just do the research and then hand the assignment over to Joseph."

Max asked again, "What happened to Brando? Deshi was interrupted when I asked before."

Jackson said, "That, my friend, is a long story that deserves more attention than I can offer with this feast waiting in front of us. After dinner let's build a fire on the patio, and then I'll tell you what Joseph and I found when we went into the bowels of Scampia to find young Brando."

Anna said, "That sounds good." Then she lifted her glass and said, "But before we begin ..." She looked at everyone. "I want to say that everything I love is around this table."

Her family and friends smiled at one another and lifted their glass in agreement.

―⊂∘⊃―

Outside of Montalcino, Italy, the seven new partners had just finished a harvest of one of Pascal's vineyards that same evening. Pascal removed a big pork shoulder roast from the smoker he had started earlier that day. His picnic table was set with candles that lit the table for their late supper. The sparkle lights hanging from the trees complemented the bright stars above. Lia and Gina stoked the bonfire. Pascal carried the pork shoulder to a side table and yelled, "Lia and Gina, come here and help me plate this meat."

They walked his way as Joseph sat down on the bench seat of the picnic table next to Claire. Sophia and Luca sat across the table from them. Joseph put his phone away and said, "I had a message from that architect in Rome. He's meeting us tomorrow morning at eleven. According to Hans Brekman, his firm specializes in restoring these old monasteries for other wineries and hotel chains. He should be able to tell us the scope of this project."

Joseph looked at Claire, arched an eyebrow, grinned, and said, "We may have to make another trip to Buenos Aires, Double-O-Ten."

Joseph asked Pascal, "What's that light on top of the hill?"

"It must be that real estate agent coming back to lock up the castle."

—◦◦◦—

The breeze in Paso Robles became just cool enough for Deshi, Mandy, Anna, and Sophie to accept wool knit shawls. The light and warmth from the fire set the mood for Jackson's story of Brando Bruzzelli. Anna had one eye on the baby monitor and the other eye on her wine glass as Armando poured from a bottle of last year's vintage of the Tobin family's Carménère.

As he poured the wine for his family and friends sitting around the fire pit, he said, "This Carménère wine is a perfect pairing for Jackson's story about his trip into the ghetto of Scampia. Before he begins, taste the wine, savor its soft, gentle flavor and long finish. The Carménère grape is one of the original Bordeaux grapes that is now very rare there. Our estate kept a plot of these vines producing for decades. The hot days and cool nights, along with the deep calcareous rock formations located just under the topsoil here in Paso Robles create the perfect terroir for these delicate grapes. Our vineyard represents almost ten percent of all the Carménère grown in California."

Armando finished his trip around the fire by pouring his own glass and sitting next to Anna.

All eyes swiveled to Jackson. "Before I can begin the story of Scampia, you have to know Brando. Brando is Joseph's second cousin. He looks and acts just like Joseph. Brando's father was the godfather of the Naples mafia organization. He kidnapped Brando's mother when she was fifteen, and he abused her until Brando was born. He then banished them to the slums of Scampia in Naples. Brando and his mother grew up together. She schooled him and did her best to keep him away from the mafia influence.

"Brando was an excellent soccer player, one of the best in the city at the age of fifteen. He accepted a scholarship at a private high school in the ritzy part of the city and excelled in soccer and his studies. But he dropped out of school after two years there and went to work at a bank. At the age of nineteen he was considered a very successful businessman."

Sophie said, "Does Joseph have any other cousins we should know about?"

Jackson and everyone else laughed. He said, "I'm not sure about that."

He went on, "At some point Brando was pulled into the mafia organization because of his name. A few weeks ago he was forced to attend a meeting of the mafia bosses that we were secretly monitoring.

"Joseph identified him and later turned him to our side. Brando gave us the mafia's plan for going into Scampia to kill competing gang members. We passed that information on to the Naples police and the Anti-Mafia squad.

"While Joseph, my men from The Agency, and I were taking care of business at the mafia's headquarters, Brando was embedded with the more than one hundred soldiers of the Bruzzelli faction for their planned slaughter of the rival gang members.

"Later that night, Joseph and I couldn't contact Brando. His phone was stationary, so we decided to leave the yacht and go to Scampia to find him. It was after two o'clock in the morning by then.

"We took one of the inflatable Zodiac boats from the yacht to go to Naples Bay. We tied up the boat in the small-craft docks and followed the ping of Brando's phone location. We heard sounds of gunfire coming from the location where we hoped to find Brando. There was an epic gunfight in the streets of Scampia. Total chaos. The Naples police and anti-mafia squad had been waiting for the Bruzzelli soldiers to take out the rival gangs. After the Bruzzellis had killed their competition, the authorities moved in to arrest the Bruzzelli mafia men.

"We held back until the police force got everything under control. Then we carefully moved closer to the spot pinpointed by Brando's phone. The streets were clogged with ambulances and squad cars with their swirling lights. The GPS signal coming from Brando's phone indicated his phone was right in the middle of a large pile of body bags full of dead gangsters. That was when two police officers approached Joseph from behind."

Chapter Forty-Eight

IN MONTALCINO, LIA PLACED PLATES OF SMOKED PORK IN FRONT OF Sophia and Claire. Gina came in right behind her with more food for the group. Luca asked Pascal in broken English, "How much of the new ground could be planted with additional grape vines?"

"Almost all of it." Pascal pointed off in the distance. "We'd start with the south-facing slopes that are currently being used as pastures for the neighbor's sheep. We could—"

Joseph jumped to his feet and shushed them. He peered into the darkness, then bolted away into the night.

Chapter K

BRANDO STRUGGLED TO SEE IN THE BLACK NIGHT. HE HELD HIS HANDS out in front of him and took short, slow steps. He was lost.

There should be a way out of here. When he heard a noise, he instinctively crouched and listened hard.

A speck of light pierced the darkness in front of him, and then it was gone. He stood up. *I'll head in that direction. Maybe that light is the way out of here.*

He inched slowly forward, trying to find a way to his future, to escape his past. But pitch-black darkness hindered his progress. He felt himself being pulled down a slope toward a flicker of light. *Is this the way to the start of my new life?*

What was that? He heard voices.

Chapter Forty-Nine

<hr/>

Back in Paso Robles, Jackson continued, "Even though Joseph is fluent in Italian, we couldn't take the chance the police officers would understand or believe us. We were forced to take down the officers and drag them out of sight into a dark alley. Brando surprised us. He was hiding from the police and from two Bruzzelli men he'd just escaped from.

"A few days before, the mafia bosses found out that Brando was a Cairo descendant, just like Joseph. That gave the green light to anyone who wanted to kill him. Two mobsters cornered Brando when they noticed he wasn't shooting their enemies. They confiscated his weapon, money, and phone. Luckily, a group of policemen interrupted them. Brando escaped when the two Bruzzelli men attacked the police officers.

"The man who took Brando's phone must have been killed in the shoot-out. He and Brando's phone were in one of the body bags we saw piled on the street. Brando was hiding from the police when we stumbled onto him. We made it back to the yacht without a problem."

Chapter Fifty

———◦◦◦———

J OSEPH INSTINCTS WERE CONFIRMED WHEN HE HEARD THE SOUND OF someone tramping through the brush. He crouched and waited. When the intruder stepped close to him, he launched himself at the shadowy figure. They both hit the ground with a thud. The man cried, "No! Stop! It's me, Brando!"

"Brando?" Joseph took a close look at his face. What the hell are you doing here? He helped Brando to his feet.

Brando brushed himself off and said, "I wanted to surprise you."

Joseph said, "You surprised us alright." He put his arm on Brando's shoulder and guided him to the picnic table.

When they stepped into the light of the bonfire, everyone gaped at Brando.

Sophia said, "Brando! You scared us half to death. We weren't expecting you until tomorrow."

"I couldn't take another day at that bank knowing you all were together. I escaped, and I've decided to retire from the banking profession. I'd rather be here. He sat down between Lia and Gina and smiled at all his friends. Brando said, "Everything I love is at this table."

Joseph said, "I know that everyone here feels the same way. They all lifted their glass of wine and smiled at Brando.

Brando turned to Pascal. "Isn't there a path down from the monastery? I had a lot of trouble fighting through the brush getting here."

"There's a path, but it would be hard to find in the dark. What were you doing up there?"

"I saw a car pull out of the monastery's driveway when I drove up and thought you all were up there."

Lia brought Brando a plate of the smoked pork. Brando smiled at her. He asked Joseph, "So … did you buy the old monastery and a bunch of Italian farmland today?"

"No, but it's looking pretty good. We'll meet with an architect from Rome tomorrow morning to get his take on the project."

Brando laughed. "Nice. If we're going to expand Pascal's wine operation, we'll have to get him a tractor to help out his old mule." Everyone at the table laughed.

"Mama, did you pick out your bedroom yet?"

She laughed. "No, not yet."

Gina said, "We want to fix up that stone barn next to the monastery for our place."

"That's a really cool idea," Claire said. "Why that building?"

Lia replied, "It has a big open loft area with a large door we can slide open to see the night sky." Lia and Gina giggled. Brando blushed.